ALSO

The Ladies of Bath

The Duke's Daughter ~ Lady Amelia Atherton

The Baron in Bath ~ Miss Julia Bellevue

The Deceptive Earl ~ Lady Charity Abernathy

The Hawthorne Sisters

The Forbidden Valentine ~ Lady Eleanor

The Baggington Sisters

The Countess and the Baron ~ Prudence

Almost Promised ~ Temperance

The Healing Heart ~ Mercy

The Lady to Match a Rogue ~ Faith

Nettlefold Chronicles

Not Quite a Lady; Not Quite a Knight

Stitched in Love

Other Novels by Isabella Thorne

The Mad Heiress and the Duke ~ Miss Georgette Quinby

The Duke's Wicked Wager ~ Lady Evelyn Evering

Short Stories by Isabella Thorne

Love Springs Anew

The Mad Heiress' Cousin and the Hunt

Mischief, Mayhem and Murder: A Marquess of Evermont

Mistletoe and Masquerade ~ 2-in-1 Short Story Collection

Colonial Cressida and the Secret Duke ~ A Short Story

CONTENTS

THE DECEPTIVE EARL

The Deceptive Earl

Lady Charity Abernathy

Ladies of Bath

Isabella Thorne

A Regency Romance Novel

The Deceptive Earl ~ Lady Charity Abernathy
Ladies of Bath
A Regency Romance Novel

Cover Art by Mary Lepiane

2018 Mikita Associates Publishing

Published in the United States of America.

www.isabellathorne.com

Part 1

Artifice

1

Lady Charity Abernathy, the only daughter of the Earl of Shalace was in her dressing room with her mother and her maid. It was a beautiful and fashionable dressing room, but Lady Charity could think of nothing but escaping it, and her mother's fussing.

"Mother, please," Lady Charity Abernathy said. "Enough."

"My dear Charity," her mother said as she rouged the valley between her daughter's breasts so that they looked like round melons barely contained in her dress, "men, even gentlemen," she continued, "must be enticed to see what you want them to see. They are not quite as intelligent as they would have you believe; or as we women, would have them believe they are."

"But mother," Charity began again, and her mother tutted as she so often did, hustling Jean, Charity's lady's maid, out of the way so she could tend to her only daughter.

Charity threw her maid a pleading look, but of course, there was nothing Jean could do once Charity's mother got a thought in her head.

"Your face is quite passible, my dear, but not quite as beautiful as your friend Lady Amelia's. She will outshine you at every turn unless you give the gentlemen something else to look at. Even the scandal cannot dim her beauty."

Charity glowered. "Amelia is married," she reminded her mother. "Her year of mourning is past."

"I am aware," her mother said with her usual centure. "Lady Amelia is already wed and with child despite a full year's engagement."

Charity sighed. She did not even want to think about Lady Amelia right now, or whether or not her friend had truly found love. They had not parted on the best of terms, and if Charity was honest with herself she was still a bit jealous of Amelia.

"Amelia is not even in Bath," she told her mother as she made a sweeping gesture toward the window of her dressing room. On the other side of the panes of glass lay the cobbled streets that boasted fountains with the medicinal waters. Lady Charity and her family had removed to Bath for the summer holiday to take their leisure in her father's townhome. Amelia remained in London. Charity was not like to cross her path for another week or two, at least.

Lady Shalace blew out a breath as if in disbelief of her daughter's ignorance, before launching into a lecture on Charity's lack of enthusiasm to tie down a proper suitor.

"Charity, you have dawdled in your engagement and will quickly find yourself upon the shelf. Alone."

Charity turned away from her mother under the guise of adjusting the pleats of her gown. She had had enough of this conversation, day in and day out. How often had she been told that Lady Amelia was first engaged and Lady Patience first to be wed? She could almost speak the words before they slipped from her mother's lips.

"Lady Patience married well enough, the first born son of the Earl of Blackburn," Lady Shalace hooked her daughter's shoulder and spun her back around to continue her ministrations. Charity bit her tongue rather than remind her mother that the opening ball was not for another week yet, and there were few enough in Bath whose notice would matter before that day. "Even with all that garish red hair, she managed to capture a son of an earl and has already given him an heir," her mother continued.

Charity stared out the window and only half-listened to her mother's prattle. Mention of Patience had presented the opening that the countess had needed for the reminder that Lord Barton, Patience's elder brother, was still wholly unattached, and that he was also the son of an earl.

Patience's brother, Reginald had escorted the three friends so often upon their previous excursions, that he felt more brother than suitor to Charity. Still, there was no use telling her mother that.

"How is it that my daughter is the last to be married?" Lady Charity made no attempt to conceal her distain for the situation. "Even those others, the Misses. What are their names? They are married before you, titled and all."

"Julia and Lavinia," Charity provided in monotone to appease her mother's rant.

"You ought to have been the first, if only you would listen to my instruction."

"Mother," Charity sighed. "I am not the last. Nor have I years enough to be shamed for it."

"Oh?" Lady Charity mused. "Who remains? The Poppy sisters, all the dozens of them? It is no wonder that so many daughters cannot be married off."

"That is a gross exaggeration," Charity replied. "Six children in all to the Poppy's and only four of the fairer sex, and do not forget Constance is married."

"Very well, then. Half dozen," her mother corrected. "Still, our families have long been friends, but what a shame it is that the sons must suffer their income be divided by so many dowries."

Charity knew better than to suggest that there might be more to marriage than income or status. Her mother valued little else and took pride in the fact that her daughter could boast possession of both.

"Don't frown so," her mother said. "It makes wrinkles." She ran her fingers along Charity's brow, smoothing it, and brushed a blonde curl back from Charity's blue eyes. "You must put your best self forward. You are beautiful and personable, but do not be too forward. Men do not like pert women. Save your opinions until after you are married, dear. And mind your tendency to gossip."

"I do not gossip," Charity retorted. "Nor am I pert." A

single arched brow on her mother's fine face revealed her disagreement with the latter statement. For the most part Charity, would rather speak her mind, and was uncomfortable with the subterfuge her mother and many other ladies seemed to thrive upon. She wondered aloud, what if men practiced the same deception. She explained that she certainly would not like it.

"Dear, men have only one thought when it comes to women," her mother said. "And it is not how to deceive them. They are at their core simple creatures," her mother continued. "Don't complicate things. Let them see what they wish to see...within reason of course, and they will do what you wish them to do."

Charity shuddered at her mother's machinations but there was no help for it. The *Ton* had despised her mother in her youth, and she viewed them all through those wounded eyes.

"Mother," Charity protested. "I cannot really disguise the fact that I am an heiress. Everyone in the *Ton* already knows that. I wager they will only see my money anyway..." although she herself could barely tear her eyes away from the apparent ludicrous size of her bosom in the glass. Charity shot a small smile to Jean, her maid, who waited patiently. Jean would help her to fix this.

"And that is exactly why you want them to see *you*, Charity, dear." Her mother pinched some color into Charity's cheeks, because, according to her, paint on the woman's face was gauche. "And not just your father's money," her mother concluded with a smile.

Is this really all that I am? Charity mulled over the thought as her mother attempted to tug the neckline of her gown ever lower. Thankfully she had been laced to an inch of breath and the garment would not budge.

"Ah well," Lady Charity sighed. "It shall have to do."

Charity stood in obedient silence as her mother instructed her to laugh more and scowl less.

"Your face shows every moment of disapproval," her mother tweaked Charity's chin and enacted a perfect example of false laughter. "You must learn to hide some of it. You'll not fully approve of any man, though they must never learn the truth of your thoughts."

Charity sighed. Agree always, fawn, and be ever in need of some service or another. Those were her mother's strict instructions. In all, Charity determined that she must be anything a man might desire of her. Anything, that is… but herself.

Charity was not sure it was an improvement to have the man drooling over her breasts instead of her money. At least, a gentleman who wanted to marry her for her money would be honest in his aims. There was little he could do to hide poverty. It was a scent that carried far and wide among the *Ton.* A lecher was in Charity's opinion, harder to bear, and certainly harder to ignore.

But, Charity gave in to her mother's ministrations with the understanding that as soon as she could excuse herself, she would scrub the rouge off of the tops of her breasts, or Jean would help her to camouflage the paint with powder. This was a ritual that she and Jean had perfected.

Mother would take no notice once they had made their departure. She would be too busy making her flirtations to men nearly half her age; on Charity's behalf, of course.

"If you shall not make yourself appealing," her mother would scold, "then I shall cast the hook by singing your praise."

She couldn't really blame her mother. Lady Shalace had begun life as a poor somewhat distant relation to a peer, and used her own bountiful assets to catch Charity's father. She had never been accepted by the *Ton*, and she wanted more for her daughter. Her mother was convinced that no one was truly who they said they were, and in that, Charity supposed she was right. Truth was hard to come by in the *Ton*.

Charity certainly knew that gossip distorted every bit of news, but she longed for honesty in her own marriage, honesty and love; even her mother had that. She knew her father loved her mother to distraction, and she thought her mother loved her father too, in her own way even if it was only caring and mutual respect. There had never been a question in their devotion to one another, even when her father's illness had bound him to the house. Her mother remained faithful and had simply directed her energies toward their daughter instead.

"I want to marry for love," Charity had once said when she was very young.

"Don't be ridiculous," her mother had retorted. "Do you wish to be poor as well?"

Charity didn't think it would be awful to be poor, not if you had love. It seemed rather romantic to her to have nothing but one another and told her mother so. Only once more had she broached the subject. When Lavinia married, Charity had been overcome with happiness for the lovers. Mother had said that Lavinia, who often spoke in wistful fancy, was naïve and childish. Perhaps it was so, yet her friend *had* married well, and for love. Was it really such an impossible dream?

Mother had laughed heartily in a most unladylike manner, the picture of coarseness that the *Ton* despised in her, and Charity had never again brought up the subject of love with her mother. Charity had however spoken with her father, before his mind began to wander.

She loved the easy camaraderie that existed between herself and her father, and wished at least that regard from her husband. She wished for someone she could talk to that required no rouge or guise; someone that could see the truth behind the trappings and still want her for who she was inside.

"I want to say good night to Father before we leave," Charity told her mother as she completed her own toilette. They were off to a private concert held by her mother's dear friend, Mrs. Thompson, one of the greatest gossips in Bath. Charity knew there would be little chance of escaping the plotting of the two older women. The night would be a bore at best for even the musicians were little more than local names.

"Hmmm," her mother had said, as her maid came into the room carrying one of the gigantic turbans her mother loved so well. Lady Shalace put the monstrosity on her head and began to pull out artful curls to frame her face. The turban was turquoise and had several large diamonds studding the front of it so that her mother could show off her wealth. It was beautiful if a bit ostentatious. Charity supposed her mother had inured herself to the gossip of the *Ton* and decided to give it a path to follow. "Don't be long, dear," Lady Shalace muttered as Charity exited the dressing chamber. "I shall wait for you in the carriage."

After her last minute ablations to remove some of the rouge her mother had applied, Charity hurried to her father's room. She hoped he wasn't asleep already. He usually was abed early, but he liked to look at her before she went on an outing.

Charity was of the opinion that her father, was at one time, and perhaps still, deeply in love with her mother despite the discrepancy in their ages. Now, however, his mind was failing and he sometimes mistook Charity herself for her mother. Still, the best part of many a day, was spent at his bedside reading to him or doing needlework while listening to his stories.

"Father?" she whispered as she visited his sick room.

"Come in, Charity. Oh, you are a vision of loveliness. You look so like your mother when she was young," he told her and she smiled as she twirled before him. His skin was thin, but not without color. It was the look of a man who rarely ventured out yet was not so far gone that his mortality was of immediate concern.

"Only the best for you, dear one" he said, clasping her gloved hand with his liver spotted one and bringing it to his lips for a kiss. "Only the best; do you hear me?"

"Yes, Father."

"Has a man been chosen for your fancy?" he asked with a gleam in his eye that made Charity giggle. Her father often teased about her mother's goals, knowing full well that Charity would not be pressed.

"Not yet," she winked. "For, as Mother says, not all the gentlemen have arrived for the summer. We must view the whole selection before we set our mind."

All of a sudden, her father's expression lost its humor and turned serious. "Find a man who can look past all the trappings and see the woman inside; as I did your mother."

Charity wasn't altogether sure that was true, her father seemed blind to her mother's flaws, but she took him at his word.

"Yes, Father," she said as she kissed him on the cheek. "Tomorrow we will take the waters," she said. "Rest well." She hoped the healing waters of Bath would make her father feel better. She blew out the candle and let him to sleep in peace.

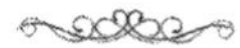

2

The concert that evening was attended by no more than twenty couples. Still, it was overcrowded for Charity's taste because most of the guests were not her friends. Her mother was overjoyed with the new selection of acquaintances, for there were several gentlemen to whom her daughter had yet to be introduced.

Charity was not certain what rock her mother found these rogues under, but none were husband material. Even her mother had to agree to that, but she did insist that Charity practice her wiles. She had been out for three seasons and was well on her way to being a spinster, if she could not manage a bit more effort. When her mother was finished cataloging what was wrong with her manner, Charity hardly felt in a joyous mood to attend the gathering.

Oh how she longed for the gay parties with Lavinia

and Julia, but both were now married and Charity was left to her own devices and her mother's machinations. "I wish the Poppy sisters were invited," she told her mother and Lady Shalace replied that Charity should cultivate more friendships among the daughters of the Peerage.

"Yes Mother," she intoned. She missed her friends to distraction, but she did her best to be cordial with the gentlemen to whom she was introduced.

Charity attempted to appear intrigued and even forced a wide smile whenever her mother's fingers would pinch the back of her arm. The sharp gesture was the matriarch's covert way of guiding her daughter's behavior and correcting her mistakes.

Charity was glad for the length of her gloves which would cover the red mark that must be developing after a half dozen moments of such instruction.

If only she were chaperoned by Julia's elder sister Jane. Then she would have no need to fake a smile. She would be truly gay.

She longed for the days when Julia and Lavinia were at her side. Even Amelia's company would be preferable. They had such fun. Charity had always surrounded herself with a bevy of friends. Now there were none and she simply felt lost without them. The hollow feeling inside, she realized was loneliness, even amidst the small gathering at the soiree.

Her mother taunted her with the possibility that she may remain a spinster and truthfully, the thought brought a spark of fear to her breast.

The other ladies were married and although Lavinia

was in Bath, she was not at this soiree. Julia would not arrive in Bath for several days, and even if she did, she was never one to enjoy outings. She had her own husband and household to attend to now. They had little time for their unencumbered friend and everything had changed.

This year was nothing like the pleasant summers past when the young women had been nigh on inseparable and mostly left to their own devices. Now that they were busy with their own homes; she rarely saw them. She so missed her married friends. Charity sighed with sudden debilitating melancholy.

"Darling," her mother offered an arm and a false smile though her tone suggested annoyance. Charity allowed herself a shamed grimace as the most recent gentleman turned away to find a more willing partner. "You really must do better. Once the crowds descend upon Bath I shall not be ever present to guide you. How can I trust that you will not go brushing aside every gentleman who offers you a cool punch?"

"I have a glass," Charity replied cheekily, raising her drink to prove that she was not in need of another.

Lady Shalace's eyelids flickered as she collected her temper. "Then you might have set it aside or watered the ferns," she groaned. "Anything but deny the offer."

"That seems a waste," Charity mumbled too low for her mother to hear. The truth was that Charity had wanted neither the libation nor the gentleman who offered it. Sir Charles Marbury was a loathsome creature who lost more to the tables than he had to spend.

Charity's dear friend, Mr. James Poppy had warned her of the scoundrel two summers past and she was certain the man saw little more in her than the weight of her coin.

Mother might have been aware of that if she spent more time learning of a single gentleman rather than tossing her daughter at them all. Charity felt a frown forming between her brows as her mother gave her a slight push towards the growing crowd.

"Wrinkles," her mother whispered, and Charity smoothed the frown from her face. "Charity," her mother informed her seriously. "There may be none here that have caught your interest, but you might hone your charm for the evening." Lady Shalace then informed her daughter that she would be watching from across the room. Charity expected a full report on her failures when they reconvened in the carriage later that evening.

With another sigh, Charity tipped her drink into the nearby potted plant and turned to join the fray with as much false pleasantry as she could muster.

She scanned the crowd obediently, though there were few of worth in attendance. That is until Charity's gaze was drawn by a young gentleman who was surrounded by doting women. Although his back was to her at the moment, he seemed to be quite the center of attention, flanked by Miss Macrum and another woman she did not know.

Lady Charity's eyes narrowed as she took in the gentleman. He looked familiar, though she could not immediately place him, that is until he turned and she caught sight of his startling green eyes. Then she could not mistake him: Neville Collington, the Earl of Wentwell.

They had danced this summer past and his emerald gaze had burned over her skin. Now, those same eyes brushed over her like a physical touch, and she looked quickly away lest he see she was watching him.

She peered at him from behind her fan. He was dressed in the finest silk coat which had been trimmed to perfection. Charity could almost see the muscles beneath the silk. She felt her heart beat increase with just the appearance of the man. Every inch of his stature exuded charm and nonchalance. Lord Wentwell was too beautiful to be real. His smile was confident as he stood entirely at ease amongst the party guests.

He gave all appearance of being engaged in the conversation with the lady he was with, yet his mind was elsewhere, other than on the lady before him, Charity was sure. He looked every inch the rake the *Ton* accused him of being. She was not usually so cautious, but she remembered Julia's conundrum with rakes last year. In truth Lady Charity only danced with Lord Wentwell, to distract from her friend, Julia's troubles.

The fact that he was embroiled in rumor for most of last summer, made the dance even more sensational. Charity recalled him clearly: his broad shoulders and his hand warm upon her glove as they danced. His firm yet confident attitude bordered on arrogance as he led her around the dance floor. She and the gentleman had only danced once, but that once had made an impression. She had found herself quite out of her depth with his banter. She was breathless in his arms, afraid she would disgrace herself and could barely answer his quips. She was no better than a tongue-tied ninny held captured by his deep green gaze.

When the dance ended, Lord Wentwell had been spirited away by some other female before Charity could regain her poise, and ever since she had avoided his company for fear that she might next be caught in a rumor, or perhaps it was because he made her feel naïve and childish.

Charity dropped her shoulders and prepared to slip away when a slight cough reminded her that her mother's watchful eye would not waver. She pasted a smile on her face, and without ado, turned in the opposite direction of Lord Wentwell to find a safer partner for her conversation.

That partner appeared in the form of Colonel Ranier, a portly gentleman of uncertain age who made her feel comfortable. She needed no guile to entertain him. Colonel Ranier, was a decorated war hero and a genuinely nice man, if a bit boring. Charity greeted the man warmly and was welcomed into the conversation.

The opening ball was the topic of choice. Charity found that she was a willing participant, for she too had looked forward to the event, if only to see who might be summering in Bath this year. Surely there would be some younger girls she could befriend. She would enjoy helping them on their way to matrimony. She beamed at the sudden thought. The summer was not wholly a loss.

She might still enjoy her holiday if she could find someone with which to share it.

She was just starting to enjoy herself, and became engaged in an animated conversation about Captain Beresford's and Amelia Atherton's nuptials, when she had the uncanny feeling that someone was watching her. She glanced behind to see none other than Neville Collington, the Earl of Wentwell studying her. For a moment, she was flustered and had to ask the colonel to repeat himself, but she rallied. Neville Collington had disconcerted her last summer, but she was better prepared now. She would not let him unbalance her again. He was just a flirt and a pretty face. She was a lady of the *Ton*. She would remain cool and aloof.

Colonel Ranier was telling a particularly funny story about Captain Beresford and Captain Jack Hartfield. Luckily she heard the story earlier from Lavinia, the new Mrs. Hartfield, and could nod and smile in all the right places without paying the colonel much mind. All the while she covertly watched Lord Wentwell from behind her fan.

NEVILLE COLLINGTON WAS USED to being the center of attention. As an unmarried member of the Peerage he attracted more than his fair share of female notice. It was no surprise that the earl found himself engaged in conversation with several young ladies. He often found such diversion entertaining, but none present were enough to hold his attention today. He wondered how he might manage to extricate himself from their company including that of the grasping Miss Macrum.

The woman was tolerable when accompanied by Miss Danbury, but no longer. He sighed and scanned the room, wondering if he should just take his leave. His brother Edmund had been unwell all week, and Neville could not enjoy himself when his thoughts were with his sibling. He hoped that his mother did not have issue with his brother this evening while he was away. Danvers was ill-equipped to handle the situation.

Wentwell had just finished his drink and was searching for the hostess to give his regrets when he spotted the lovely and curvaceous Lady Charity Abernathy speaking with a woman who, from the similarity of form, could be none other than Lady Charity's mother the Countess of Shalace. The Lady Shalace was equally curvaceous, but certainly not as lovely in deportment or in disposition as her daughter.

Lord Wentwell knew his own mother disliked Lady Shalace for exactly the sort of maneuvering that Miss Macrum attempted with him. It was well known, according to his mother that the Lady Shalace, the former Miss Lovell had caught herself an earl using less than proper methods. Trapped was more like.

Well, the lady's daughter was certainly not going to manage the same with him, Lord Wentwell thought, no matter how beautiful she was. He was wise to the feminine maneuverings. Still he did find Lady Charity intriguing. Watching her, she seemed nearly as frustrated with the evening as himself, or perhaps that was just her mother's hovering.

Last summer Lady Charity had all but thrown herself in front of him when she thought he might ask her shy friend for a dance. Contrary to her expectation, Lord Wentwell had not been about to ask the reticent lady to dance. Timidity did not interest him. One had to admire the bravery of throwing one's self into the proverbial line of fire for the sake of a friend, and yet once dancing Lady Charity seemed to lose her nerve. At least she seemed a bit more subdued as he brought her blushing into the conversation and the flush on her pale skin had been most alluring.

Once she found her voice, Lord Wentwell realized the Lady Charity had a rapier wit and a fresh perspective on the pomp of the *Ton*. His quips were met with such stark honesty. He found the Lady amusing and laughed aloud not once but several times at her candor. It had been a long while since he had felt such joy. Lady Charity had provided a refreshing outlook, and in the paucity of lively attendants at this particular soiree, she was the brightest among them.

Lady Charity turned abruptly from her mother. If possible, her eyes were brighter than he remembered. She blinked rapidly, and with a quick glance around the room, chucked the entirety of her drink into the decorative fern that graced the archway. With her cup still in hand, she turned and joined in conversation with the Colonel Ranier.

Wentwell paused. He knew Colonel Ranier from the short time he was engaged in His Majesty's Service. It would be easy to insinuate himself into the conversation if he wished to reacquaint himself with Lady Charity. He decided he did.

She snapped her fan open bearing it before her as if it were a weapon. In fact he decided, she was perhaps the most enticing woman he had seen for quite some time. He would be remiss if he did not renew their acquaintance.

3

Lady Charity glanced again at Lord Wentwell and realized he was moving in her direction. She felt dizzy, like a small bird about to be pushed from the highest branch. Charity ground her teeth. Her palms had begun to sweat beneath her gloves in a most unladylike way, and she felt as if she could not get a full breath around her stays, which were not in any way too tight.

"I say, Wentwell," Ranier said jovially. "You have met the Lady Charity Abernathy, have you not? Her father is the Earl of Shalace. Marvelous chap."

Charity held out a hand, but narrowed her eyes. She expected the gentleman to fail to recall their dance last summer. Surrounded by ladies as he often was, it would be a surprise to Charity if he could recall more than one pretty face in the myriads with whom he danced and flirted.

"Of course," he offered, a slight bow in Charity's

direction. "I was honored to partner the fair lady this summer past. Though I am afraid we have not had the occasion to renew our acquaintance since."

Charity smiled, flattered that he remembered her. "It is lovely to see you again, Lord Wentwell," she replied inanely while her muddled brain tried to think of something more worthwhile to say. She could hear her mother's voice in the back of her mind, even though Lady Shalace was well outside of speaking distance, the coaching gave Charity something to latch onto. She obeyed the instruction that she knew would be given.

Charity straightened her shoulders, and took a breath. The action thrust her bosom forward and she held her empty glass in both hands, just below the sightline of her breast. One glance by the gentleman would give ample view of both. As predicted, Wentwell's gaze took in the sight, and in fact lingered there until his gaze bordered on scandalous. Luckily the neckline of the dress was fairly sedate by her mother's usual standards. Mother wanted to save the truly titillating dresses until the opening ball. Thank heavens Charity had managed to have the most revealing of the garments altered before arriving in Bath.

Lord Wentwell, face broke into a grin showing perfectly even teeth and a dark glint in his eye, but instead of offering to fill her cup, he simply commented upon it saying, "I see that you are without refreshment, Lady Charity."

"So I am," she said, raising the glass slightly and Colonel Ranier hastened to say that he would oblige her. Taking her cup, he made haste to see it refilled.

Charity could nearly feel her mother's triumphant grin behind her. Rather than bask in her success, Charity felt soiled with the ease of manipulation as the colonel hurried away. She was of the opinion that Lord Wentwell had also manipulated the situation to be alone with her.

She disliked the façade and Lord Wentwell was certainly in the thick of such things. It would not do to tempt him, or herself considering his rakish reputation. Still, as far as Charity was aware, no official scandal had taken place around the gentleman, only whispers of impropriety, but nothing proved. Besides, he was good friends with Lord Barton, Patience's older brother, and no one was more upright than Reginald.

A little flirtation would not cause harm so long as scandal did not ensue. She took up the fan at her wrist, waving it artfully in front of her breast, both drawing Wentwell's attention and hiding herself from view. His gaze followed the path of her fan and burned across her skin like a physical touch. He was absolutely solid beside her in that moment. She could smell the scent of him and feel his heat even in the summer evening. She was quite sure that Neville Collington was capable of ruining a woman. In fact, she was sure he could manage it without even applying much effort and that was the issue. One look and a woman could find herself lost in those penetrating green eyes.

LORD WENTWELL BROUGHT his eyes firmly back to Lady Charity's face. Hers was quite a beautiful face, with full lips and eyes as blue as the sea. He smiled down at her. "Are you terribly parched, my lady?" Wentwell asked expecting to catch her in a falsehood, and apply his charm.

"A drink would indeed be pleasant," she replied smoothly. Not exactly a lie, he realized, as she tossed a look over her shoulder to her mother. "It is uncommonly warm, and Colonel Ranier is kind to fetch me a drink," she said as she fanned herself.

"Implying that I am not kind?" Wentwell replied, one eyebrow raised.

"A lady would not say so." She fluttered her fan artfully, or perhaps she was just a bit nervous, her eyes passed over the other guests, perhaps looking for Ranier. An unaccustomed stab of jealousy flashed through him. He wanted her eyes on him.

"And yet you think it, do you not?" He said drawing her deep blue eyes back to his face. "Oh, Lady Charity, you wound me."

"By my thoughts? I think not." She laughed lightly, falsely, with just the right amount of levity for a lady. "In fact," she continued. "I think it would take more than my mere words to do you harm. I believe you are well protected by hubris."

"I would not wish you any ill, even an ill thought, Lady Charity. An inspiring thought I would hope to stimulate. An amusing word I would cherish, but I would never wish you ill." He took a beat as he twisted his signet ring on his hand. "Nor would I get you a drink," he said, raising his eyes to hers.

"Then you are unkind," Lady Charity said.

"Quite the contrary. It is only that I would not wish to be absented from your beauty, not even for a moment, as you are quite the most lovely and vivacious in attendance here tonight." Lord Wentwell looked at her expecting to see the preening debutante, but instead, there was a smolder in her eyes; fire upon the sea.

"Do you think to turn my head with your cleverness? Your words are rehearsed, Sir. Do you repeat them to each young lady you meet?" the lady said lifting her chin a bit. "Or does the delivery vary?"

She studied at him through narrowed eyes. "I warn you, your honeyed tongue will not work on me," she said, but the flush of her cheeks belayed her words.

"As you will. But if we shall speak of honey and tongues," he said softly. "I shall be very kind, indeed." His voice was a low purr.

Lady Charity took a step back, snapped her fan shut and brandished it before her as she spoke. "You are a rake, sir. Both unkind and dishonest in truth," she said loftily, but he noticed she did not move significantly away, and her color was high, but not a true blush. He gathered that she was enjoying the interplay as much as he, and he wanted to test the limits of their interaction. It was, after all, not her first season.

"You *do* wound me," he intoned.

"You are easily injured then," Charity said. "I would not have thought a gentleman of your experience would be so fragile."

"And I would think a lady of such verve would thirst for more than punch," he said.

The heat of a blush colored her face fully now. "You

are too forward," she said bringing up her fan to hide her face and turned as if to leave.

"Is that so? I think I am not forward enough, but upon your word, I shall desist. But do enlighten me. How do you find the soiree, this fine eve?"

She stuttered for a moment at the swift change of subject, and then caught her balance. "It is pleasant," she replied.

"Ah, for a lady bent on honesty, you do bend the truth. Tell me, what does my lady truly wish for this night?"

"An honest conversation, perhaps an honest gentleman, but I despair. I shall find neither here, certainly not in such trappings as you employ."

"Am I not honest when I extoll your beauty?"

She ignored the complement entirely and said, "Even if you are honest, you hide it well."

"And I venture, that your plea for honesty is but a ploy."

"I assure you, it is not."

He pulled a handkerchief from his coat, and waved it about, affecting a much more foppish manner than he usually employed, as he whispered conspiratorially, "Oh, but what a cad I would be if I said that a lady's dress was ill fitting or that her maid ought to be flogged for the bird's nest that she left upon her mistress' head."

Charity nearly snorted with laughter as she followed his eyes to Mrs. Thompson, who did indeed look as if she wore a grey tangle of a bird's nest upon her head.

"For shame. She is our hostess," Charity said with little censure.

His voice lowered to a secretive whisper and leaned close. She did not pull away from him this time, and he breathed in the scent of her. "I shall keep your secret," he said.

"What secret?" Her face was wrinkled in that quizzical frown that he had begun to enjoy.

"I know you are not parched as you implied to Colonel Ranier, but rather, perhaps as floating in punch as that poor potted plant."

"Now, that is surely not honesty, but cruelty," she said.

"To the flooded plant, for certain" he said. And her lips quirked in amusement.

"Still, you should not say it."

"And the lady craved honesty."

Lady Charity tossed another look over her shoulder to her mother. Wentwell realized that she was indeed closely chaperoned, and he wished to see the unencumbered girl who was so bright and forthright last summer, without her mother standing by. His heart went out to Lady Charity as he realized her predicament. He attempted to walk with her a bit, to move her out of her mother's direct line of sight, but she side stepped him, staying in her mother's view, and he smiled indulgently. "Perhaps then, you would take it upon yourself to teach me," he said.

"Teach you? What would I teach?" she asked, her face screwing up in the most adorable frown of confusion. Almost immediately she wiped the expression from her face, and the cool mask was pulled upon her face once again. She was once more as bland as the rest of the *Ton*. Oh how he wanted to see that unguarded wonder upon her face again, and perhaps more.

"Why, to be honest." He said earnestly.

"I think that lesson is an undertaking for an expert," she quipped, with a slight laugh.

"Are you not up to the task? In all honesty, then what do you see when you look at me?"

"I know you are a rake sir, and honesty is the last thing to pass your lips." Charity made mock to turn away from him, and she caught sight of Miss Macrum who was standing nearby, perhaps coming to join in the conversation. "Oh," Charity exclaimed in surprise. "Miss Macrum."

Miss Macrum pursed her lips in a sly grin. She seemed well aware of Charity's game and Charity felt a moment of embarrassment, as if she had been caught out, for what she was not exactly certain. Charity wondered at the sudden tension. Surely, Wentwell was not one to be hurt by a bit of banter and they were in full view of her mother. There was no scandal here.

Charity brought a smile to her lips. She was never particularly friendly with the lady, but she was also never one to give another the cut. She stepped aside to allow Miss Macrum to join them, but the woman sported a particular scowl. Charity felt as if she should tell her, as her mother had often done, that such frowns cause wrinkles, or perhaps, that her face may stick that way. Charity would never have had the nerve to say so in polite company, still she bit her lip, a quirk of a smile escaping.

"We meet again, Lord Wentwell." Miss Macrum said

as Lord Wentwell gave her a stiff bow. “Miss Macrum,” Lord Wentwell said shortly.

He did not take Miss Macrum’s hand and for just a moment Charity wondered if he was annoyed at Miss Macrum’s intrusion. No, that could not be, she thought as Miss Macrum renewed her acquaintance with Lord Wentwell, and leaned upon his arm. It appeared, according to her familiarity that they were old friends.

Miss Macrum pursed her lips in a sly grin. She seemed well aware of Wentwell’s unsavory reputation, but it didn’t seem to bother her. She sent a condescending look towards Charity. She appeared to be aware of Charity’s game as well as the fact she was more proficient in its playing.

“Look at you, Lord Wentwell, ” Miss Macrum said after introductions were finished. “The pinkest of the pinks wearing a scowl to frighten tomorrow.” Although the words were said with a smile, Charity thought Miss Macrum a bit forward to speak so. This only heightened her assumption that the two of them were familiar with one another.

“Tomorrow is not what I hope to frighten,” he said in a dry voice.

“Why you will frighten the young lady away with such a countenance. There must be a demon at your heels, for such a black look,” she said simpering.

“No doubt,” he agreed. “It is called matrimony.”

“Surely, it is not so,” Macrum said. “I have heard that a titled man must be ever seeking a wife.”

“You are misinformed,” Lord Wentwell said. “It is only

a man on the rocks who seeks a wife, and then only a woman flushed of pockets."

"Could the woman not be flushed of face?" Charity added.

Wentwell turned from Miss Macrum to Charity. "Indeed she could, but flying one's colors is a maiden's ploy," Wentwell said.

"It is no ploy," Charity said, feeling the heat of a blush on her cheeks. She wished she could stop the coloring, but Wentwell smiled indulgently at her before turning to Macrum.

"Now, flying to the time of day is more the established game," Wentwell said, "For those more world wise. Do you not think so, Miss Macrum?"

Miss Macrum opened her mouth, but did not speak. A moment later she found her voice. "I am sure I do not know what you mean."

"Then why are you here?" Wentwell asked reasonably.

"Here?" she said a bit confused, and truthfully, Charity was also not sure what Lord Wentwell meant.

He clarified.

"Here," he said again. "Here in Bath; here at this soiree; here speaking, in this conversation."

"Why it is customary, I believe for unmarried ladies to place themselves in the company of unmarried gentlemen," she said with a small smile for Charity before her eyes went back to Wentwell.

"Ah yes, the marriage mart, the torture chamber of unbounded gentlemen, to the unbounded pleasure of all unmarried ladies."

Charity thought he was over dramatic, but she too did not find the façade enjoyable. "I do not find it particularly pleasurable," Charity interjected. It grew tiresome to be paraded before every eligible young gentleman in the *Ton*, although talking to Lord Wentwell was beyond exciting.

"Are you not seeking a husband, Lady Charity?" Miss Macrum asked.

"My mother is completely engaged in the matter," Charity replied.

"But you are not?" Lord Wentwell asked.

"If you knew my mother, you would know she does not require my help in the endeavor."

He laughed a short bark of joy. "I do know your mother, or at least my mother knows the lady. So the Lady Shalace is to do the choosing? Have you no say in the matter, Lady Charity?"

"Apparently," she said. "I must bow to her opinions."

"Of course you must," Miss Macrum interjected. "The opinion of a countess must be obeyed."

Lord Wentwell gave her a look, and then turned back to Charity. "I am not generally interested in other's opinions," he said and Charity was aware of a sudden coldness in his voice.

Miss Macrum seemed stunned to silence.

"She is my Mother," Charity said into the gulf, but she was not at all sure her mother was still the topic of conversation. "Her opinions are important to me."

"Of course they are," Miss Macrum said, reaching out to pat Charity's hand indulgently. "I am sure she is doing her very best for you. In fact, I have never seen a more stunning depiction than the one you present this evening, the picture of ingenuous charm."

Charity was not sure why Miss Macrum suddenly found her interesting. A moment ago, her eyes were all for Wentwell. Nonetheless, Charity was gracious. She expressed her gratitude for the complement and groped for one of her own in return. Unfortunately, Miss Macrum's garments were quite obviously a remake of last season's style. No doubt the lady was saving the best for when the rest of the *Ton* arrived in Bath. Charity latched onto the topic of the dress, which although not quite the height of fashion, was expertly sewn, and Charity did so often need the services of a good seamstress.

"I must say, your dress fits you perfectly," Charity said. "I must have the name of your dressmaker. She is a miracle worker."

"Indeed," Wentwell intoned.

Miss Macrum's eyes narrowed momentarily, whether for Wentwell's comment, or suspecting that Lady Charity was making fun of her outdated dress, Charity did not know, but Charity's bright smile caused her to reconsider and her lips stretched into a smirk.

Wentwell looked away seeming somewhat distracted, and Charity took the moment to answer Miss Macrum's silent question.

"Truly. You have no idea how often I need the services of a good seamstress." Charity leaned in to speak softly to the woman, while Lord Wentwell stood, his shoulders stiff and still. "The dressmakers so often misjudge my size and that of their tape," Charity said.

Miss Macrum tittered as if Charity had shared secret

of worth, and Wentwell turned back to them, his eyes appraising Miss Macrum for a moment. She preened in the attention. "I take it you like my gown," she said, her voice honey sweet, and her hands passing slowly down the front of her dress, and playing with the buttons along the bodice.

Charity thought that Miss Macrum's fishing for a complement gauche, but expected Wentwell would accommodate her.

He paused, giving her another slow appraisal which Charity thought might be uncouth, but that was before he spoke and proved himself a rogue.

"It looks a fair bit of muslin to me," he said, his voice flat and matter of fact.

Miss Macrum sputtered and blushed, at his crude comment and then pursed her lips, but before she could respond, he continued, his commentary in a cold and businesslike manner. "I should think that the buttons on the front of the dress, should be a great time saver, Miss Macrum," he said. "In the event that you do not have a lady to attend you."

Charity very nearly asked when she would possibly lack such service, but she was so appalled by the comment that she bit her lip and the hush extended between them like the calm before a storm. Charity felt herself color darkly in embarrassment.

Wentwell laughed aloud, breaking the awkward silence. The sound was sharp and entirely false but Miss Macrum joined him with her own shrill twitter. "You are so very droll," she said, laying her hand back on his arm.

"And you Miss Macrum. Are simply unbelievable."

Charity threw a glance to her mother to see if she was still watching. She felt so out of her depth. She knew she was meant to be flirting, but somehow she could not summon the same lightness that she had before Miss Macrum joined the conversation. She did not think Wentwell droll. She thought him a callous, full of artifice and insensitivity.

Wentwell smiled at the ladies, but the light did not reach his eyes. He gave a short bow, and excused himself with barely concealed haste. "I see some friends I must speak to before the night ends. Excuse me." The excuse was so flimsy as to border on rude and Charity wondered what she might have done to remedy the matter.

"Of course," Charity murmured. She wondered if she had done something wrong at his abrupt departure. She was supposed to hold the gentleman's attention. She tried not to notice that her mother was frowning at her. She discovered that she did not care.

Charity felt soiled by the conversation. Both Miss Macrum and Lord Wentwell had such counterfeit personalities that Charity told herself she was glad to be rid of all their intrigues, but she found her mind going back over the conversation to try to figure out where she lost her way. It was all pretense. How could anyone follow it? And yet she had for a moment. For a moment, she thought that she and Wentwell shared...something. Tonight perhaps, or perhaps during their dance last summer.

No, she reminded herself. All of his charm is fake, it is simply hard to remember such things when dancing with him. One must wonder what it is that he seeks so hard to hide beneath the mask. Although the thought intrigued Charity, she decided that she really did not want to know what lie beneath Lord Wentwell's smooth façade. She did not care. I am sure it is something horrible, or perhaps it is nothing at all, she thought. Perhaps he is just empty.

She just did not notice how empty until Miss Macrum joined the conversation, but Charity thought, when she watched the dialogue, rather than participating in its exaction, she saw a different side of him, a side that was coarse and biting. Yes, she decided. Miss Macrum had revealed his cruelty. His rakish façade may hide some true decadence, and if that were so, she would have nothing to do with him. Still try as she might the Lady could not quite convince herself the smile Lord Wentwell had given her was entirely false.

4

"Shall we stroll?" Miss Macrum asked, looping her arm with Lady Charity, and startling her out of her reverie. Charity felt trapped at once, but she could not deny the offer now. "I see that the Earl of Wentwell has caught your eye," Miss Macrum said.

A flutter went through Charity's midsection at the thought. Had he? Were her thoughts so transparent? "I haven't surely. Or he hasn't," she said glancing over her shoulder at the man.

"Don't look now," Miss Macrum cautioned tucking a gloved hand into her own and patting it as the pair moved along the floor.

"It is alright, my dear. I quite understand." Miss Macrum crooned, leaning close as if she and Lady Charity shared a secret.

The truth was, Charity never quite got on with Miss Macrum. She was exactly the sort of female that her mother would have wished Charity to befriend: full of artifice and cunning. Miss Macrum would have been called plain, if she were not so skilled in the presentation of self so as to make herself wholly appealing. Charity listened while Miss Macrum made conversation, telling her how she was on good terms with the Collington family; how she and her good friend Miss Danbury would often partner with Lord Wentwell and his younger brother, Edmund at events. Charity's heart sank. Lord Wentwell did have a brother. She remembered now. "Still, he is the most challenging fellow in the room," Macrum continued. "It will take far more than a simple flirtation to earn a proposal from The Rake of Wentwell. Never have I met a man so against the institution."

Of course, Miss Macrum was right. Charity was quite out of her depth considering the earl. She knew that, but Miss Macrum annoyed her, even though she was only repeating much of what Charity had thought of herself. She had known Lord Wentwell was not a suitable marriage partner. Charity felt her cheeks grow red with embarrassment. Still, she had encouraged the flirtation. Never had she thought that Miss Macrum would think Charity and herself of similar ilk. The thought made Charity's throat tight, and yet, what other young miss might she befriend for the evening.

"I..." Charity searched for an excuse to not walk with Miss Macrum. The woman made her uncomfortable, but no reason was forthcoming.

"Is that not what you are doing?" Miss Macrum asked. Had Charity been so forward with another lady, in the company of her mother she would have been scolded for her cheek. Lady Shalace would have taken offense, but Charity although she was loath to admit it could not deny that Miss Macrum had read the situation with expert eyes. "Were you not thinking to gain favor with the earl here amongst lesser company before the true test of the opening ball?"

"I really just meant to be sociable." It was perhaps the most genuine statement Charity had uttered in quite a while, but at the mention of marriage to the Earl of Wentwell, she could not contain a flutter of excitement. Still, she would not trap a man.

Miss Macrum laughed, a soft titter that was meant to draw the eyes of gentlemen, and it did. Charity smiled at the room careful to give no gentleman the feeling that he might be favored over the others.

Charity did her best to extricate herself from Miss Macrum, but the woman had now laid a hand on her arm, and leaned in to speak as if they were fast friends. Charity craned her neck searching for some escape which would allow them to cease this prowling though Miss Macrum had navigated them well outside of view of much of the room. Her eyes lit upon Colonel Ranier who had returned to their previous position with her drink in hand and was now searching for her.

"Truly I have no designs upon Lord Wentwell," Charity said. "Now if you will excuse me, I see Colonel Ranier. He went in search of a refreshment for me, and I must be returning."

"Nonsense," Miss Macrum laughed again. "One of

your status is not sociable with an earl without aim, and not with a colonel unless absolutely necessary. There is no future there. He is far too safe for you, Lady Charity. Truthfully, I seek a finer catch myself and I am not a lady."

"I do not think there is such a difference between ladies and misses," Charity said. In fact, some of her best friends were misses before their marriages...their happy marriages, she thought. Ones they achieved without subterfuge.

"In any case," Charity said added loftily in an effort to forestall any more of Miss Macrum's prowling. "I would rather avoid rumor."

Miss Macrum gave Charity a long, telling look. Her eyes flickered over to Lady Shalace, who was watching her daughter with avid interest amid the gossipmongers, Mrs. Thompson and Mrs. Sullivan.

"I do not think that safe shall be allowed," Miss Macrum laughed. "Besides, there is no fun in a safe fellow."

Charity had had enough of this conversation. Miss Macrum was far too worldly for Charity's taste. In fact, Charity wanted nothing more than to remove herself from the woman. She normally loved social events, but without her real friends, Charity wished she could return home to finish the book she had been reading to her father. If there was anything that was safe, that was it, but a single glance at her mother reminded her that she, unlike her friends, was still unmarried.

Her mother lifted her chin and inhaled dramatically,

which Charity knew meant that she was to put her shoulders back a bit more to accentuate her feminine figure. Her stays did not actually allow her much leeway in the matter. Mother already had her way, but Charity artfully used her fan to obscure the gentlemen's view as she took a breath.

"Come." Miss Macrum giggled in Charity's ear as she leaned close and caught her sleeve. "If Wentwell is not to your liking, let us join Mr. Fulton. He is a special friend of mine and quite a lot of fun."

At that moment, Colonel Ranier made his appearance and Charity had never been more pleased to have a gentleman fetch her a drink. The poor man must have been searching for ages for her. She offered him an honest smile of gratitude and thanked him for his duty. Miss Macrum raised one shoulder in defeat as if Charity had somehow disappointed her. She then wandered off towards the entertainment for the evening, presumably to find Wentwell, or some other man she meant to net for her titled husband.

Charity remained by the Colonel's side for as long as was appropriate before returning to her mother. The Colonel had been nice enough, but she was forced to admit, Miss Macrum had been right in her proclamation that he would not hold Charity's interest for long. Charity had done her best to test her appeal, but she was halfhearted in her attempt. Even the Colonel could tell that she was unimpressed, and they parted on cordial terms. Neither would search the other out in the future, but neither had they caused offense.

Charity made her way back to her mother, wondering why she should be envious of Miss Macrum? She did not want to marry Lord Wentwell anyway. He is a rake and a cad, she reminded herself. A rake is a charming lecher, nothing more. Marrying a rake or a lecher is inviting a lifetime of misery no matter what Mother said. In that regard she had to agree with Julia. After talking with Miss Macrum, and seeing how callously Wentwell treated the lady, Charity was reaffirmed in her duty to avoid Wentwell, no matter how beautiful he might be. He is not genuine, she reminded herself. He is in fact, the gentlemanly version of Miss Macrum herself. Indeed they deserve one another. Charity was not that sort of person, nor would she ever wish to be, conniving and deceitful. And yet, is that not what she had done to poor Colonel Ranier? She felt a hint of unease. She did not want to be fake. She did not want to be the person the *Ton*, or perhaps her mother, was making of her. Or perhaps what she was making herself. That thought was even worse.

Charity's mother sighed as she relayed her daughter's missteps. She knew it was wrong of her to admit defeat so easily. "Proper words and actions would have kept the gentleman entertained," her mother insisted.

"But Mother," Charity argued. "I would have been unable to find appeal in the gentleman. What was the point of dangling?"

"If Colonel Ranier was not to your liking, Charity, what of the other young gentleman to whom you were speaking? You seemed to be doing quite well with him until Miss Macrum interrupted."

"Mother, that is Lord Wentwell," Charity said, with an air of disinterest.

"Wentwell?" her mother asked. "The young earl?" She sniffed with disapproval.

"Yes, an earl," Charity confirmed confused. Normally her mother was all in for a title. Charity was quite upset that she had misread her mother's wishes. Lord Wentwell seemed to be in possession of all of the qualities her mother desired in a suitor for her daughter: wealth, title and all. Yet Lady Shalace had turned up her nose. Her mother was simply never satisfied, Charity thought angrily.

"Mother, whatever is the matter with Lord Wentwell? He is young, wealthy and an earl in his own right." Charity broke off as she realized she was defending the man. She told herself she wanted nothing more to do with him. "I thought you would be pleased," she finished lamely.

"Well, his mother leaves much to be desired," Lady Shalace replied. "Still, you are quite right, Charity. He is the most eligible bachelor in attendance tonight, though if rumor is to be believed he is also a rake." Lady Shalace paused thoughtful. "How is it that you know him, Charity?" her mother asked, presenting all appearances of shock and horror though with a slight upturn in the corner of her mouth as if she were secretly impressed by her daughter's flirtation.

"It was Lady Beresford who introduced us," Charity admitted. "Lord Wentwell is close friends with her brother, Lord Barton. I only danced once with the gentleman during the summer last," she clarified. "That is all."

"What did he say?" her mother pressed. Her need for gossip was like the thirst of a desert flower.

"Nothing Mother," Charity replied.

"Not then," Lady Shalace persisted. "Now, in your most recent encounter."

Charity thought a moment how to explain to her mother, but she could not. She ended, just shaking her head. "We exchanged only the most necessary words. I laughed once and then moved on without a backward glance." Or rather he moved on without a backward glance, she corrected mentally. "There was nothing to recall, Mother. I certainly would not waste my effort on Neville Collington. Miss Macrum may have fallen under his spell, but certainly not I."

"Ha!" Lady Shalace laughed. "It is a gentleman who will fall to your spell, not the other way."

"Of course, Mother," Charity intoned.

Lady Shalace patted her daughter's hand as Charity glanced toward Lord Wentwell, and suppressed a sigh. "Do not worry, Charity," she said in an unaccustomed moment of understanding. "All will be well."

Lady Charity knew that it was not that the mother and daughter did not love each other. Charity and Lady Shalace were as fused as any maternal connection might be. However, the differences in their personalities made it difficult for the pair to relate to one another. Although Charity had her mother's lush form, she had much of her father's open and friendly attitude. She simply could not manage to do what her mother wished of her. No matter that they loved one another, neither could have what they wished without the other suffering for it.

Charity's only hope was that she might find a suitable match as her mother wished. To do so she must find someone so endowed with rank and wealth, who somehow would also satisfy the yearnings of her own heart. The task seemed impossible, at best.

5

Neville Collington had given his valet the morning off since the man had been awake so late dealing with his brother Edmund last night. After Neville had managed to calm his brother, and bring him back to the present, Neville and his mother had been too upset to sleep. They had a cup of tea together to settle their own nerves, after sending the servants away.

"Do you think he will ever be right again?" his mother asked tearfully. "Or will he forever fight phantoms in his head? What does he remember do you imagine?"

"You do not want to know, Mother," Wentwell said. "Did you write to the physician in Austria? What does he say?" Wentwell sank into the chair exhausted. His brother's episodes took the very life out of him.

"Of course I did, but the man did not offer much hope, a combination of chamomile and caring. We have been corresponding. I shall fetch his latest letter." His mother started to rise, but Neville laid a hand on his mother's arm. "Later, Mother."

"Perhaps I shall write to him again of this latest incident," his mother said. "You can post the letter on the morrow."

"Very well." Wentwell rubbed his face. "We should be abed. We will speak of it in the daylight."

"It is day," his mother said gesturing towards the window where the beginnings of dawn peeked in. "I hear the sound of the lark."

"I do suppose it is," Neville said with a yawn. "Nonetheless. I am for bed right now. Perhaps I should take a trip to Austria to see what might be done. It pains me to see him so."

"I as well," his mother said. "No matter that he is a man grown, Neville, he is still my son, my youngest and I would spare him this pain."

"And he is my brother," Neville had said. He wished he had an answer, but he did not and so he went to bed disgruntled and awoke mere hours later unrested.

Now, Neville stood in the blinding light of late morning, with the awful night behind him. He was trying without success to choose his clothing for the day. Neville wondered why he was not still abed himself, dreaming of Lady Charity, remembering what delight she had been, both last night and at the ball last year. Could it be that she was truly what she presented herself to be? While still half asleep, he reminisced about her while he dressed for the outing with his friend Lord Barton and his friend's sister, Lady Beresford.

Neville had considered begging off, but he had promised to accompany Reginald this morning to attend his sister Patience. However, that was before his brother's episode had kept the whole house awake until the wee hours of the morning. Reg was also a good friend and knew of his brother's condition. He would understand if Wentwell chose to remain at home this morning. He was not fit company for any lady at the moment, but Lady Beresford was married and not one he had to impress, unlike Lady Charity who had kept him on his toes yesterday. He smiled as he thought of her.

He realized the cravat he had chosen did not match his waistcoat, and tossed it aside. He searched for another that would match the blue embroidery of the coat. The color, he thought as he selected it, was just the shade of Lady Charity's eyes. He ruminated over the thought of her eyes, and her form, and her uncommonly sweet disposition for an overly long period of time before at last shaking himself out of his revelry and tying the tie.

He knew why he was unhappy with the gentler sex just now, and it had nothing to do with Lady Charity. He paused in the tying of his tie as he became again caught up in the thought of her. She was brilliant last evening, meeting every quip with one of her own, and laughing at all of his jokes. He almost forgot that she was one of the devious sex. And dear heaven, she was beautiful.

In fact, the two of them were getting on quite well until Miss Macrum arrived. At best, the ladybird was a busy body, at worst...well he had already thought the worst of Miss Macrum, her and Miss Danbury both. He could have possibly forgiven the pair for their meddling, and conniving. It was understandable that Macrum wanted a title, he could forgive her for himself, but the fact that she, along with Danbury, had hurt his younger brother was more than he was willing to bear.

Danbury had thrown his brother over with much the same callousness as Lady Katherine had done to him all those years ago. Such callous action could not be forgiven, and if the Macrum puss thought she could wheedle a title from him now she was dead wrong.

Wentwell heard his friend Reginald downstairs greeting his mother, the dowager Countess Wentwell. He was actually surprised that his lady mother was awake and dressed before noon. After his brother Edmund's episode last night, Wentwell expected his mother to be indisposed for most of the day. Apparently she was made of sterner stuff.

Wentwell was still tying his cravat when Reginald came up the stairs to his friend's room. "There's tea if you want some," Neville said nodding towards the side table.

"No. Thanks. Its good to see you smiling at least," Reg commented. "Did you enjoy the concert last evening?"

"It was more enjoyable than I had expected, until that viper showed her face. It is a pity she was not remanded to the country with her vile friend."

"Now, Wentwell, let it go. There is nothing to be done about it, and picking at a scab will not allow the wound to heal." Reginald sank into the side chair and watched his friend fuss with his cravat, adjusting the tie, and then pulling it loose to retie it again.

"Fiend seize it," Wentwell swore at the thing and began again.

"You primp like a woman," Reginald complained.

Wentwell threw him a look. "Are you in a hurry?"

"I told Patience I would take her to the shops and perhaps the waters this morning. I did plan to do so before noon."

Wentwell paused in his tying. "I am not fit for feminine company this morning," he said.

"Tell me something new," Reginald said, drumming his fingers nervously on the armrest.

"You should go on without me," Neville said.

When Wentwell was finished tying his cravat, he found his slightly wrinkled waistcoat and brushed ineffectively at it before Reginald commented. "I know you have a man for that. It looks like you slept in the thing."

"There are reasons a man should take care of himself," he told his friend with a wink.

Reg laughed aloud. "So have you decided? Are we going to the Pump room or not?" Reginald asked.

"I see no reason to do so," Wentwell said. "I would much rather to the races. Why would you volunteer to ferry your sister about? Doesn't she have a husband for that nonsense now?"

"She does, but he is still in Town, and the vapors of Bath will cure what ails you," Reg said.

Wentwell snorted. "I have found the air in Bath to be quite noxious lately."

"Which is exactly why you should take the waters," Reg urged. "It will cure this melancholy of yours."

"I'll tell you what will cure my melancholy," Neville snapped. "Unfortunately I am sure the *Ton* would take exception to my strangling the source of it."

"I meant something which would preferably keep you from being remanded by the law."

"Humph," Neville said as he gathered his jacket. "Come on then. Let us to your sister, but I warn you, I promise to be vile company."

THE MORNING FOLLOWING THE CONCERT, Lady Charity left her mother still abed, while she took her father to the healing waters where he might be lowered into the steaming pool by his manservant, Wilson. Charity's maid, Jean Davies also accompanied them. The morning bathing hours for women had ended an hour prior. Charity was not at all displeased that she had missed her opportunity to soak, for she cared not one bit for the earthen scent of the hot spring and always felt a wash was in order afterward, which was of course absurd.

She and Jean took their seat in the gardens as they awaited the return of the earl from his dip.

"If you shall not bathe, my dear," her father had murmured as he was led away, "at least you must collect a vial to carry in your purse. I find a few drops in my tea to be quite pleasant."

Lady Charity nodded, though she had no intention of adding the limey water to her drink. There were enough quacks and peddlers milling about boasting their herbal and mineral tonics, all boosted by the healing powers of the waters. While she did not deny that the warmth of the water was a relief to sore muscles, especially after a long evening of dancing, she was not entirely convinced of its miracle benefits. Her father, however, did seem to do better after a long soak, so perhaps there was something to it after all.

Jean settled on the bench with a bit of needlework, but Charity was restless. The air in Bath was hot and a bit sticky with the humidity from the waters, but nothing at all like the closeness of Town in summer.

Charity didn't mind summering in Bath so her father might benefit from the waters. She knew many of the *Ton* visited Brighton by the sea, but the gardens and architecture of Bath were beautiful. She was perfectly happy to sit on a garden bench with her needlework or a book. She felt she was back in time when the Roman artisans worked their magic, and thoughts of Romans reminded her of Julia's paintings and their giggling. She felt desperately alone, even with Jean by her side. Perhaps she could convince Julia to go shopping with her once she arrived in Bath, that is, if Charity could escape her mother's ministrations.

Charity enjoyed beautiful things and was always mesmerized by the exquisite style, where everything had its place. The simple symmetry of Bath calmed her. She loved the mosaics set with glittering stones. When she was doing needlework, one stitch at a time, she often wondered at the patience it must have taken to construct such beauty one tiny stone by tiny stone. She admired the fine sculptures as well as the street crafts and often found some little treasure made by humble hands. She had always been drawn to the artists, sculptors, painters, potters and metalworkers who constantly visited Bath to share their talents with the gentry who summered there. She was a constant patron and a few of the merchants even recognized her.

In the past, Miss Julia Bellevue would have strolled with Charity through the streets as they admired some beauty of manmade design. Julia's eye for art was unparalleled, and Charity longed for the artist's companionship. Now that she was married, Julia was more like to stroll with her husband, Godwin Gruger, the Baron Fawkland. Perhaps one day, when Charity had acquired a husband of her own, the pairs might take their leisure together once more.

Prior to their matches, the ladies had chittered about their futures as wives. Laughing and wondering about the men they would love had occupied countless hours. Now that the reality had begun, Charity found herself quite outside of the loop. The others had found their mates, while she remained unhindered and wholly at sixes and sevens. She was completely unprepared for this reality.

Perhaps that was why she now found herself so drawn to the Poppy sisters. Through the years, they had grown close enough to call one another cousin, despite no blood link between the families. The Poppy sisters were, four in number, three of them still unwed with no prospects in sight. At least, not that Charity had heard tell of any serious suitors.

She sighed and glanced up just in time to see the smiling face of her dear friend Patience approaching upon the arm of her brother, Reginald. Her heart leaped for joy. Even as a married woman and mother, Patience did look somewhat like a waif, with her wide eyes and red hair curling around her face as it came loose from her summer bonnet. Charity could not help but smile, all of her previous melancholy melted away in the presence of just one good friend.

Charity stood and waved the siblings over with a warm greeting, and Patience caught her friend's hands with a bright smile.

"Ho!" the gentleman cried. "A bright face for this dreary morn." He greeted Charity.

"The sun is shining," Charity laughed at the absurdity of the gentleman's claim and felt instantly better than she had felt all week. "I cannot claim to compete. This day is lovely."

"That it is," Reginald confirmed.

"I thought Lord Beresford was delayed in parliament and you would not be here until next week," Charity said to Patience.

"My husband will rejoin us later. I have come with Reginald and Mother and their household."

"Oh?" Charity said concerned. "And your little one?"

Patience said laughed. "He is well on his way to being spoiled rotten by his grandmothers, but tell me, what brings you to the gardens?" Patience asked as she squeezed her friend's hand.

"Father is taking the waters," Charity announced.

"Have you time for a stroll?" Patience craned her neck toward the bathhouse which was teeming with patrons.

Charity glanced at Jean who nodded without looking

up from her needlework. “I shall be happy to wait for the earl, Milady,” Jean said.

“Yes,” Charity confirmed. “Father should be an hour yet.”

“Then you must walk with us,” Patience begged. The siblings informed Charity of their intent to stroll through the gardens and toward the town center in search of some small gift to send to London for a cousin’s wedding.

“I should rather like a walk,” Charity accepted the offer with a smile. The day was hot and the prospect of waiting upon the park bench for her father’s return promised nothing, but discomfort and unladylike perspiration. At least at a walk she might catch a breeze or even stop in the shade of a shop or sample some cool drink.

Jean would remain at the park to keep watch for Charity’s father and manservant, though there was no indication of their appearing for quite some time. Charity might walk in the protection of her friends without causing alarm, nor would her father need worry that she had gone missing. Bath was, after all, a bustling town, not quite as big as London of course, but it had its own charm.

Charity and Patience excitedly discussed about the opening ball, and made guesses about who might be coming to Bath this summer. Charity began to feel quite revitalized by Patience’s happiness. She admitted that she was looking forward to the arrival of the socialites that would be soon making their appearances in the vacation town.

“It has been nothing but a bore,” she admitted to her

friend. "There are few enough of us here to form a true party, and even then I seem the only one without a pair. It's quite ghastly," she confessed. "It appears, everyone has been married."

"And what of me?" Reginald feigned offense. "Have I been wed without my notice? My word, someone might have told me." He glanced over his shoulder as if to see a surprise wife there on his arm.

Charity laughed. "You have only just arrived," she consoled the gentleman. "For today we might be the only two to ourselves, Lord Barton." She realized that the comment might be construed as forward, but Reginald did not see her as a possible bride, and neither did she see him as a suitor. She had known Patience and her family too long. Although there was no true impediment to their marriage, she could not see Reginald so, although her mother would have had them trussed together in no time if she had her way. Still Reginald teased her as an older brother might.

All in all, they spoke more as relations than acquaintances and therefore the conversation was nothing more than a lighthearted banter to pass the time as they made their way to the shops.

"I am undecided," Patience mused. "A new parasol, or shall I trim a fine shawl for the bride?"

"Something for the house," Reginald offered, but Patience shook her head.

Charity shrugged. She had no need for such items for her mother kept her armoire bursting with such finery. She always wondered what a marriage might provide that she did not already possess. There was only one answer, she thought as a flush filled her face, for it was not something that could be gifted by a guest.

Reginald stood kicking his fine kid boots in the dirt as he listened to the women debate the usefulness of each item. Charity bit her lip as she thought him rather like a school boy who itched to run in the fields rather than sit for his lessons.

"Why don't we peer into this shop ahead?" Charity suggested.

"If you wish," Patience agreed, but "But I find I am parched."

"Perhaps your brother might fetch us a refreshment," Charity said, but Patience shook her head. "Let us but glance in this next shop, and Reginald might procure our drinks while we browse. Then we shall meet him to sit a while in the café. This is the café, is it not?" Patience inquired of her brother, gesturing towards the corner establishment.

Lord Barton lit up at the suggestion of a pause in the shopping. "It is," he agreed.

"It is far too hot to walk very far without a sip of something cool," Patience said. Charity looked at the establishment. As evening drew nigh, the room, may become more of a pub, but in the light of the morning, it was respectable enough.

"We shall meet you in a few brief moments," Patience promised.

"Moments turn into hours," he teased his sister.

"Go on." She shooed him away.

The gentleman raced away before the ladies could change their minds. No doubt he would have preferred a pub, but nonetheless, the room gave a small respite from both the heat and the women. He flashed Patience a grin before he left the ladies.

Patience laughed at her brother's retreat, knowing full well that he had no interest in shopping other than that his sister, needed a companion for the excursion.

A short while later the women exited the shop with little to show for their efforts save a string of pearls that Charity had purchased on a whim. Perhaps, she had thought, they might be woven into her hair or artfully placed along the crown of a hat she had been thinking to commission.

The two ladies went into the neighboring café to rejoin Reginald. It was all that Lady Charity could do not to groan aloud when she saw what, or rather who, awaited their return.

Their request of libation had been met with vigor, though it appeared that Reginald had acquired a stray along his journey. The gentleman at his table was an addition to their party, which made Charity start, though she said nothing and hoped her face did not show her unpreparedness.

Neville Collington, the Earl of Wentwell, looked relaxed as if he were in his own home, with one arm draped over the back of the chair and his trousers pulled tight. He and Reginald both stood at the ladies entrance and seated them at the table. Wentwell offered Charity her drink. Charm spilled around him and his smile was all too appealing. The same eyes roved her as if he could see more than she was wont to show. She picked up her drink and was reminded of the empty drink cup and

Wentwell's flirtation at the soiree. She put down the cup and immediately fanned herself, artfully using the contrivance to obscure his view. He raised his eyes to hers and grinned at her. She had the uncanny feeling that he was remembering the same conversation.

Charity pursed her lips to keep from admonishing the perpetual flirt. Mother would scold her for not participating and, to be fair, Charity had no direct grievance with the gentleman. Perhaps it was the heat that was making her irritable. Or, perhaps it was the pressure that she had been receiving to engage in such conversations with those of the opposite sex, when she just wanted to enjoy her summer in Bath. Charity was not annoyed with Neville Collington in particular. Only, all that he stood to represent, rakes in general and the artifice which kept ladies from finding a man's true nature.

"Lord Wentwell!" Patience said smiling. "It is good to see you again. Reginald said you had a letter to post."

"I do hope I did not inconvenience you, Lady Beresford, Lady Charity," Wentwell said with a nod. "It was an important matter that I did not wish to leave to a servant."

"Not at all, Wentwell," Reginald said, answering for the women. "We were all ready for a sip of something to cool our palate."

"Yes," Patience said. "I do hope you will join us for the rest of this morning."

Charity nearly groaned aloud. Her hope of an uneventful and relaxing morning just disappeared.

"I have already promised Reg I shall do so," Wentwell

said, with a slight nod of his head to his friend, and Charity wondered if he had not promised, would he have slipped away to some more gentlemanly pursuit.

Reginald was grinning like a madman, but he hid his smile in his cup.

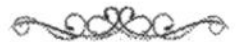

6

There were few men who frequented Bath that were not familiar with Lord Wentwell. Somehow they all seemed to take favor with him despite his ways among the ladies. Charity wondered if it was some sort of vicarious longing that the other gentlemen had for his loose morals. Lady Charity could not see the earl's appeal: refused to see it, in fact. Of course, Neville Collington was in possession of a dangerous array of features. The Earl of Wentwell was altogether too handsome, and he knew it. Every fiber of his being shouted the knowledge as did his artful grin and his glinting eye.

Patience was already on to a new topic, recounting their shopping excursion to Lord Wentwell while they enjoyed their slight repast.

In no time at all, Patience expressed her desire to continue shopping, and she led the way, guiding the foursome toward a neighboring shop, where various novelties were sold.

Lady Charity found herself flanked by the two gentlemen and she did her best to devote her undivided attention to Lord Barton and ignore Lord Wentwell entirely. Despite her determined focus, she could not cease to be aware of the pair of devilish green eyes that burned her from behind.

Whether she had intended to or not, she had somehow piqued Lord Wentwell's interest. Charity refused to be another challenge for the gentleman to best. She did not doubt that he notched his bedpost with his conquests. She would have none of it. She would not allow herself be so used.

"Reginald," Patience called to her brother as she browsed an outdoor booth that was bursting with bolts of fabric. "You must help me find something similar to Mother's evening shawl. I am certain that this style is just the thing for her."

Charity strolled after the siblings wishing that she had never agreed to this excursion. At this moment, she would rather be sitting at home or upon her bench with simple Jean than partnering Lord Wentwell through the streets of Bath.

"My dear Lady Charity," Lord Wentwell spoke her name as if merely capturing her attention were enough to make her swoon. Charity had to admit his voice was deep and smooth as butter. She turned away from him, determined not to hear or let the man affect her.

"Are you often in Bath?" he continued, this time close enough that she might not continue her pretense without offense. She could smell the scent of him, a pleasant sandalwood smell. Only a scoundrel would overstep personal boundaries so. Still, she had to answer or be proclaimed rude.

"Only in the summer," she replied shortly. Her response was honest, but not forthcoming. She picked through a box of trinkets, weighing each in her hand and holding one up for inspection.

"Do you not prefer Brighton and the sea?" he tried again.

"My father prefers Bath."

"Then you do prefer the sea." He smiled as if he had gleaned some great insight into her character with the assumption.

"I have not been often enough to make a determination," she admitted with a simple lift of her shoulder. She turned back to her examination of the trinkets with aplomb. She would not give him a moment's regard.

"You should try the sea," Lord Wentwell leaned against the table of baubles and Lady Charity tried not to notice how the artful cut of his clothing clung to his fit frame. He looked a bit rumpled this morning as if he slept in his clothes, and yet somehow his disheveled appearance made him all the more appealing. Charity turned abruptly away, a blush coloring her face.

Lord Wentwell began to regale her with tales of the waves and the salt spray. At one point he lay his hand, warm on her elbow and she nearly dropped the bauble she held.

"Here in Bath, the heat of summer air is heavy with

moisture and the scent of the mineral waters. I find it to be somewhat cloying and I do not enjoy the taste. The sea, on the other hand, ah, the sea sends quite a different message to the senses. It is freeing and quite overwhelming."

She turned to him startled at his passion.

"I should like to take you to the sea," he said fervently.

To speak so ardently was not seemly, but he continued, almost as if he were not speaking for her ears, but for himself alone. "The sound of the waves as they crash against the shore is intoxicating. It fills one up, pulls one in and rolls over the skin, like an ever present heartbeat." His voice was soft and sensual, and Charity felt a moment of unease with the conversation, though she could not quite put her finger on the reason. Goosebumps appeared on her skin although the weather was uncommonly hot.

"The clean salt of the air is quite unlike any other taste one can imagine," Wentwell said. "It lingers over the lips and leaves an altogether delightful languidness trailing in its wake." He looked at her then, his green eyes altogether darker in color than she had imagined earlier.

Charity pulled away from his touch, anger rising like a bright flame. She gasped thinking of the telling way that he described the coastal town. Their conversation of lips and waves and heartbeats was not inappropriate in any overt way; however his words sent strange feelings through her. He affected her sensibility in ways which made her insides twist.

Charity did not miss the earl's subtle context, nor his hand pressing on her elbow. She looked up and met his startlingly green eyes. They were a vivid shade of dark emerald, and he was looking at her with an interest that seemed to burn across her skin. Still Charity attempted to not take it to heart.

Instead, Charity cultivated a feeling of annoyance, for herself, and indeed for all of the young ladies who would soon begin their first season and in their innocence fall prey to Lord Wentwell's honeyed tongue. She reminded herself that Lord Wentwell was a dangerous man. He was a flirt through and through: a rogue and a scoundrel. He used his wit and smooth speech, much like one would tread a garden path. He took the path without thought of his walking. His speech, like the traveling of said limb was altogether immaterial. He used speech without effort, without thought and without sincerity so intent was he upon the destination.

It was as if his flirtation were a reflex, a muscle that must be exercised but that took no effort or care on his part to maintain. The habit was so ingrained that Charity wondered if the gentleman could make untoward statements in his sleep and dishonor a woman with the same nonchalance.

"Lord Wentwell," she began. "You need not play your games with me. I assure you, I have neither the time nor the inclination to participate. Walk alongside me, if you must, but you need not waste your breath on convincing me of the benefits of... of the sea."

Lord Wentwell laughed. He threw his head back and let forth an honest bout of laughter that caught Charity off guard. "Now you are incensed," he said. "How like a woman to get her dander up when a man would be droll.

I only meant to engage in a bit of witty discourse, not to cause you emotional upset, Lady Charity." He paused. "It is I suppose a woman's nature to be emotional when it is a man's to be logical."

Charity narrowed her eyes. "That is surely a falsehood." Certainly, he did not believe the dross he spouted. She did not understand Neville Collington, and although she told herself she should pay him no mind, the puzzle that was Lord Wentwell had engaged her interest and despite her best judgment, she found herself torn between wanting to know more and brushing him aside altogether. "And I care not for your tricks and games," she said loftily.

"Tricks and game," Lord Wentwell mused. "My lady, you think me so base as to imply nothing but subterfuge to meet some foul end. Oh fie! Again you wound me."

Still his words seemed disingenuous. It was as if he expected her to require his banter, and that he would dutifully oblige. At no point had Charity ever witnessed the gentleman let slip an inclination of true interest, in any female that she knew, Charity controlled her features and matched him, revealing little more than disinterest. She felt as if she were walking on moss covered stones and at any moment she may be plunged into the cold water of a pond, but still she kept on, excited by the conversation in some odd way.

"Quite base," Charity spat back, though her teasing tone belayed the seriousness of her words.

"Come now. I do not think all the ladies consider me so dreadful." As he leaned close, she could feel the power of his presence, but she refused to be cowed. She would not back down.

"Perhaps, they do not know you."

"Perhaps *you* do not know me," he quipped.

"Ah, but I know of you, Lord Wentwell."

"Do you think so?" he questioned, somewhat amused. "Then tell me, what is it you think you know of me?"

"I know that you are said to be a rake, and as such, I should have nothing to do with you."

He chuckled in a deep masculine way that put Charity on edge.

"From the look of you, I had not taken you for the pious type."

Charity fumed at the insult, so carelessly placed he had no idea what he had done, or perhaps he did. She fluttered her fan in front of her bosom.

"Pious?" Charity scoffed. "Which do you call me, Sir, frigid or forward, and then pray tell when flattery lost its appeal so that you now seek to deliberately insult me?"

"Not at all, my dear lady." Lord Wentwell smiled, and the action lit up his face. "It is only that I have found that there are two types of women." Lord Wentwell leaned close to taunt her. The scent of him was fresh and filled her senses. It was not often a gentleman smelled so delightful. It was some expensive cologne, of that she was sure. "The pious sort who tremble in fear at my rakish ways..." Lord Wentwell's voice had dropped to a whisper, his breath trailed silkily over her ear. With difficulty she brought her mind back to the conversation at hand. "... and those who have the bravery to engage in a little lighthearted flirtation; those who understand a bit of fun."

"Fun! Lighthearted flirtation?" Charity repeated with obvious disbelief. It struck her that he had willingly labeled himself a rake. Charity wondered what that meant. Was he shameless or might there be some level of awareness in what appeared to be a callous unfeeling man?

"Of course," he teased. "But what harm is there in a hint of verbal intrigue?"

"I fear the problems arise when the intrigue veers off the verbal path," Charity retorted.

"I shall follow where my lady wishes to go," he said smugly.

"I assure you, *my lord*, I do *not* intend to go anywhere with you."

"So you are pious," he repeated.

"I am neither pious nor party to your tricks. Rather, I myself lay somewhere in between. A pity that you have only met two sorts of female. Perhaps you might consider expanding your outreach."

The sound of his laughter was the music of the angels, but she had no fear of his appeal for it would be lost upon her. She knew his tricks. She was raised as witness to the most skilled of falsehoods. She would not be made a fool by some gentleman at play.

"Ah," he grinned.

Charity could see how many a Lady had felt a fluttering of the heart at such a sight. His teeth were so even; his lips so full. Oh, lud, why would she even be considering his lips?

"Then you are a secret member of the second group," he continued.

"Which group?" She had lost the thread of the conversation, much to her chagrin.

"Those skilled with words and savvy enough to withhold your attentions in an attempt to increase appeal," he said. "A difficult challenge, but not beyond my effort."

Charity's instinct was to roll her eyes and pommel the fellow for suggesting that she might be playing hard to get, but she would not do so. She told herself that his arrogance was getting on her nerves.

Neville Collington was an uncontrollable philanderer.

"I assure you that there is no artifice in my words," she answered with a cool smile. "It is in all honesty that I call you a rogue."

The slight lift of the corner of his mouth told Charity that Lord Wentwell was not offended. Far from it. In fact, he was enjoying their little spat, not because there was any sense of flirtation, but Charity assumed that it was not likely that the gentleman had ever been challenged so directly.

"But Lady Charity, there is always artifice when words are exchanged between men and women. Indeed, I do not believe that those of the *Ton* can converse without it. Mine is at least an obvious pretense, and therefore, an honest one."

The man spoke in riddles. How could a pretense be honest? The Earl of Wentwell was an enigma. Charity felt she must unpuzzle his perplexing behavior, but she could not see the way of it. He must find it amusing, she realized. Yes. Lord Wentwell was so bored that he played these word games as a form of entertainment. "You admit then, that you toy with ladies' hearts for your own amusement?" Charity asked, proud that she had deduced his aim. "What a gentleman might call a light hearted flirtation often left a lady in tears, or worse, ruin. The gentleman is rarely the worse for it."

"If a lady should choose to gamble her heart am I to blame if she would lose it?" Lord Wentwell retorted, a wicked gleam in his eye.

Lady Charity wanted nothing more than to spout her dissent. She controlled her reaction by applying pressure to the inside of her cheek. She felt her hackles rise as she faced the over-confident gentleman. She might not fully approve of the games this gentleman played, but she understood their execution. Her mother had seen to that. A lesson might be taught here.

Charity raised one shoulder and allowed it to drop in a show of nonchalance as she stared the gentleman dead in the eye. "You think yourself so skilled. Perhaps it is only you have yet to meet your match."

Lord Wentwell had the gall to laugh. It was an open joyous sound, but it was clear the he thought no lady up to the challenge. He, so skilled in the art, could not possibly be susceptible to the charm of one so inexperienced as Lady Charity Abernathy. It was all she could to do suppress her grin. His assured nature would cause him to play right into her hand. Lady Charity had no tolerance for toying with people's emotions and that was often why she found it difficult to aimlessly flirt as her mother wished. This, however, had nothing to do with emotion. Charity would prove to Lord Wentwell that he was not so in control. The gentleman had far too much certainty. It would do him well to be brought down a notch.

Charity glanced toward Patience and Reginald who were now bickering like two five-year-olds over whether their mother's aged shawl had a pattern of flowers or fern and which she preferred, and indeed if either of them had the gall to pitch the thing out without their mother's knowledge.

7

Lord Wentwell thought of the interaction with Lady Charity as he lingered about the booths. Of course, he was not truly offended. She was pretty enough to catch his eye, and he enjoyed the banter, but she was the friend of his friend's little sister. If anything he thought her ingénue rather endearing.

It was not long afterwards, when a slight dark-haired shop girl fluttered her eyelids coquettishly at him. Wentwell noticed that Charity was watching, and he smiled down at the shop girl who was all too open with her charms to ignore. She spread the fabric before the ladies with aplomb but her dark eyes were shuttered, and in a moment she glanced up, first at Lord Wentwell and then at Lord Barton. Her gaze settled on Wentwell, as he expected. He had a moment of pity. Poor Reg and that blasted red hair.

His eye strayed momentarily to the shop girl as she brushed her fingers over his, straightening the fabric, but his gaze went back to Lady Charity. Aside from her beauty, Lady Charity was witty and fun. Still, he was sure that Lady Charity was not so unlike all of the other dozens of ladies that he had come to know. She offered a challenge. He liked her quick wit and ready smile. She met him quip for quip without inane giggling, and that was refreshing. She did not seem to be enraptured by his charm, but he was sure that could be remedied if he wished it so. He was quite confident in his abilities.

She was lush and beautiful, but she was not a dalliance, and he was not for marriage. So what did he care what she thought of him? He knew his own worth. He was an earl in his own right, and he knew what that meant among the ladies of the *Ton*. As far as Lady Charity was concerned, it did not matter. It was not as if they would be wed. In fact Neville would do all in his power to avoid such a trap for as long as possible. He intended to remain a bachelor until convention demanded marriage of him, and as an earl, he was allowed quite a bit of time.

For the moment, Lady Charity was an appealing distraction. Certainly she was pleasant to look at, soft in all the right places. Still she was a lady of the *Ton*, not a light skirt. Neville had always harbored a soft spot for women of deep and particular softness. He was not attracted to women who were long of limb and fine boned like the shop girl who was batting her eyelashes at him or for that matter, Miss Macrum who seemed to think that she was making headway with him.

He could not see why a man would want to bed a woman who was nothing but bones and angles. He liked the feel of flesh in his hands. And of course, there was her glorious golden hair. He wanted nothing more than to bury his face in that mass of silken curls. However, barring that impossibility, he doubted Lady Charity, or any lady born and bred to the *Ton*, would hold his interest for long. Even practiced widows were only a short amusement at best. He had grown to expect little else. Still none had offered the honest discourse that Lady Charity offered. He found her intriguing.

By now, the skinny shop girl had grown bolder, leaning in to him, promising more than the wares in her hands, but she held no interest for him. If the gentlemen had been alone he would have told her directly that she might be more to Reginald's preference, but of course, he could not make his wishes known in present company.

The heat of the sun had reached its peak and Neville was beginning to wonder how much longer they were to remain at the shop. He was bored, and the shop girl, his station and wealth in mind, was all too interested. Neville was beginning to feel the pressure to disengage as the girl brushed her hand against his several times in obvious invitation. If she became much more bold it would be gauche. It was the light of day, and he obviously was with ladies of the *Ton.* Perhaps she expected him to promise to return tonight, but he made no such promise. He would have told her bluntly to desist if the ladies were not in attendance. As it was, he had to endure and ignore to keep with convention.

Lady Charity suddenly insinuated herself between him and the skinny shop girl, and lay her gloved hand on his arm.

"Oh Lord Wentwell," her soft voice crooned at his

elbow. The very sound of it was like the clear ringing of bells and her eyes were bright, so earnest, that he could not look away. "I saw a seller across the way with a brilliant emerald broach that I cannot forget." She leaned into him giving all appearance of a lover. Her voice was low and coaxing, her breath hot against his neck. "May we go?" Her fingers tightened on his arm.

Neville looked down into her clear blue eyes. There was a gleam that would go unnoticed by any save himself. A gleam that was there to speak a message just for him. She was all too aware of the shop girl's attention, and rather than being incensed, her lips quirked in an almost smile. She found humor in his predicament. Still she had appeared just in time to extricate him from the situation, as if an angel from a dream, or was she jealous of his attentions to the shop girl.

He opened his mouth to speak, and she blinked at him, long and slow. Sweet heavens, her lashes were long, and her eyes as blue as the sea. The shop girl was forgotten. There was only this seraph in front of him.

"May we go?" She repeated.

He breathed in the scent of her. "Of course we may."

Charity giggled lightly, a sound like music. Strange how the sound was not grating on the ears. No. It was a charming sound of real happiness.

The shop girl sized up the lady, and determined that there could be no competition. Wentwell realized there were few that could hope to best one with the combined position and form of Lady Charity Abernathy.

He tipped his hat to the lowly maiden and offered his elbow for Lady Charity Abernathy's grasp. He placed his hand over her gloved one, inching up to rub a thumb across the skin at her wrist. "Whatever you wish," he said in a low voice meant to entice her.

"My," she giggled in a low whisper for his ear alone, "I had expected you to be more skilled at the retreat. You have had the practice."

Neville's eyes glanced down upon the coy female. He refused to admit that he required the assistance. Yet, she had come to his aide. Why?

"You might thank me later," Lady Charity added in a husky voice as she clung to his arm in a moment of sudden clumsiness, forcing him to tighten his hold to keep her upright, the softness of her brushing against him as she stumbled. The sudden and profuse blush that filled her face had him believe that she had not tripped on purpose, and yet she failed to clarify in what manner he might thank her as she offered. A number of very inappropriate ideas flitted through his mind as he breathed in the scent of her perfume. It was the softest hint of lavender. Neville could not help but think that she had meant to imply some sort of clandestine payment was in order. He wondered at the slight upturn of the corner of her mouth, almost a smirk. Her lips were quite pink, as if she had been recently kissed, or wished to be kissed. He dragged his eyes away from her face.

After their removal from the shop, the pair made their way across the lane. Still, there was something in Lady Charity's manner that made Neville wonder if she understood the effect of her manner. True to form, few ladies could maintain their cool facade in his presence.

He had perfected the art of appeal, although she had proclaimed herself immune.

"An emerald broach, you say?" he asked in hope of redirecting the conversation.

Lady Charity released a frustrated sigh.

"I should never choose such a color," she revealed. "Green is my least favorable color." She faltered a bit as she looked up at him, and caught his wandering gaze. "But then," she continued, haltingly. "It should only diminish the effect of my eyes," she said finally.

She made the statement with aplomb, as if she had been told the fact a hundred times. She was neither proud, nor boasting. The statement of blunt fact seemed to reveal that her claim had been a ruse, and then she lowered her eyelashes in a coy gesture and he was uncertain. It was as if she had pulled the very earth from beneath his feet.

"I am sure any jewel would look lovely against your fair skin," he offered as she shyly avoided his gaze, taking special attention to admire a collection of embroidery swaths on display for the commission of crests. It was a bland complement, but a truth. One of the display counterpanes was bright and beautiful, reminding him of the *broderie perse*, his mother had bought, imported from India, an elegant and elaborate piece of embroidery for the guest bedrooms' done on whole cloth quilts. Yes, he thought, Lady Charity could wear nothing but a bit of bed linen and still look fetching. In fact, she would look very appealing clad only in said linens with his own crest embroidered upon it, or perhaps only in emeralds. Heat blistered through him at the thought.

Though her eyes were a deeper blue than the summer sky after a heavy rain, even a green gem could not diminish the effect. She seemed not the type to encourage compliments and so he kept any further comments to himself, save what had already been said.

She offered no response. It was a strange thing, he thought, that a lady would not do what she could to continue his commentary on her person. Most women never tired of complements. Lady Charity seemed bored by the prospect. Had she been a man, Neville thought, they might have been friends, but as a woman they had no recourse to such friendship, at least it was very rare. He knew several men who had befriended women, but those ladies were either one's own wife or the wife of another. The thought of her as the wife of another shot a spark of anger through his veins. Why he would care if she were another man's wife? He asked himself. There was no answer.

"I have no interest in a broach," she admitted. "Nor am I aware that any such bauble even exists."

"Your ploy then is to separate me from the crowd?" he teased. "Are you aiming to find yourself alone in my presence? You, my dear lady, play a dangerous game." Perhaps, he thought there was a quiet corner where he might steal a kiss. The thought was uncommonly exciting as it was broad daylight.

"Lud," she said, and her lips broke into a smile revealing a slightly crooked tooth. He found it strangely endearing. "I would not stoop to such measures," she said. "My ploy is to have someone convey my package," she said placing her boxed and paper-wrapped pearls in his hands.

He grinned at her. "Your package is my pleasure," he said with a slight bow, and he waited for a blush that did not come. She had already turned away as if his banter meant nothing to her.

Lord Wentwell agreed with her statement that according to convention, she needed accompaniment, but he did enjoy teasing her. He followed in her wake as she perused the market. She gave the appearance of no tolerance to his flirtations, yet neither did she do anything to dissuade his antics. It was as if she might handle his attitude with good humor and yet, somehow, at the same time cease to encourage any further relations. He was unable to gauge how he was affecting her sensibilities.

She looked up and then off into the distance where other wares were set up for sale. "In truth, I too should like to move on from this place, though I am much in need of your services," she said.

"Indeed," he intoned, and she ignored the innuendo. Instead of rising to the bait or even blushing shyly, she was direct to the point of bluntness.

"You see," she continued. "If I am to stroll across the way, I shall be in need of a worthy companion."

"Am I not a worthy choice?" Neville asked with a grin.

"What other choice might a lady have?" she asked. Again, her words were vague and enticing, yet demure at the same time.

"But surely an heiress such as yourself, must have a long list to choose from," he teased.

“The last of my list, to be sure,” Lady Charity lifted her chin and sniffed.

She was indeed a daughter of an earl, he thought, but what a countess she would make.

“Still, you shall do, however, in lieu of a better sort,” She intoned. Neville found himself smiling alongside her. She left no pretense as to her opinion of his character, yet she would not be put off from her own tasks. She took his arm and they put some distance between them and Reginald and Patience. He was curious now. What was she about? Surely all this was not simply for a shopping escort.

Wentwell glanced back to his friend and his sister. Reginald and Lady Beresford still stood in their argument with the seller of some bolt of fabric that had caught the lady’s interest. To barter the price was to be expected, yet Lady Beresford seemed offended by whatever it was that the shopkeeper refused to negotiate.

“I feel a bit faint,” Lady Charity breathed

Neville, immediately tightened his grip on her to keep her from falling, but she did not swoon. She only looked up at him, and said in a breathy voice, “The heat is stifling”

Her words were to draw his attention, he was sure, as was the movement of her fan. Yet it was the faraway, dreaming look in her eyes that captivated his soul. Beads of perspiration had indeed appeared on the lady’s skin. A single drop made its wayward journey from the hollow of her throat down...down to the cleft of her breasts. It was all that Neville could do not to stare as she fluttered her fan over the sight. He looked back to her face, wanting nothing more than to taste the sweetness of her lips.

Lady Charity had the form of a goddess and the mind of a minx. Neville was certain that she could take whatever she wanted from whatever man she chose, if she set her mind to it, but most of the time, she seemed oblivious to her charms.

Lady Charity's blue eyes lifted to meet his own and she seemed little more than bemused. She pressed the pads of her fingers to her neck as if she might pat away the heat with her bare hand.

Neville cleared his throat and released her unsure of what he should do.

Then in a stroke of sheer brilliance, for his brain was clearly addled, he recalled that he was in possession of a handkerchief which might provide the Lady some relief.

With the offer of the napkin, Lady Charity graced him with a benevolent smile.

"I am most grateful, Lord Wentwell," she said in a tone that was at once soft and endearing and held a husky edge of sin. Though he did not often consider himself tempted by women of the *Ton*, he could not deny that Lady Charity seemed to be a cut of a different silk. She was no slip of a girl. No. Lady Charity was all feminine. Her curves and stature were nothing less than those dictated for the angels by the Lord Himself. She did not immediately use the handkerchief to mop her face as a man would have done, but instead snapped her fan shut and waved the aforementioned handkerchief above her bosom and then delicately dabbed at the damp trail along her neck and chest. The motion only served to draw his attention to her flushed skin.

Neville had never wished that his hands could replace those of another, but this time, he did. She was both soft and steady, calm and cool, and most disconcerting of all, seemingly completely unaware of her appeal.

Lord Wentwell felt as if he needed a General to force his thoughts into line. It was a novel feeling, one which he had little practice when it came to management of such issues. Neville had faced the most precocious and sensual women of the *Ton* and emerged unscathed. He began to fear that Lady Charity's lush body combined with her innocence would be his undoing.

"My lord," she whispered, catching his arm. "I have a... particular request."

"Yes?" he asked. *Anything, he thought.* He could not be sure as to her thought, distracted as he was by his own wandering mind. He shook his head to clear it of immoral images.

Get ahold of yourself Wentwell, he thought. Ladies were not easily capable of causing Neville to lose track of his aim. The truth was that he had one focus in mind, whilst among the ladies of the *Ton,* whether they were aware of it or not, and it was not what most ladies might guess. It was not licentiousness. It was avoidance. He would not be led to matrimony. He had trod that path nearly to his own detriment. He was now wary.

Yet, Lady Charity Abernathy was such a strange combination of contradictions. She was both in need of his care, and firm against his ways. She was strong and soft, hot and cold, captivating and standoffish, but above all, she was a lady of the *Ton,* a lady to be wed, and not bedded until that holy blessing.

"I should like nothing more than to collect a potion for my father," she admitted with a slight blush. "You see, he is often much improved by the waters here in Bath, and I would like to give him a gift to relieve his spirits. Something, perhaps, that he might sip at night when he is weary. He is alas, unwell."

Of anything he expected the lady to say, Neville did not expect her to speak of her father. It should have been a douse of cold water on his passion, but it was not. He was genuinely concerned that her father was ill. He understood, more than most, how disconcerting it was when a loved one was out of sorts.

A portion of his heart broke at her words. She was so sincere and honest in her approach. Neville understood the desire to soothe the pain of a loved one and how disconcerting it was when a family member was out of sorts.

"I am sorry to hear that," he said.

Lady Charity's commitment to her father caused him a level of unease that he had not expected. It seemed such a noble request. Such a selfless request, threatened Neville's cool posture.

"Will you help me to find some seller of the waters?"

"Of course," he capitulated.

They wandered down the lane in search of some item that could be taken back for the relief of Lady Charity's father.

"What ails him?" Neville asked after a short while of silence.

"It is nothing," she said, as if suddenly thinking she had already told too much. Her father was a Earl. One did not let loose the news that a peer was unable to fulfill his duties. One did not say that his wife and steward had been running the earldom for some time now. No. One did not confirm such rumors especially to one such as himself.

Lady Charity blushed furiously. Much more flustered now, than she had been, she turned from him, and he did not wish her to turn away.

"I am sorry for your pain," Neville said catching her gloved hands in his own.

She sighed and for just a moment her eyes brimmed and her thoughts were far away from him.

She turned her direct gaze back upon him with a dazzling smile and the moment of weakness was gone.

"I am sorry," he repeated. "And will help if I am able," Neville offered while replacing a small bottle of smelling salts that Lady Charity had deemed unworthy upon the seller cart.

"Do not feel pity for me," she replied. "My father and I share a great love, a bond beyond illness and time. He is a great man."

"I am sure that is so."

Lady Charity finally selected a small vial of perfumed water that might be sprinkled upon her father's bedclothes.

"There," she nodded. "Now he might rest easy when I leave for an evening. He worries so for my welfare. It is only right I worry for his."

What did Lord Shalace have to worry for his

daughter? Neville asked himself. She had everything, and more. Or, was it something that he could not guard, such as her heart, which might be at risk? For the first time, he found that he cared for the answer.

Neville warned himself that those thoughts never ended well. It would be best to remember that Lady Charity Abernathy was no different than the other ladies he had encountered as of late – fleeting at best. He had no need of anything more permanent. More than that as a daughter of an earl, a dalliance was out of the question. Any misstep would lead only to marriage. And that he would not allow. Still he silently wondered if perhaps a bit of lavender water might be just the thing for Edmund's troubles.

Lady Charity dabbed once more at her glistening skin while she made some further comment that his mind could not gather. Her neck and the regions southern occupied his mind without exception as she attempted to find some reprieve from the heat.

She looked up at him with heavy lids. It was then that Lord Wentwell recognized that they were standing, quite alone, in an isolated way that bridged the distance between two of the most populated shopping centers of Bath.

If the Lady stepped forward but an inch, their bodies would be a mere breath from touching. Lud, she was so very soft. She turned her face up toward his; their lips, but a second from colliding if he simply chose to lean down upon her. Her breath was heavy, which sent every fiber of his being into chaos.

Lady Charity did not close her eyes in anticipation, as

he had expected. Instead, she watched him as he stood with a question in his eyes. Would she allow his kiss? He wondered. It was a bright afternoon. Even so isolated, he could not risk it.

Her teeth, the one ever so slightly out of alignment, clamped down upon her lower lip and as she worried it, he realized that was what made her lips so pink and alluring. A moment later her tongue darted between those lips, moistening them. The action did more to Lord Wentwell's control than he cared to admit. That tender flesh was trapped beneath her teeth while her pale eyes bore into his soul. For the first time in ages, Lord Wentwell felt as if someone could see the truth in him, rather than what he chose to reveal.

"I..." she gasped but did not continue. She licked her lips again, and dragged the handkerchief up from her bosom to her chin. She lifted her chin a little and met his eyes.

He stood over her, unsure of how to proceed. Lud, he want to kiss her. His hand snaked forward to settle, ever so gently, upon her waist. Yet, he did nothing further to invade her space. He watched her with shuttered eyes, leaning forward ever so slightly, willing her to turn her face an inch or so upward and invite him to press his lips to hers. He could not recall the last time that such an urge has so fully possessed him. All had been an act until now.

"Lord Wentwell," she breathed. Her words rippled across her full lips and he could think of nothing else. He nearly told her to please call him Neville, but he restrained himself. To do so would imply a familiarity that he could not allow himself.

He let his eyes close and reopen languidly to see her still hovering an inch or so away. He would let her come to him with her lips. He could not take, but only sample what was freely given. Only a breath of wind might bring them together now. He waited for her tacit approval. One small, delicate hand crept forward to rest against the beating of his heart, her gloved hand, so small upon his chest.

Their eyes connected and it was as if the world stood still. She saw him, the truth of him, he was sure.

"Lord Wentwell," she repeated.

His name upon her lips did something to him that he could not explain. It was like a branding of his soul. She had laid claim, and he was willing.

"Call me Neville," he said wanting to hear his given name fall from that sweet mouth.

"Lord Wentwell," she said again, with purpose, and the air about them suddenly cooled. "Do not ever doubt that a woman is capable of the same pretense that you pedal. She is no more or less capable than a man."

Her words were like a dagger in his heart. He knew that. God be good, he knew, and yet he had allowed himself to forget. The softness of this woman had beguiled him. Women were not sweet and helpless things. They were vipers. Now, this one, this soft angel had proven her point, a point that until this moment he had forgotten. How had he ever forgotten?

"Now," she stared up into his eyes with all the heartfelt care that her tone promised, yet her words and eyes were ice cold, "let us not dally any further in these games. I believe that I have made my point."

He moved his hands to her shoulders, and set her aside, with finality, though not ungently. He took his hands from her as if he had been burnt. It had been a close thing, but he remembered. He felt his own cool mask descend and once again he was safe.

"Excellent," she revealed a cool grin. "Now, the next time you are so certain that you are capable of winning any female heart, I only ask that you recall this moment. Women, of any status and fortune are no less capable of achieving their ends than a gentleman who is in search of temporary entertainment. Women are not toys for your amusements. We are people. Are we understood?"

Neville found himself nodding, much like he might if he had been schooled by his tutor at this ripe age of eight and twenty. A memory bubbled to the surface, one that left him feeling flushed and bothered. Lady Charity had nothing to do with the negative reaction that cooled his veins like ice. However, she had reminded him of the calculated ability of another determined female, one that had taught Neville how to guard his own heart against the supposedly gentle sex.

In his heart a rage burned for the woman who had left him nearly at the altar, and for this woman who so callously reminded him of his sin. He ground his teeth together.

Lady Charity strolled away with the confident gait of one who expected him to follow with no rebuttal, and he did follow, because it was custom, but he was wiser now. She rejoined her friend and continued her conversation with Lady Beresford as if nothing out of the usual had occurred.

Neville knew otherwise. He had to shake his head to process the matter. He had met women of high confidence; he had nearly married one of those calculating vipers. He had met those with pride in their form or position. He had never, until this moment, met another female so capable of duping him, save one, and both he had almost fallen to. He would not fall again.

Lady Charity had played him like a fool. Her skill and charm was both appealing and devastating, leading him to believe she was honest. Only upon her exit had he learned that each calculated word was an act, and although he was filled with a cold rage, nothing could have made him want her more. The need to chastise her as she had done to him was almost a fever within him.

There was little that made Neville's blood boil, but falsified encounters such as what he had just experienced were at the top of the list. Though he was expert in their exaction, he had only once before been the recipient of such gameplay. Until this very moment he had thought himself immune to such tricks. He had learned his lesson. He would not ever again be made the fool.

He had been young and naïve when Miss Katherine Dubois had toyed with his heart. He knew Katherine wanted to be a countess, but he also thought she had some tenderness for his person. She did not. She was beautiful, and buxom and entirely false, just like the lady before him.

It was Katherine who had kissed him, and it had been the first time he had kissed a woman. His mother had warned him: ladies did not allow such kisses unless they were bound for marriage, and he was willing to offer it for the sweet taste of her, but that taste turned bitter when he realized that he was only a means for her to catch another. She had used his young and tender heart as bait to catch another older, but Neville thought, perhaps not wiser peer, for that man now had a viper in his bed.

Neville had cried like a child when he lost her. The last time he cried so, he had been eight, when his father died. It was Reginald who had pulled him out of his doldrums. Reg told Neville, he had not lost her; for Katherine was never his in the first place. You are better off without the strumpet, Reginald had said.

Then the two of them had gone to a club and gotten roaring drunk. Neville had bedded a skinny dark-haired wench who was much more Reg's type than his own. Before his friend dragged him home and practically poured him from the carriage at dawn. Neville remembered nothing more from that night except for the first time in his life, he had apparently rang a fine peal over his mother when she attempted to chastise his behavior: a fact that she reminded him of in subsequent days.

While Neville might wish never to see Katherine again, Lady Charity had caused him to dredge up the past. As he considered her calculated attack, he became aware that the truth of the pain came more from that long ago encounter than any action with the present lady. She thought she had taught him a lesson, yes, but she had also wounded him deeply without realizing it. She had caused him to recall a grievous injury that had not and could not be repaired. He had thought himself in control. He had thought himself well armored. Now he realized he was not. He remembered that the dangers of the female sex were far beyond the physical damage that might be done by a gentleman. He walked in silence as the ladies prattled and Reg joined their laughter until they found their way back to the Grand Pump Room where Lady Charity's maid still waited for the Earl of Shalace.

A short wave and nod ended their encounter as Lady Charity rejoined her maid upon a bench outside the bath houses. She allowed fulsome farewells to her friends, while offering little else than a single raised eyebrow to Lord Wentwell.

He bit his tongue and refused to allow her willful approach to cause him anger. He smiled, but the smile did not reach his eyes. He would go and tomorrow, he would never have to think of Lady Charity Abernathy again, unless he wished to...unless he wished to teach the little chit a lesson. He knew, it was best if the pair avoided one another as a whole, rather than continue this game of which might hold the relative power. But there was a part of him that would not let the game end here. He had been bested, but he would not take the defeat easily.

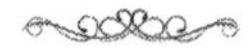

8

Charity returned to the house in the early hours of the afternoon. She was still shaking her head at the memory of her encounter with Lord Wentwell. It served him right that she had given him a dose of his own character. The gentleman needed to be reminded that his actions had consequences that would not be tolerated by all of the gentle sex, certainly it would not be tolerated by one, Lady Charity Abernathy. Still, she felt remorse for her action.

She liked Lord Wentwell more than she cared to admit, and regretted that she had, perhaps taken her lesson a little too far. He had seemed hurt by her revelation, more so than she had expected. Perhaps she had touched upon some sensitive issue. Charity had only meant to wound his pride a bit. Lord Wentwell was entirely too prideful. But she was not an intentionally cruel person, and it seemed that he had been genuinely hurt. She had not enjoyed how his lips tightened and the tic in his jaw jumped. She lamented how the light had gone out of his eyes, and he had looked at her with icy coldness.

Ah well, she thought. It mattered not now. Charity had no intention of interacting with Neville Collington again. In fact, she prayed that she might never cross the path of the charmer for the rest of her life, though that was likely impossible. All of the *Ton* knew one another, and as a daughter of an earl, she was unlikely to avoid Lord Wentwell entirely. She would meet the members of the Peerage and their families on occasion.

ON THEIR WAY home from the Grand Pump Room, Charity's father made a comment while they rode in the carriage that she had thought seemed out of sorts. "Do you feel better, Father?" she asked him, but he did not answer, and before they had driven a block, he was snoring. She hoped that the waters helped him. At least he seemed to rest easy.

Charity had not explained to her father the drama of the day. In fact, she thought it best that she not mention it. Though her father was less likely to ridicule her behavior, than her mother, he would not have expressed compliance with her interactions with such a gentleman. Charity also knew that he would have been right. She was playing with fire. Lord Wentwell was best avoided. The last thing that she needed was a rumor about her involvement with the ne'er-do-well. She resolved she would put him from her mind. His opinions did not matter in the least. Neither did his strong arms or his gentle touch or even the light in his very green eyes, green with darker flecks, like bits of fire.

THAT EVENING in Charity's dressing room, while Jean brushed out her hair, Charity shared the encounter with her maid. "The gentleman shall get himself in a scrape if he continues to toss his affections around to land where they may," she grumbled to Jean who was listening with half an ear as she set Charity's curls for the evening. "I want no part of it."

"Nonetheless, you seemed to have shed your melancholy, my lady. Did you enjoy your outing?"

"I did," Charity agreed. "It was wonderful to share the afternoon with Patience."

"Only Lady Beresford?" quipped the maid, and Charity launched into an explanation of the morning's events, laughing aloud as she told of their antics, and soon the conversation centered on Lord Wentwell.

"Your mother would scold you for your boldness," Jean surmised. Of course she was well aware that even her mother's censure would do little to dissuade Charity once she had set her mind to the act.

"You cannot deny that Lord Wentwell was in need of a lesson," Charity said.

"No, but few ladies have the gall to confront a gentleman as such," Jean said as she arranged a particularly stubborn curl.

"He is no gentleman," Charity intoned.

"Still, he is an earl," her maid said. "Do you not fear repercussions?"

Charity shook her head. "He is a member of the Peerage. He will not sully himself with outright lies and we did nothing which can cast aspersions upon my character. He has no recourse."

"Truly, you have no fear?"

"No Jean. I have no fear, for I care not what Neville Collington thinks of me. In fact, if he dislikes me it will encourage him to keep his distance."

"Your mother would not approve of this action."

"No. Mother would not approve," Charity agreed. "Yet the gentleman is such a rake I cannot stand to be near him and pretend as if I must allow his fawning for no reason other than that he is a man."

Charity paused thinking of how Lord Wentwell complemented her. He seemed sincere, but a man such as he, could not be.

"He did not seem the fawning type," Jean observed.

"Well, perhaps not." Charity paused thinking of the commanding way he had directed her as they walked, and his hand on her own gloved one. She shook her head abruptly. "But still he is not for me." Charity waxed long about how a lady would be run from town if she behaved half as badly as Lord Wentwell. To be sure, her reputation would be little better than a hoyden if she flirted with as many gentlemen as he might ladies. The thought brought color to her cheeks.

"He is a cad and cur. I do not have anything further to say about him."

"You do seem to have exhausted the topic," Jean said.

"I have not. He is quite despicable."

"Indeed. You have done him a service, I think." Jean added after Charity had calmed down.

"Yes. Now, let us wash our hands of him," Charity said.

"I think you are right. It will not do to dwell on one so base as Lord Wentwell," Jean added.

"Certainly not." Charity agreed and vowed to set the gentleman from her mind. Such a vow was much more easily made than accomplished.

Part 2

Disgrace

9

It was the evening of the opening ball in Bath. Charity still had not spoken to Julia, but some of her other friends had arrived for the ball. She was excited to meet them all again and exchange stories from when they last were together. Lady Shalace entered the dressing chamber, to make her approval or disapproval of her daughter's appearance for the evening, but Charity was nearly finished with her toilette. Jean had curled her hair into a mass of golden ringlets atop her head, with pink roses and the string of pearls she had bought in town last week.

Charity had already donned the lovely Parisian dress her mother had purchased for the event. The flounce around the neckline was truly exquisite and unique. The silk of the flounce was actually pink, not ivory, but so pale that it blended well with the ivory of the gown, and tiny pink roses, each made with intricate care sewn onto it. It felt heavenly against her skin. Charity felt beautiful.

She also felt blessed that her mother had made no attempt to accentuate her daughter's features on this eve. Perhaps her mother thought that the rouge may mark the silk now that the garment was on her person, or perhaps the countess was distracted with some rumor or other that her friends had been whispering about all day. Charity did not hear much else than that some lady of moderate means had been ruined. She did not care to hear the gossip that pervaded the streets of Bath. She tried her best to ignore it. She remembered how often gossip was untrue or certainly an exaggeration. One would think her mother, of all people would know that, but Mrs. Thompson, Mother's dear friend was a forever spouting fount of gossip and Mrs. Sullivan was hardly better.

"Do be careful, dear," her mother said. "It will be more difficult for me to keep a watch on you, with the crush of people arriving for the summer season."

"Don't worry, Mother. Every summer someone or other is ruined or has some severe misfortune to overcome. It shan't be me enmeshed in such rumor." Charity found that keeping one's sights on a happier note was much more pleasant than dwelling on others' misfortunes. Charity was neither surprised nor intrigued by her mother's information, but in a few moments, the topic turned to Charity herself and she was forced to listen.

"Charity, You were out in the sun for far too long this week. Really, when will you listen to me? Your cheeks have too much of a hint of color to be called rosy, and Miss Davies mentioned you spent an entire morning walking with Lady Beresford. Did you even take your parasol?"

"I had a bonnet, Mother."

Lady Shalace huffed.

"I promise I will be more careful in the future."

"Lud! What if you should develop freckles, like Lady Beresford? Can you imagine a more debilitating fate?"

"I shan't get freckles," Charity said. "I doubt they are catching, Mother." Though her cheeks did have more color than usual, Charity thought that the effect made her look bright and exciting. She allowed her mother to call for the application of a soft powder to return her skin to its porcelain hue, but when she began adjusting her daughter's bodice, Charity rebelled.

"Mother," she huffed. "We must be off. We are late as it is."

"Fashionably late," her mother said.

Charity sighed. "In any case, I am sure, there is little else that can be done to repair my features."

Charity had meant the words as a witticism, but her mother had only nodded as if resigned to the fate of her daughter's inadequacy. Charity refused to let her Mother bother her tonight. She was strangely filled with elation. It was going to be a wonderful evening. She just knew it. It was the opening ball! Everyone would be there. Charity could hardly contain her excitement, and even her mother's diatribe could not dispel her happy mood.

Charity expressed an interest in speaking with her father before they went out for the evening, but her mother informed her that he had been abed for several hours.

"Oh, no! But he so loves when I show him my dress before we depart, and this one is so very beautiful." She twirled around to show it off.

"I know, but your father has not been feeling well," Mother said. "I am afraid the miracle of the waters has not set in yet."

"Oh but it will," Charity said. "I know it shall."

Lady Shalace nodded. "I do hope so."

Charity was sad to leave without her father's words. It was not often that she ventured to an event without his approval and advice. Today, more than any other, she had wished to speak with him. Still it could not be helped and at least her father might have his rest.

Charity descended the stairs and found Mr. James Poppy waiting in the parlor. Charity had known him for ever so long, as had her family.

They had played together and called one another cousin from the time they were children, but she hadn't seen him, or any of the Poppy family since last summer.

"James," she said, hurrying to greet him. "I haven't seen you in an age. How are you?"

"Very well, cousin. I have come to escort you and the countess to the ball. I must say you look particularly lovely this evening."

"Thank you, James." Charity said and she asked after his family and sisters.

"They will be at the ball, I assure you," he said. "Francesca was fair bursting with excitement. It is her first time at an evening event."

Charity laughed thinking that it was hard to believe young Francesca was of an age to come to an event like the opening ball in Bath. "And is your father escorting your mother and sisters?"

"Yes," he replied. "Along with my brother."

"Your brother? Michael is in Bath?" She laughed. "Has there been a fire in London that I have not heard tell of? Has his townhouse burned to the ground?" Charity enjoyed teasing the Poppy brothers about their peculiar ways. "I thought he must love the smell of London in the summer."

James laughed. "He has indeed joined us here in Bath for the summer. Father insists he take a bride. He is not pleased."

"Why ever not? A man of quality must ever be searching for a wife."

James just shook his head. "My brother is a strange and moody man," James said. "He abhors fun."

"Perhaps we might change that," Charity suggested.

James Poppy raised a dubious eyebrow.

Michael Poppy was a resolute bachelor who preferred to be left to himself. In fact, Charity very much doubted that he took any enjoyment in social engagements. It was his serious nature that led him so. Every action or reaction must have a purpose and, unless with good cause, frivolous socializing was beyond his ability to justify. Charity had always thought this strange because his younger brother and sisters were all very open and friendly. Though the Poppy ladies preferred their quaint life on the country estate, they were always thrilled to mingle with the crowds of London or Bath when given the opportunity.

"And what of you, cousin? Are you searching for a wife?" Charity asked.

"I may have my eye on a certain lady," he said enigmatically.

Charity smiled. She had never truly considered the Poppy brothers as potential suitors. Mother would not approve for they were neither titled nor in possession of enough wealth to suit her fancy. However, Charity could not deny that their character was pleasing and even their features were the sort that were pleasant to look at.

She accepted the offer of Mr. James Poppy's arm and wondered whether she might become a permanent fixture there at some point.

More than anything, Charity was attached to James' sisters. Alfreda, Roberta, and Francesca had long passed letters back and forth between their country home and Charity's London townhome or her father's country seat, depending upon where she and her parents were in residence. It was not until the summer of her tenth year that she spent with the ladies that she truly began to improve as a horsewoman. Truth be told, there were few that could match the Poppys in that skill, and it was their eldest sister, Constance who had taught Charity to sit a horse. Charity had learned enough to make her claim to competence, and although she did not enjoy the hunt. She did love a leisurely ride through the pastures or park alongside one of the sisters.

Her knowledge of the Poppy brothers was less extensive. Often they had been away on some business or other on behalf of their father's estate. They were both educated and successful in the management of their house, though their prospects for improvement seemed to have reached its zenith.

Charity wondered aloud if she might again visit their estate. Lady Shalace, who had joined the young pair as they climbed into the carriage, harrumphed and made a disparaging comment about the dust and wind that whipped through every inch of the countryside. Charity did not mind, for in her opinion, the beauty of the land more than compensated for the dirt.

James assured her that his sisters would be more than willing to host Lady Charity for a month or so and Charity made a note to speak with Francesca on the topic. Besides, Charity thought, it was always a relief to have some time away from the watchful eye of her mother. The Lady Shalace would find some excuse or other to avoid the trip. Jean should accompany Charity as long as she was not yet wed. Charity felt a pang of distress at the thought. After she was wed, she would only visit at her husband's whim. Of course, she might visit with her husband. Or, perhaps, he might chose that they would not visit at all.

Charity closed her fan and held it in both hands, twisting it nervously between her fingers.

Lady Shalace's hand snaked out as she rapped her daughter sharply on the wrist. Startled more than hurt, Charity looked up, abashed, for she had not even realized that she had given in to her nervous habit of twisting her fan. She had cracked several of the delicate fans in her first season, but she thought that she had broken the habit. She wondered what worry had reared its ugly head to bring it back. The thought of worry brought to

Charity's mind picture of Lord Wentwell's face, though his features were far from ugly. She sighed wondering if the earl would be in attendance tonight. It was most likely; no one in Bath would choose to miss the opening ball.

A sharp glare from her mother was all the chastisement that was necessary. The countess had timed her correction for the moment when Mr. Poppy had been gazing out of the window, and the entire exchange went unnoticed for his part.

10

As Charity and Lady Shalace, with James Poppy as their escort, descended from their carriage after the short ride, a slight breeze carried the blissful scent of flowers to them. The Assembly Room was where the ball that generally opened the Bath summer season was held. Still the name was a misnomer, because unless it rained, the ball was rarely contained within the room itself, but instead spilled out on to the beautiful grounds and gardens. Charity had been here before, but the venue could not help but amaze. The place was awe inspiring in both beauty and size. Outside in the courtyard were gardens and palisades and arches all reminiscent of the Romans who built much of the city. Pools and fountains and flowers adorned every inch of the place. Balconies lined the outer edge on a second and third floor, where mosaics depicted ancient stories.

Although the smells in Bath were mostly pleasant, Charity touched a perfumed handkerchief to her lips.

She was warm and felt she would have a slight pink glow by the time they reached the Grand Pump Room Hotel; no rouge needed, but sweat collecting on her upper lip would be gauche. As she used her own handkerchief to pat the sweat from her lip, she thought of the handkerchief that Lord Wentwell had shared with her at the shops. She found herself glancing around to see if he was in attendance, and then she stopped her wandering eye. She did not care. It could make absolutely no difference at all to her if he was in attendance or not. James escorted her forward and she commented that the refreshment served at the ball would be pleasant. She was parched. There was also a fountain inside where one could drink the medicinal waters, but she found the taste off-putting.

The room was a crush. Even spilling out of doors, the place was full to overflowing. Hundreds of ladies and gentlemen were gathered around pools and fountains. The place was lighted as if it were daylight with lanterns hung everywhere. In a daze, as her eyes skimmed over the heads of the crowd before her, she wondered if somewhere in that crowd was her future husband. The thought gave her pause. One glance over toward her mother revealed a similar line of thought in the lady's head. Pursed lips with a slight lift at the corners meant that the countess was pleased with the sheer number of gentlemen in attendance. Charity would be expected to be accommodating to someone or other. If she played her cards right, she might be able to hide amongst the crowd outside of her mother's range of influence. Then, she might actually enjoy the evening in the presence of her friends.

Her mother's whisper in her ear naming several introductions that she must wheedle out of the crowd left Charity feeling less excited for the evening that she had hoped. There were tasks to accomplish, despite the heat, that would take all of her focus and charm to achieve.

Still once inside the ballroom, Charity and James slipped away from the Lady Shalace, who was caught up by a snare of busybodies recruiting for some philanthropic venture. Mrs. Thompson was in the midst of it, so Charity thought her mother would be some time extricating herself. Charity found some friends of her own, including the Poppy sisters, among the crush of people. The Poppy sisters greeted Charity with a warm embrace and they began to share plans for the rest of the summer in Bath.

Lady Beresford joined their number, while several other ladies scanned the crowd for prospects. Charity didn't comment on the subject until Patience prodded her gently. "And you, Charity? Has a gentleman caught your eye?"

Charity startled at the innocent question, as if Patience knew she had been thinking of the Earl of Wentwell. Charity would have quizzed Patience upon her companion for the strange bit of shopping they had done, but Reginald appeared at his sister's elbow, and Charity felt uncomfortable talking about Lord Wentwell with the gentleman's acquaintance here at hand.

Instead, she changed the subject. "Is your Lord Beresford still not arrived in Bath?" she asked of Patience.

"My husband arrived earlier today with his brother, Samuel and Amelia although they are staying with her Aunt Ebba. The Beresford townhouse was getting quite crowded."

"And my own Captain Hartfield has arrived with the fleet," Lavinia added as she appeared at Charity's shoulder. The former Miss Lavinia Grant had married the dashing Captain Johnathan Hartfield of the Royal Navy.

Charity smiled brightly at her friend, and turned to see that she had also arrived in the company of Julia, the newly made Baroness Fawkland.

Charity barely suppressed a squeal at the pair's arrival.

Julia greeted Charity warmly and asked after her mother.

Charity grimaced.

"Still quite the same then," Lavinia teased, her laughter bubbling from her. All three women had to smile. The young Mrs. Hartfield resembled nothing so much as a small blond China doll. Lavinia had traveled to Bath with Charity to await her husband, but Charity had not seen Julia since her wedding and she had missed her quiet friend these past few months.

"Married life seems to agree with you, Baroness." Charity said with a grin.

Julia blushed shyly still not used to her new title as Baroness Fawkland.

Julia was quite tall with a vast quantity of dark locks which normally tumbled to her shoulders in unruly curls. Still nothing could dispel her stately beauty. Today her hair was caught up in a more matronly style. It still curled, but it was pulled up in jeweled comb. Charity always wondered how long it took Julia's maid to arrange the curls just so. She must have to sit for hours. Charity shuddered at the thought. She was glad that Jean was deft and quick with her own locks.

"Why didn't you send word you were in Bath?" Charity continued. "We might have had tea and talked." The girls had always had tea together when Julia arrived in Bath, and they talked about their plans for the summer. It was practically a tradition.

"Lord Fawkland and I got in after tea time yesterday, and we had so much to do," Julia admitted and Charity suppressed her pang of sadness at the broken tradition with the promise that they would have tea another afternoon. Julia was married, but still she knew how little Julia liked large gatherings, and the ballroom was particularly a crush.

"I did not really expect to see you here, Julia," Charity said. "I know you hate crowds."

"Lord Fawkland reminded me that as a baroness, I have a duty to be seen. Anyway, I could hardly stay away," Julia said. "Lavinia twisted my arm most ardently. After all, what sort of friends would we be to leave you here alone for the opening ball, when it has always been us three?"

For a moment, Charity felt almost at home. She had her friends around her, but when Baron Fawkland returned with drinks for his wife and Lavinia, and the topic turned to redecorating Julia's townhouse in Bath, she felt somewhat out of place in the matronly conversation.

Charity watched with no small amount of jealousy as her friends held on to the arms of their new husbands. Charity was amazed at how quickly things might change. Only last summer the three ladies had been giggling and weaving though the crowds in pursuit of love together. Now, Charity felt like a spinster, left behind as the two of them shared secrets with their spouses. In no time at all they would have children and she feared they would grow even more apart.

She shook that thought from her head. Charity was nowhere near the age of a spinster. Her mother's lectures must have been taking hold of her thoughts because Charity knew well that she still had many years before she was past her prime.

She turned her attention to the unmarried ladies in their party: the three younger Poppy sisters, Alfreda, Roberta and Francesca, as well as their friend Miss Flora Muirwood. Flora was shorter than the Poppy's with a sallow complexion. She had dark hair and dark eyebrows that resisted being arched which gave her a serious expression. With the crowd of chattering females around her, Charity learned a great deal of the gossip running through the summer season as they waited and weighed the different gentlemen who had come to Bath.

"Mr. Crafton, over there," Roberta Poppy gave a covert nod to the gentleman across the way, "made quite a fool of himself today. I heard tell."

"What source?" James gasped in mock surprise.

"Why, you, of course!" his sister replied giving her brother a little push. "Go on then. Tell the tale."

James went on to share that this afternoon past he witnessed one Mr. Crafton being bodily expelled from the gaming room at nearly midday.

"For shame, Mr. Poppy, spreading gossip," Julia admonished him. "You should know better."

"I shall bow to your chastisement, Lady Fawkland," he said with a literal bow, and Charity found herself smiling.

"Mr. Crafton has a...more sober countenance tonight," James observed. "It is astonishing that he has managed to join us." His tone implied that he was not fond of Mr. Crafton, though Charity knew few who were. The gentleman was known well throughout Bath as one who fell too far into his cups, often making some scene or another. True ladies knew well to give him a wide berth.

"It appears the fleet has landed," Baron Fawkland said as several men in naval dress uniforms entered the ballroom.

Patience's eyes took in the new arrivals and she caught Charity's arm. "Oh, do look! Amelia and Captain Beresford have arrived. Let us go speak to them. You might offer your congratulations." Charity nodded to Patience but hesitated as several of the men moved to greet the new arrivals. When Charity has last spoken socially with Lady Amelia, she had cross words for her. There was of course, the event of the Duke of Ely's funeral, but Lady Amelia had been too distraught to truly speak, and Charity had yet not apologized.

"Go on," Charity said. "I will join you shortly." In

truth, Charity could not find it in herself to approach Lady Amelia until she apologized for her unkind words, and that would not happen in so public a place. Charity turned back to the Poppys, determined to have a good time and put all the intrigues of finding a husband in the background for the moment. She was inundated with offers to dance and laughing, she accepted. After several dances she returned to the section of the ball room the Poppys had claimed for their own.

She noticed Miss Macrum, and wondered aloud, "Where is Miss Danbury?" The two women were not often seen apart. The detail was notable. Neither Miss Macrum, nor Miss Danbury would wish to miss such a varied array of gentlemen for single evening. No one who was anyone missed the opening ball of the Bath's summer season.

The crowd fell silent around Charity. The buzz of the room carried on, but Charity's circle of friends stared back at her with wide, shocked eyes as if she had said something scandalous.

"What is it?" Charity asked with a shake of her head. "Have I missed something?"

"Something?" Francesca laughed. "Only everything!"

The youngest of the Poppy sisters linked her arm through her friend's and moved close to whisper the tale of intrigue and scandal.

"Miss Danbury has removed from Bath," Franny murmured. The others stepped closer to hear the sweet gossip retold, adding their own nods and details as she went.

"No!" Charity gasped. There were only two reasons

why a lady might remove at the height of the social season, death or dishonor.

"She has returned to her country house," Alfreda said. "Practically flogged by that dragon of a chaperone she has. Although it is no wonder..."

Dishonor it was then. "Mrs. Mott?" Charity was having trouble catching up to this particular bit of gossip, and how far along it went.

"Tis true," Lavinia nodded. "Their townhouse is across the road from my aunt's and it stands empty. The entire family has left: her sisters, and her elderly aunt. Her father seemed in quite a rage at the time of their departure."

"They never even bid farewell, though they had borrowed our horses the day before," James added with a shake of her head.

"How rude," Roberta commented.

"This is all very suspect," Julia said. "But I will not add to the rumor, nor should you Lavinia. You know how these things take on a mind of their own."

"True," Charity said. "Perhaps Miss Danbury expected an offer?"

"Perhaps," Alfreda said, "but such things almost always turn out badly for the lady."

"I suppose we shall not see her again for a year," Roberta said as she took a sip from her cup, and Charity's question was answered.

Charity felt her jaw drop in unladylike shock. She snapped it closed before she might be seen catching flies.

Every year there was a rumor that some lady or another had become with child, but more often than not it turned out to be false. Charity was not truly friends with Miss Danbury, but she would not wish her ill.

"So is it suspect or confirmed?" she asked.

"Confirmed as to her condition," Flora added. "Her maid would walk to the market with ours, and she let slip that the lady had been quite ill in the mornings. A doctor had been called so I would suppose a babe is within."

"Are you sure this is truth, Flora," Julia asked. "It is possible for a lady to be ill with some ague or even tainted food." Julia was ever the one to err on the side of caution, but Flora shook her head sadly.

"I cannot believe it," Charity shook her head. Though, she did believe every word. Miss Danbury was well known for her forward nature and widespread flirtation. She had quite the reputation though Charity had never suspected that her behavior would have gone so far as to have relations with a man. The thought made Charity's stomach churn. Miss Danbury would be ruined forever. Surely the gentleman would do the right by her and marry her.

"And what of the gentleman?" Charity asked. "Is he known?"

"No," James interrupted, shaking his head.

"Yes," Lavinia and Roberta stated in unison.

"Well," Charity laughed. "Which is it?"

"It has not been formally acknowledged," Francesca provided. "There has been no talk of a union. All the more shame to his character for it."

"To whom do you refer?" James challenged the ladies in general and his sisters in particular.

"You know who," His sister, Francesca blurted.

"Not Lord Wentwell. We have discussed this and I cannot agree."

"Lord Wentwell!" Charity gasped aloud. Only earlier this week, she had found herself in close quarters with the rake. Now, her encounter at the marketplace seemed all the more cause for concern. What if someone had been seen? What if she might now be labeled by his follies?

The Poppy's argument flowed around her and Charity could make no sense of it. The Poppy sisters seemed adamant that the gentleman was Wentwell, and James seemed just as adamant that it was not.

"That you would take his part," Alfreda shot at her brother. "Is more shame to you, James."

James harrumphed and stalked away.

The ladies began to titter and seemed that before the family's hasty departure, Miss Danbury's father had been to see Lord Wentwell and all were suspicious of his involvement. James and the other gentlemen defended the earl with vigor, though they could provide no proof to dispel the ladies' claims. Even James' own sisters were having none of it. Surely there must be some truth to the tale then.

Charity shook her head. She had tangled with the devil and come out unscathed. A sigh of relief was all that she could muster. Miss Danbury, or any lady for that matter, was at risk of falling for Lord Wentwell's varied charms. Charity would not be surprised that one, or many, ladies had found themselves falling into his arms… or his bed. He was a silver tongued serpent, but he was also so exceedingly handsome.

She felt her cheeks flush at the thought and made a comment about the heat of the room to divert any suspicion.

Roberta interrupted. “He had already gained a reputation as a rake. Now being caught alone with him, even though I doubt he would be a villain, could still… um…be detrimental for ladies of our stature.”

Charity’s eyes flew wide. “But Miss Danbury is the daughter of a Baronet. She is not some commoner’s daughter, and this is an earl we are discussing. Should he not be a gentleman?”

Alfreda Poppy said, “I’m sure he realizes we are commoner’s daughters, but that does not make the act less reprehensible, earl or no.”

“Oh,” Charity said realizing she had been insensitive.

The others glanced at each other and scoffed. “He certainly is insistent to have his way. I would not dare be caught truly alone with him,” Flora said suddenly serious, her color high. Charity prayed that none would hear tell that she had already shared a moment alone with the gentleman. Nothing had happened, of course, but rumors, spread like fire, once caught.

Charity sat fanning herself vigorously, and thought that it could just be the summer heat, that had caused her to flush, but she didn’t think so. The conversation made Charity more hesitant, and cross, by the minute. If only she had known the gossip but a few hours sooner. While she sat here in agony, the other ladies giggled about his fine form and impressive stature.

She was relieved when the conversation took a more agreeable turn. The few remaining gentlemen went in search of libations. It was far too hot in the crowded room to not have something to sip on for relief. Charity's fan was doing little but moving the hot air around.

After the gentlemen's removal from the conversation, the topic would not be squashed. The whispers were too rabid to be put to rest. "Ah, there is the reprobate," Flora whispered.

"Is he here?" inquired Charity looking from Lavinia to Flora "Surely not." Perhaps he had not the gall to show his face in a crowd after such a recent revelation.

"He is. No, don't look now," Lavinia warned as Charity attempted to look over her shoulder. "He is walking with your brothers," she informed the Poppy sisters. Her tone revealed that she was displeased that James had run to speak to the object of their conversation, perhaps to warn him of the rumor. "I would have thought better of your brother."

James, as if aware of their speculation glanced in the ladies' direction.

Flora smiled down into her cup, a blush coloring her cheeks. She lifted her brown eyes and met Charity's sharp blue ones.

"James would not be friends with him if he were such a villain," Flora defended Wentwell. "He is forward and roguish, but I do not think he would..." Her voice dropped to a whisper. "I mean, there is Miss Danbury, but she has always been a bit of a hoyden, hasn't she?"

"You only have to look at how she dresses," Roberta added.

Charity suddenly felt self-conscious of her low cut neckline and obscured it with her fan.

The girls tittered their agreement.

"Well," Charity said sharply, snapping her fan shut, she folded her hands primly around it. "If he is so roguish, I shall have nothing at all to do with him. I am looking for a husband, not a dalliance, and so should you be." Charity tried to put on a serious face for the young ladies. After all she was several years the girls' senior, save for Alfreda.

Charity assured herself she wanted nothing more to do with the gentleman. "We shall not risk our reputations for his entertainment," She reopened her fan and wafted it in from of her face as if she could wave the entire matter away as easily.

"Thank you, Charity," Julia put into the conversation. "We are married ladies now. Lavinia and I are under obligation to set an example for the young ladies, especially those in their first season." Julia threw the young Francesca a look.

"You are quite right, Julia," Lavinia said primly, as if finally realizing what they had been discussing. "It is not seemly for any lady to engage in gossip, and this is not at all proper genteel conversation for a lady, especially, an unmarried lady."

Francesca giggled.

"What is so funny?" Lavinia demanded.

"You, a proper married lady," Francesca said.

Captain Jack Hartfield and Baron Fawkland had returned to the group with cups of lemonade to go around. "Who is a proper married lady?" the captain asked as he offered a cup to his wife, and the other ladies.

"Why, Lavinia," Charity said, thinking that she

wanted most of all to be a proper married lady herself. "And of course, Julia, but Julia has ever been proper."

Lavinia feigned dismay and slapped Charity with her fan. Charity grinned at her.

"Yes," the baron said, as he touched his wife's shoulder. "And although it is not quite the fashion to dance with one's wife, I would like to borrow this married lady for a twirl around the floor." He caught Julia's hand and she looked into his face with such unabashed love, that it hurt Charity's heart. Was it possible for her to find such a true love, or was it already too late for her?

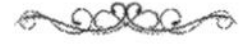

11

It was with a heavy heart that Charity partnered with Mr. Fulton, one of James's friends. He was a perfect gentleman throughout, and when he escorted her back he bowed politely, but Charity's eyes were already on the dancers that were lining up for the next set, a quadrille. The rogue, Neville Collington, the Earl of Wentwell, had apparently asked Miss Macrum for a dance. It would have been impolite to refuse, but Charity thought she would have done so, if she had been a dear friend of the woman he had so recently ruined. Flora Muirwood joined Charity; and James and Michael Poppy appeared, most solicitously, with refreshment for the two girls. The ghost of a frown passed James' face as Michael asked Flora to partner him for the dance, and Charity expected James to ask her to dance as well. He did so with an affected pomp that made Charity smile.

Upon the arm of her friend, James Poppy, Charity

allowed herself to be led to the floor. With the Poppy brothers lined opposite, the other positions were soon filled in with nearby dancers. Charity averted her eyes and raised her chin as she saw Lord Wentwell and Miss Macrum join the adjacent set.

Let them, she thought. At least I shall not have to clasp hands with him for he is not my opposite.

The music began and Charity allowed James to parade her in the circle alongside his brother and Flora. Whenever they passed Lord Wentwell and his partner, it was polite to give a small nod of acknowledgement, but Charity could not bring herself to smile. Instead, she narrowed her eyes, gave her nod, and moved on as she might if she had never met the man. He seemed surprised, at first, by her ability to ignore him in such a smooth manner. Charity did not care. She would do nothing to encourage any further interactions.

She focused her attention entirely on her partner, and their friends across the way.

It was not until the set was nearly complete that she sensed something amiss. The pair, Miss Macrum and Lord Wentwell, had appeared to get on well enough during the dance. The lady had showered her partner with smiles and whispered words. Charity imagined she was passing some secret message from her friend, to Lord Wentwell. However, Lord Wentwell seemed rather put out by the exchange. Instead of encouraging the flirtations, he gave hardly a response and a tic began to jump in his clenched jaw.

James lay a hand on her arm as the quadrille ended. "Walk with me and take a moment to catch your breath. I have something I would like to ask you." James murmured.

Charity glanced briefly back at Lord Wentwell, and then smiled up at James and took his arm as the quadrille ended. She would be glad to be absent when Neville Collington brought Miss Macrum back to the group of women seated on the outskirts of the hall. She did not want to see him.

Miss Macrum had her claws dug into him for the set, but as soon as it ended, Charity noticed that he did not escort her back to her chaperone. Instead, the strangest thing occurred. Charity caught sight of the lady's flushed face as Lord Wentwell, turned and left her standing on the dance floor unescorted. He hurried out of the room altogether.

"What a cad," she murmured, but James did not deign to answer. He appeared to be deep in thought. Walking together, the two moved away from the others and made their way out of doors towards a large fountain.

"First Miss Danbury and now her dear friend, Miss Macrum. She must be more careful. The man has no shame. I tell you, I would not have danced with him. I would have cut him direct."

"Who?" James asked.

"The Earl of Wentwell," she replied. "With such rumors flying, I would not have danced with him at all, Earl or no."

"Truly?" James said. He stopped and looked at her.

"Truly," Charity replied. "Even you could not dispel the rumors about poor Miss Danbury."

"I have heard the rumors, but I am not sure that Miss Danbury is entirely innocent."

Charity considered the fact. Innocence or no, Miss Danbury's intention could not absolve a gentleman from taking what should be left to the sanctity of marriage.

They walked in silence until they came to a foot bridge. As they started across it, Charity stopped her eyes wide, her body suddenly tense and ready for flight. James glanced at her in surprise, but then he followed her gaze to the center of the bridge where none other than Neville Collington, the Earl of Wentwell stood with his head bowed, leaning on the rail and looking away from them. He seemed lost in thought and shadowed in frustration. If Charity had not seen what had just occurred she might have felt sorry for him and asked what was the matter.

"Shall we change directions?" Charity asked, looking at the earl.

James patted Charity's hand and spoke lowly to her. "He is my friend," he said. "I think he may have unduly suffered from these ill-advised rumors."

Charity looked up at James. The word of a Poppy meant much to her. If James trusted Neville Collington, though she might not agree, she must at least consider his opinion. "So he is not a rake?"

"Well, perhaps, but he is not one to be afraid of. Believe me; he has no need to force a woman." James' face reddened. "I'm sorry," he said. "I forgot myself; to speak so frankly to a lady."

Charity hid her own blush behind her fan. That the earl had no need to force a woman had never been up for debate. Women seemed to fall to his feet, or wayside more like. No, the earl might not have forced Miss Danbury, but that does not mean that their encounter was altogether pure. That in itself was a crime in Charity's book.

James voice dropped even lower. "He has enough trouble as it is," he muttered. "Why less than a fortnight ago..." James broke off, patted her hand again and said, "I will not leave your side, but I am eager to speak with him. I want to ask after his brother."

As James had not left loose of her hand in the crook of his arm, Charity really had no choice in the matter. Oh she supposed she could have protested and James would have relented, but it seemed silly with her cousin by her side. What harm could a simple conversation cause? They were not, in fact, alone. No scandal could be had for she was upon James' arm, and not the earl's.

Charity took advantage of the earl's distraction and observed him more closely as he looked off of the bridge and into the distance. His handsome face was dark and brooding; his brows drawn together in a frown. She wondered at how different his face looked when he was smiling, as if there were two versions of the person inside of him, the mocking rake and a more serious man.

James and Charity were nearly a stride from Lord Wentwell when he heard them and abruptly turned to face them.

"Poppy," he said greeting James, but his eyes were on her.

"Hello, Wentwell. I believe you know my cousin, Lady Charity Abernathy."

"We have been introduced," Lord Wentwell confirmed acknowledging her with a nod.

Charity breathed a sigh of relief that he made no mention of their earlier encounter. Let James think they had made only bare introductions. Charity found her manners and curtseyed prettily, and the earl took her hand to kiss it and greetings were exchanged.

She felt the scrutiny of his eyes upon her like a physical touch. Even through the gloves she felt the heat of him. His voice was a deep rumbling baritone that went straight to her heart and pounded in her ears. She felt a strange churning sensation deep in her belly.

Why now was he so able to influence her? Was it because she had not taken charge from the start. Truly, Charity's resolve was always stronger when she was fueled with purpose or anger. It was strange that only minutes ago, she had been determined to scold him. She had not felt this breathless abandon. In the moment she had none of that righteous anger, and perhaps the gentleman had the upper hand. That was it, she thought. It could not be that he made her breath or her heart race for reasons other than that she was without control of the situation. Certainly she could never care for the man, and she would not let him get the better of her.

She bowed her head and tried to make a show of social grace, but by then his attention was already back to James. She felt bereft, and a bit peevish at being so suddenly ignored. She snapped her fan open.

"James, old chap! It is so good to see you here today. I thought to find Lord Percival Beresford and ask him what the duce happened in London, but I haven't seen the

Beresford brothers. In fact, in all this crush, I have found no one I know. Can you believe it?"

"Now that is an untruth," Charity replied without thinking. She fluttered her fan artfully, drawing Wentwell's eye. No doubt he meant that he saw no other gentlemen, that he knew, but now that she had spoken, she had to continue with discrimination, or look the fool. "You know Miss Macrum, surely," Charity said. She did not bring to mind their past conversation, but instead referenced the dance just past. "Just now, I saw you dancing with her."

He turned those burning green eyes back on her and she fell silent, squirming under his gaze. His voice was rather tight, and she found the deep timbre unsettling now. "I do not believe I know Miss Macrum at all," he said. "And even if I did, I fear she has grown rather...irksome."

"Irksome?" Charity repeated incensed for the lady. How could he deny her when he had so easily ruined her friend? She wanted to chastise him. She wanted to gain the upper hand that he had gained back from her with only a look. "Was it not you who just spurned her on the dance floor? Now you call her irksome? You are unkind, Sir." She fluttered her fan artfully, waiting for his apology, both for his lie and for his mistreatment of the lady.

James tightened his grip on her arm. "Charity," he began, but she just gave him a look and he was still.

"No, James. It is quite all right," Lord Wentwell interrupted. "Lady Charity is correct. I spurned her friend, but I think, perhaps, you do not know Miss Macrum as well as you believe."

His arrogant, superior, attitude annoyed her, and Charity wanted nothing more than to prove her point. She was after all, not blind, nor was she a liar. Just days ago she had spoken with Lord Wentwell and Miss Macrum in the same conversation. She assumed from his current lie, that lies were his routine practice. What had begun as a bit of flirtation, now was joined in earnest.

"I know that every rumor has a bit of truth in it. Now you say you do not know Miss Macrum, and I know that is not true." He was lying plain and simple, and she would not let the lie stand. It went against her grain to do so.

"I only said I did not know her at all considering..." He broke off clenching his jaw. "Considering," he repeated.

Charity felt him falter and pressed her advantage. "Considering? Considering what?" Charity urged. When Wentwell did not answer at once, she continued, sure in her victory now. He would certainly apologize for his base behavior and perhaps he would do right by the Miss Danbury. The thought gave her a moment's pause, and for just a second, she could not breathe with the thought, but she pressed on. She did not want the man for herself. She did not. Any man who could treat a lady so would never make a good husband. She took a breath and continued her attack. "Still in as much as leaving a lady on the dance floor is an ill piece..."

"I left no lady," Lord Wentwell remarked, interrupting her in a rude fashion.

Charity fired back. "Leaving one to her own devices

when the gentleman is just as much a part of the act as she, is vile beyond what I thought even a rake capable of."

Wentwell set his penetrating green eyes upon her and in a moment spoke. "Be plain," he said tightly, and Charity blushed to speak of it, but she pushed through regardless to her embarrassment. If she could help the poor lady, she must do so, mustn't she?

"You know of whom I speak," she said lowering her voice.

"Charity," began James again, but she shook him off with a shrug.

"All of the *Ton* saw her in your company. Both Miss Danbury and Miss Macrum and both are covered in rumor."

"That is not my doing."

"Then whose?" Charity challenged him.

He turned to her, his jaw still tight, and his green eyes flashing with anger. She had felt the chill in the conversation with him and Macrum, but she had not thought how it would feel to have that cold directed her way. Something inside of her shivered at the biting rejoinder he delivered.

"Perhaps you should talk to your good friend Miss Macrum," he said coldly. "She seems to know everything you need to know, and all the *Ton* believe her like gospel," he muttered under his breath.

"Miss Macrum should know what happened to Miss Danbury. Miss Danbury is her friend."

"That woman doesn't know the meaning of the word friendship," he said. "And I purport that Miss Macrum is not Miss Danbury's friend, if she ever were, she would certainly be no longer."

A frown crinkled Charity's brow. Did he mean that Miss Macrum wanted a title so badly that she was willing to try her hand at Lord Wentwell even after he ruined her friend Miss Danbury? The thought gave her pause, but even if Miss Macrum was false, that still did not excuse his villainy with Miss Danbury. No. He was simply trying to confuse her to be exonerated of his crime. She would not have it.

"Still, you further the destruction of a good woman's name. You are the cause of this rumor. Why will you not put it right?"

"I am the cause of nothing," he insisted. "Miss Macrum is a busy body who should mind her own business."

Gads, he still stubbornly denied the charge, Charity thought as he continued.

"Has it occurred to you that Macrum is after a title and does not care who she tramples to get it?"

She was right then, about Macrum, but that did not excuse the issue with Miss Danbury. "What of Miss Danbury?" she asked directly.

"What of her?"

Charity gritted her teeth. The man could not be so dense. He was only being stubborn. Stubborn and obnoxious and arrogant. He deserved to be castigated. She stepped into him, and looked up into his face, trying to find the measure of the man. "You speak harshly of Miss Macrum. I understand you do not like the lady, but what has that to do with Miss Danbury, and the deed done? Miss Macrum has no control over that surely, but you do, and will not speak to it. You are a coward as well as a reprobate."

James tried to step forward at her words, but they were toe to toe now. Wentwell's green eyes darkened in anger. He was so close she could smell his scent, and feel the solidity of him. "Upon Miss Macrum," he said. "If she had one shred of class in her wretched body, she would not have spoken."

"Spoken?" Charity replied. "My discourse is not of speech. My discourse is of the deed and you take no responsibility for you actions? Shame."

"Miss Macrum had deeds enough to defend the devil. She and Miss Danbury both." He bit his lip, a tic in his jaw jumped. "As you said earlier it is not only gentlemen who have leave to act, but ladies as well, much to their folly."

He would turn her own words on her? She would not allow it. She straightened her shoulders.

"How dare you plead innocence when this stain has ruined poor Miss Danbury? You are steeped in the mire sir. Do you lie to save your own honor when you have besmirched that of another? I have nothing more to say to nor to do with you. You are a cad and a reprobate of the lowest order." She narrowed her eyes and looked upon him like he was some offal that she had stuck to her shoe. "You are so bored, that you must accost innocent ladies for your own amusement."

"Accost?" he repeated, and she knew she had over stepped the bounds of polite society but she would not take the words back. He had clenched his jaw and the tic moved in his cheek, but she pressed on.

"Innocent ladies," she repeated, gripping her fan tightly between both hands.

"There are no such creatures," he spat. "You do not know the difference between lies and truth. You are but one of your sex, filled with guile and falsehood to the brim. You claim honesty, but you would not know an honest word if it bit you like a snake. You would cozy up to Macrum and Danbury like birds of a feather."

"Which am I now? Snake or bird?"

"Viper, if you must know; and ladybird as well for they are one and the same and both as filled with falsehood as the devil himself."

Wentwell looked like he might explode. "Miss Macrum should have kept her mouth shut and Miss Danbury should have kept her legs shut, and that is the end of the matter." He snarled.

"Wentwell!" James interrupted. "You forget yourself! Go cool down before a new rumor is brewing. Lady Charity, come with me."

But Lady Charity pulled from James. Her temper stoked, she was determined to get the last word. "Shame, sir," Charity shot back.

"My only shame is that I should have hired a more respectable stable master," Wentwell spat

"We will speak at the club," James said as he practically dragged Charity from Wentwell, who stood gripping the railing as if he would break it in two.

It occurred to her that James never got the chance to ask after the earl's brother. For that, at least, she felt remorse. Charity felt the tension in her stomach roil and she clenched her fan in her fist. It snapped like a twig. Why was it that every man who was the least bit attractive seemed to be a rogue?

"Charity," her cousin said. "You were quite rude."

Well, that was certainly the understatement, Charity thought. But Wentwell was just as rude, or more-so. He made her blood boil. She turned to James and stared up at him gesturing to herself with the remains of the fan at her chest. It wobbled like a broken wing.

"Me? How can you chastise me and defend a cad like him? How can you be friends with such a man? He admits to spurning Miss Macrum. He had ruined her friend, but then goes on as if it never happened, without even so much as a by your leave. He is an insufferable man."

James smiled at her indulgently. "What do you think happened, Charity?"

She would not be swayed.

"I know what happened, James. Lavinia and your sisters told me everything."

James sighed deeply.

"What?" she demanded. "Pray tell?"

James shrugged, "Is my word not of value?"

She started to reply, but James patted her hand and led her back to the edge of the fountain. "Come. Let us not worry over these matters. It is not like Wentwell would offer for you anyway."

"I would not accept him," she said smartly.

James chuckled. "Good," he said."Because he is the last man I expect to get married."

"Yes, I agree," she nodded. "He could not limit himself to one woman."

James shook his head. "You misunderstand. In truth, he is not one to be tricked a second time and will slip free of that noose easily enough."

"Noose?" Charity repeated indignant.

"You see!" James cried. "You only focus on one part of what is told, that which might make him look a rake."

"Well," Charity scoffed, "I cannot think him the type of man to be too deeply hurt by it. Perhaps his pride, nothing more."

"Perhaps, Wentwell has the right idea," James grumbled in response.

"What say you?" she gasped in horror that James might support his friend's activities.

"I only meant; oh never mind what I meant. I am far too comfortable with you, cousin, and allow myself to speak too freely. Let me find you some refreshment and take you back to your mother and the women. Here I am monopolizing your time when you should be looking for suitors."

"I am enjoying myself. Or I was," she said, but Charity allowed James to lead the conversation from the earl although she could not dispel the thought of his smoldering green eyes from her mind.

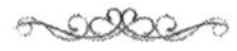

12

Reginald followed Neville's path from the ballroom to the stables where he directed the groom to get his carriage.

"Where are you going?" Reginald asked him.

"Home."

"You cannot blame every woman for the actions of one," Reginald protested.

"I'm not," Neville said. "My brother has not been well, and my mother can't handle him. I should be home."

"That is an excuse and you know it."

"She cannot see past the lies of her friend, Macrum." He said miserably. Neville did not say Charity's name, but Reg knew him well enough to see between the lines.

"I do not think they are friends. Patience has never mentioned her." Reg said.

"They are birds of a feather."

"Some birds fly alone," Reg said.

Wentwell looked at him for a long moment. "I can't do it again, Reg. I can't. I won't." He shook his head.

"I do not think that will work, Wentwell. You are an earl. You will have to get an heir eventually."

"I should just wait until I am old and grey and then take a young wife to get an heir on her. It worked for my father, and her father too as a matter of fact."

"Do you want to see your son grow up?" Reg asked.

Wentwell, sucked in a breath. "That was a low blow, Reg." Wentwell's father died when he was young and Reg knew it. Wentwell regretted that he knew his father only as a boy and not as a man.

"Come back into the ballroom. It is the opening ball. You will be missed."

"I do not care. I cannot dance with another woman. I cannot even speak to another woman. I'm just done."

The coachman brought out his carriage and Wentwell paused before getting into it.

"I don't know. Maybe when I am old, I won't care so much that all they see is a title and jingling coin."

"You know that is not what Lady Charity saw in you."

"No. She saw a rake that she hoped to reform." He thanked the coachman and took up his seat.

"Is that so bad? You can reform and she will feel proud of her accomplishment."

Wentwell threw him a look. "She did not see me at all, Reg. Not. At. All."

"Patience says she is more than meets the eye. You should give her another chance. She believed her friend. That doesn't make her a bad person. That makes her a loyal one."

"Reg, the world is not as rosy as you see it. I wish it were, but it is not." He signaled the driver and left Reginald standing in the drive before the stable.

On the ride home, Neville could not get Charity from his mind. He thought, he had never meant for the argument to go so far. He had never meant to speak so before a lady. His crude language was inexcusable. She was a lady, not some slattern tavern wench. Reginald said he should let her reform him, and truth be told, he did need some betterment. He had to admit there were times when his flirtation had gotten out of hand, and bordered on hurtful. No. Perhaps it *was* hurtful. She had accused him of being careless with women's hearts and he was. He was aware of how hurtful words could be now that his own heart was breaking. Still, he could not forgive Miss Macrum, and truthfully neither should Lady Charity. Miss Macrum had seen his attention to Lady Charity and sought to destroy their budding relationship. He realized with a start that she had done so. Miss Macrum had had her way, at least in part. He would not touch the woman, but she had destroyed the trust between himself and Lady Charity. Perhaps it was not as she had wished, but nonetheless, she had no doubt shattered any warm feelings the lady may have once held for him, but as much as he wanted to blame all on Miss Macrum, he could not.

He had lost his temper. He had acted basely and despicably. He had all but called her a whore to her face, likening her to Macrum and Danbury. If she had had a father or brother present, he would have certainly been called out. As it was, James was of a softer sort, but even

James was scandalized by his behavior. Wentwell could see no way to remedy the situation. Lady Charity Abernathy would certainly never speak to him again. In truth, he did not blame her.

"WHERE WERE YOU?" Lavinia asked as Charity returned to the ladies.

Charity certainly was not going to tell anyone, not even her friend about her quarrel with Wentwell. "I broke my fan," Charity said pouting.

"Oh," Lavinia gave her a moment of pity before telling her. "Your mother was looking for you, Charity. I sent her to speak with Ebba."

"I just needed a moment of air," Charity said.

"With James Poppy?" Lavinia asked confused.

Julia, who was hanging on Lord Fawkland's arm frowned at her and raised her eyebrows. At least, there would be no hint of rumor about her and Wentwell. The ballroom was a crush and it was not easy to keep track of acquaintances.

Charity just shook her head. She could not explain, and she did not want to speak with her mother right now. Patience came to her aid and glanced up at the doorway where Wentwell, still stood. Reginald exchanged a glance with his sister and followed his friend from the ballroom. Charity found herself pulled into a dance set with Percival Beresford, Patience's husband as her partner. He was a quiet man and did not attempt to engage her in conversation which allowed her to think as she danced.

Lord Wentwell would probably never speak to her again. She did not care. Why she should care what a rake thought of her, she told herself. She would be gay and beautiful and dance, but her heart was still beating outside where she had left it with Lord Wentwell.

Two sets later she had danced with Lord Fawkland and Captain Hartfield before being passed along back to the Poppys. She danced with Michael and with Colonel Ranier before dancing with a whole host of naval gentlemen. Her mother returned to the ballroom, but had no time to interrogate her, and she had no time to think about what she had done. She felt that she had somehow betrayed Wentwell. She did not believe him. She had believed Miss Macrum, and as she thought of her actions she realized she had no reason to believe the woman and no reason to disbelieve him. But what was done, was done.

The gentlemen she danced with told Charity that she looked beautiful, but she did not feel beautiful. She felt decidedly ugly. She had accused a man of ruining a woman, and now she was not sure she was right. He thought that she was of the same ilk as Miss Macrum, and if Miss Macrum did start the rumors then what must Wentwell think of her? She knew what he thought. He thought she was horrible, like Miss Macrum and Miss Danbury. He said as much. He categorized them together as backbiting and false. Had she become just what she had striven not to be?

She wanted to cry, but she pasted a smile on her face. Her mother didn't know it, but it was perhaps the best performance Charity had ever accomplished. By midnight, her feet were aching and she went to sit with the Poppys. Michael came to her side and brought her a glass of punch. It was a kindness, and she thanked him as she sipped the refreshment.

"Would you like to dance?" he asked. She could see in his eyes that he did not actually want to dance himself, but he asked nonetheless.

She shook her head. "I am tired," she answered. "But do sit with me."

He sat beside her but said nothing.

Wonderful, she thought. The two of us are sitting here brooding together. She pulled a bright bit from her saddened soul and managed a smile, but inside she felt only hollowness.

Michael smiled back brightly and took her gloved hand in his

Part 3

Loss

13

Nearly two weeks later, Lord Wentwell watched as Lady Charity entered the Drummond garden party amongst a large group of people including the entire Poppy family. Still, she drew his eye as if she were the only lady in attendance. She was dressed in a soft white day dress trimmed with ribbons the same deep blue as her eyes. The garment was exquisite as was the woman within it. It fit her to perfection, or perhaps she was perfection. As the day wore on, the evening sun cast pink shadows against her, and her fair hair glowed in the fading light. It ached to be touched. She looked like an angel, an angel he admired from afar.

After the words they had exchanged at the opening ball he could not approach her. To say they had ended that night on less than ideal terms would be a gross understatement. Truth be told, her censure had stunned him. He was accustomed to being pursued by women. It was a new sensation to meet one who was not the least impressed by him.

Now, Neville did not know what he might say to her. It was ludicrous. How had she managed to make him so tongue-tied? He had supped with dukes and visited at court. His manners were perfect and refined. He did not hesitate and dither like a schoolboy. He was invited almost everywhere and the ladies loved him, but Lady Charity haunted him. His own feelings vacillated between anger and desire. It was not love, he told himself. That emotion had been burned from him when he stood solitary awaiting a bride who married another.

Few enough women could see beyond those items of wealth and position to the man within. Neville had only met a handful or less in his life, all of them snagged up by gentlemen at the first opportunity. He had often thought he would do the same when he met a lady with such depth of character. Once, he thought he had done. He wooed her, revealed the truth of himself, and promised to love and care for her forever, but Katherine had been false. She had proved the wiliest of all. It had become clear that she never loved him. She had used his young and tender heart; then she washed her hands of Neville Collington and left him broken to piece the bits of his soul back together. He was determined that he would not fall for the same trick twice.

Neville Collington knew what his merits were: wealth, position, health, youth, appearance. Never again would he think that a woman could see past that. No, although his present looks and comportment were all the rage, next season a stockier man would be in fashion, or a taller man, or a dark and brooding man. Looks were transitory, youth was fleeting and fashion was fickle. Only position, and in his case, wealth would last.

He was now certain that women were far better at the act of subterfuge than they cared to admit, and Lady Charity all but proved the point over a fortnight ago. She has shown during their market stroll that she was capable of tricking him, if she so desired. It had been years since Neville had been so easily duped by what he thought was a willing female. Perhaps he had only let his guard down.

Lady Charity might have chosen to continue that act, if she had ends to meet, but her credit she did not. In light of the Miss Danbury rumor, she had chosen to ignore him instead. That meant that she did not view him as worth the effort for her machinations. That knowledge both pleased him, for sake of her character, and wounded him deeply, for sake of his pride.

Lady Charity needed neither his wealth nor his position, for she was in possession of her own on both counts. That must be why she found it so easy to dismiss him. He had nothing with which to tempt her. That begged the question, did he have nothing of himself, only wealth and position. Was he, himself, worth nothing at all? The thought pained him. Certainty his name was worth even less now. Rumor had been rife for weeks and had only grown with the retelling.

He had always thought that his rakish nature was a fun game. He joked with Reg that it kept the rabble at bay. He had never thought that anyone truly believed the dark persona. Sure, mothers cautioned their daughters, and he played the reprobate to weed out the fawning women who meant nothing to him, but he never thought that any lady he truly wanted would be swayed by the rumor, not as Lady Charity had been he thought bitterly.

He had never let rumor get so far out of hand that he could not dispel it, only now it had, and he couldn't. He found he could not shed the façade and be, in truth, the person he always knew himself to be. Somehow, the lie had become him. What was once a careless flirtation, had become the man, and he did not like what he saw in himself. Nor did he know how to correct the matter. Lady Charity Abernathy had every reason to be cold to him. He knew that now.

She had called him out and castigated him for his treatment of women and for snubbing her friend, if Miss Macrum was even her friend, her or Miss Danbury. He highly doubted that now. Lady Charity was above such petty women. She had no personal involvement with them. She had been affronted on behalf of her sex.

She had taken him to task for his treatment of womankind, and he had retaliated in the worse way possible. He had substantiated her every word by his actions. The *Ton* had called him the villain, and he had shrugged off the insult, but he had not expected Lady Charity to believe the worst of him, and when she did, he stupidly proved her word true. He had not expected the pain that her rejection caused him. Hers most of all.

Neville felt the strangest juxtaposition when he thought of Lady Charity. He did not want to feel at all. He had thought himself cool and beyond such flights of emotion, but that was the cruelest lie, because he did feel.

He was angry, for she made him furious. Yet he was drawn to her like the face of a flower reached toward the rays of the sun, asking for her beauty. She was either the purest of souls or the darkest of evildoers. There could exist nothing between. The more he thought on it, the more that he began to suspect that she was the former.

She was forthright and although her words were harsh, he now realized she voiced what all the T*on* was already thinking. Only Lady Charity had been bold enough to voice it plainly. Only she had given him honesty and he had called her viper. He deeply regretted those words now. He was so surprised, he was struck dumb that he had spoken in anger. He had never thought of himself as the reprobate she so colorfully described, but the women of the *Ton* had. All the while any of them flirted with him or laughed or smiled at him, inwardly, they all thought him capable of ruining a lady and then throwing her over. They truly believed he could be so callous.

If they really thought so little of him, then any hope of finding a lady of character was for naught, for he had so blackened his own that no true lady would have him. He knew full well why Lady Charity was vexed with him but he knew not how to remedy the matter or even if he should try. Perhaps he had played the reprobate so long he had indeed become one. If so, what right did he have pursuing the lady at all?

If the pair remained at a distance, he told himself he might soon come to forget her. His heart cried out at this decision, a sharp pain in his chest. Still, he would not search her out He would not ask after her. No Neville would go about his business as if the thought of Lady Charity as his wife never crossed his mind. He would forget her beauty, no matter what pain it entailed.

Beauty was fleeting. He would focus on other matters, and soon Lady Charity Abernathy would be nothing more than a vague memory. He told himself it was so. Had he not already made this decision? When he was old, he decided, he would take a young and silly bride, and get an heir on her. He would win her with a title, a fine home and jewels. Purchased, his brain supplied. He would then have a wife, paid for, just as one paid for a whore. The thought made him near physically ill.

One more glance at Lady Charity in her white dress, as pure as an angel in heaven sent a shiver down his spine as his mouth ran dry. He released a deep breath as he felt heat take him. He closed his eyes willing his body to nonchalance. Willing himself to forget the way her blue eyes flashed fire when she had chastised him in righteous anger. To forget the feel of her breath against his cheek, the warmth of her hand on his chest where the shattered remains of his heart still beat. The traitorous organ sped up at the very thought of her and he cursed his emotional silliness. Forget her. He would. Though it appeared that forgetting Lady Charity was going to take all of his effort and the Lord only knew how much time.

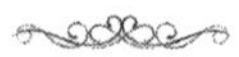

CHARITY SHOULD HAVE BEEN LOOKING FORWARD to the Drummond garden party. It was always an enjoyable event. Everyone was invited, and most even brought their children. It was a relaxed affair on a lazy summer day. There was no hurry or tension among the picnic goers, but Charity harbored a feeling of urgency in her soul. Her quarrel with Lord Wentwell still occupied her mind no matter how many times she told herself that he was of no consequence.

Why was it that he kept appearing in her thoughts? The Earl of Wentwell was not for her. She must focus upon finding a truly suitable gentleman for her husband. Yet no man seemed equal to the task. With each passing day she felt her situation grow more urgent. Charity was beginning to feel perhaps her mother was right. She was on her way to being a spinster. Maybe love was an impossible dream. Maybe her mother was right in that as well. She needed to stop being so choosy and just pick someone. Even though she had proven she could match wits with the best of them Charity simply did not want to play these games anymore. Today, Charity thought. Today would be the day, she would choose.

Charity arrived at the picnic with the Poppy family, all four sisters, both Poppy brothers, Lavinia and Flora. Even the eldest Poppy sister, Constance, her husband Mr. Nash, and her two children were there. Charity found herself sitting among friends, sharing a light conversation with Lavinia, and her captain, Flora, James and his brother Michael.

Her own mother and James' parents were conversing just out of earshot. Several other families were milling about laughing and talking. Some of the younger children, attended by governesses or nannies, were playing, most being careful not to muss their clothing.

Others were being held up as tiny trophies, dressed in their summer day attire like miniature ladies and gentlemen. It was a very domestic scene and made Charity ache for children of her own.

Charity looked back at the lively group surrounding her and James smiled at her brightly. She realized with a start that James was a good friend. She saw him almost every day in Bath and yet, she had not seen him. Not truly looked at him. Perhaps he was the solution. James would be an amusing husband. He was lively and full of humor. They had often talked and laughed in easy camaraderie. There were many couples who made a marriage on little more than that.

The Poppys were not titled or in possession of much wealth, but their estate was adequate and Charity enjoyed the country. Besides, her own father would not leave her destitute no matter how she wed. She would be provided for, as would her mother. The age difference between her mother and father was apparent to her father long before he became ill, and he was nothing if not attentive to his obligations.

Once more Charity's eyes drifted to the gentleman seated across from her. She searched her past interactions with James for any moment or inclination that there might be a future to be had with him. Nothing stood out as more than familial. Still she might do well to test the waters and see if that opinion could change now that they were older.

James was a gentleman. Charity was surprised that she had not ever really taken note of that fact. And James was handsome. Something inside of her clenched into a hard knot. Not as handsome as the Earl of Wentwell. In fact, who was? She found herself searching the picnic grounds for him, and her eyes lit upon Lord Wentwell and his party some ways away. Lord Wentwell was resplendent in his summer suit, the heat of the day making the garment cling to him. Charity forcefully put a stop to her wandering eye and looked away immediately, her heart aflutter.

She looked back at James from under her lashes and wondered what it would be like to kiss him. Her wondering brought no flurry of excitement; no feeling of glee like thinking of the earl did, but perhaps that was just the remnants of anger were still smoldering after their disagreement at the ball. No. James was the perfect candidate for marriage. Charity wondered how she did not see it before.

James was strong, able, from a good family and a gentleman through and through. Her father would be happy she was settled. She liked James. Her family liked him. Perhaps her mother not so much in status as in person, but Lady Shalace would grow to accept the union. Yes, Charity said, almost to convince herself, she liked James, and marriages were often built on less. Much less, she reminded herself, but as she thought of it, Charity still felt as if she had swallowed a bucket full of ash.

In agitation she rose to her feet. All of the men rose also. "What is it?" James asked at once.

"I—I—I'm sorry," she said embarrassed at her reaction. "I thought I saw a bee. I was mistaken. Please sit. I think I would like a bit of a walk," she said wrapping her hands around her fan and twisting it with a nervous gesture.

Michael began to offer his arm, but she turned to James, who after a moment's hesitation offered his arm instead. "Allow me to escort you," he said.

She glanced back at Michael to see his face had darkened with a slight frown, but Lavinia seemed intent on bringing him out of his moodiness. Charity and James left the group and wandered down a wide path.

"Do you think the Romans walked on this very path?" she asked.

James lifted a shoulder. "Perhaps," he said.

They wandered a bit further in silence, until Charity asked. "Do you know if there is a brook beyond those trees?"

"There is," he said.

She looked at him suddenly, wondering when he had walked so far and with whom. "Let's see if we can find it," she said.

James hesitated. He glanced back at the party gathered behind them. Then he focused on Charity. He shook his head. "Not now," he said.

"Why?" she asked.

"Is there something you wish to discuss?"

"Yes." Charity smiled at him. "You are indeed a good friend, James. I think you know me better than my family does." She glanced downward suddenly shy to make such a bold proposal to him. She should just wait. He would ask her if she gave him the opportunity. She was sure of it. Surely he could see what a good pair they made. He had been making excuses to spend time with her and her friends for the past few weeks. It was obvious he felt the same way. "So yes," she said again. "I would very much like to speak with you." She felt a blush fill her face.

James looked at her for a long moment. "Very well, then. Let's walk," he said, taking her arm, but they didn't walk as far as the brook or even the trees when he spoke. James patted her hand gently. "There is something I must say first."

"Do tell, James." Charity was actually thankful for the delay because she still was not sure how to broach the subject with James and his hesitancy made her wonder if he was already thinking along the same lines as she. Would he offer for her so soon?

"It's about Miss Muirwood," he said.

She stopped and stared at him, uncertain of what she heard. "Flora?"

"Yes. Do you think she will have me?" he asked breathlessly.

Charity opened her mouth and closed it again. "Flora," she repeated.

"Yes, Flora, although she has not given me leave to address her by her given name," he said and then spoke in a rush. "I know I am not so well off as some, and my family has my sisters to provide for, but we have a house in Bath and another residence in London, though it is perhaps not in the finest neighborhood it is no cause for shame. Our country home is small but quaint and quite beautiful...and comfortable. It is very comfortable. Do you remember it?" He did not wait for her answer but rushed on directly. "Will you speak to her for me, Charity?"

Charity was gob smacked. She stared, unable to form a single word and the silence drew out.

"Oh. She does not favor me," James said miserably. "I had thought... well, hoped..."

"No," Charity repeated.

"No? She doesn't?"

"No, I mean she hasn't said anything, but..." as Charity thought of it, she realized that Flora had let her eyes settle on James far more than once. She had also become a flustered simpleton incapable of speech quite often whenever he was nearby. "No," Charity said, again swallowing hard. "I think it is a splendid idea. I think she will be quite happy, James. Congratulations."

"Truly?" he asked with renewed hope. "Do you mean it?"

"Truly. Have you spoken to her father?"

"I have, and I've been to visit her several times this past year. Her family's home is just an hour's ride from here, and we have shared a great many correspondences."

"I see," Charity said, but then James already had Flora's approval. He only wanted to stop Charity from making a fool of herself. Did James know what she was about to say? Had he guessed? She felt a blush creeping up her face again, but she was glad he allowed her a way out of the embarrassment. She forced herself to set aside her dashed hopes, and she smiled at him warmly. "I am very happy for you. She will say 'yes'. I know she will." Charity looked away with conflicting emotions. On the one hand she was disappointed that she had no easy way out of her present unmarried situation; on the other, she was very glad for Flora that she was getting such a fine man.

"Do you love her?" Charity blurted at once and without thought.

James frowned. "Charity..."

"Oh, James. Please forgive my forwardness. I suppose I just want to know if there is hope. My mother tells me that to wish for love is a vain pursuit. Is it James? I ask because I need to know. Are my own hopes of marrying for love so far-fetched? Am I dreaming for something unrealistic and unattainable?"

James grew solemn. "Charity, I cannot answer for you. Only for me. Flora makes my heart sing. If I only give her half the joy she gives me, she will be the happiest woman in the world, for there is nothing, I would not do for her happiness. Nothing I would rather do than be with her, but it is a rare thing, love. People like us, Charity, people of stature; we have much to worry over, lands, laws, titles and inheritances. Love is often a luxury reserved for those who have little else."

Charity sighed deeply and her heart sank. "It is not fair. Why can't I find love, James? Am I too forward? Too free with my thoughts?"

"I cannot tell you," James said, "but there are many men who would do well to woo you. You will find the right person as I have. Come, now. Let us return to the others before we are overly missed."

Charity realized he wanted to enjoy Flora's company.

She looked back to James and smiled. "I am happy for you, James. I truly am."

The two of them strolled back slowly to the others

and Charity caught her friend Flora's eye. Flora blushed furiously and looked down, making Charity think that she would have to quiz Flora upon the details of her courtship with James at the earliest possible opportunity. How could she not have told Charity? But Charity couldn't ask now in present mixed company. She was forced to allow the group to enjoy the remainder of their lazy summer day, all the while observing the warm glances exchanged between Flora and James. How could she have not seen it before?

Although there was still the space on the picnic blanket that Charity and James had vacated when they left their friends, James shuffled the entirety of the party around saying they should turn to avoid the glare of the afternoon sun. He made much ado of putting the ladies in the shade. Charity thought that the movement was so that he could sit beside Flora. He unobtrusively touched his fingers to hers as he sat. The girl beamed up at him, and Charity felt her friend's smile like a spike in her heart.

Charity was happy for the pair, she truly was, but inside her heart was breaking, not because she held any romantic inclination toward James, but because he and Flora were just two more friends who were going to disappear into the realm of married couples, leaving her alone. Was everyone able to find love but her? The specter of being an old maid loomed even larger in her mind. If not James, who? Now, she must cast a wider net if she wished to achieve her goal by the end of the summer, or at least by the end of the season.

The shifting left her sitting beside Michael. She

glanced up at him through her lashes. Michael was the steadier sort. He spoke with intelligence of the war with Napoleon and his march across Europe, and yet did not make much of it, so as not to frighten the other women. Charity could have told him she had already read much of the politics to her father so the news would not frighten her. She had great faith in the English to repel all invaders. Why had she not seriously considered Michael as a suitor? She considered him now.

He was not ugly, quite the opposite. He was only quiet. Charity was not nearly as familiar with Michael as she was with James. However, it was not as if Michael had anything that could speak against his person. He was fine, in all manner, as a gentleman. Michael was the older brother, not that it mattered since neither Poppy had much in the way of wealth or position, but she had never really given Michael a chance as a person. Charity doubted his stoic personality had endeared him to many women but he was a kind man, she realized.

When she had risen to walk with James earlier, Michael had offered his arm. Had Michael been meaning to escort her instead? Charity began noting the number of times Michael had complemented her, or opened doors, or went to fetch her a drink. She realized he had been making overtures towards her, but she had not noticed. She had not given him a chance. Michael Poppy was actually quite thoughtful and she had been completely oblivious to him. She now realized the number of times she had been escorted by both James and Michael, often with Flora. Now that she knew that

James wanted to offer for Flora their foursome made sense.

The most notable plus point in Michael's favor was that he was a Poppy. She told herself this was the best plan. She wanted a family, and the Poppys were well endowed in that quarter. She would have sisters and of course, James would be her brother.

The Poppys knew her. There would be no need for subterfuge. She thought of all the others of the *Ton* and their polite masks. It was disheartening that there should seem to always be a bar to honest conversation. At least with Michael Poppy she could be herself. A lady should be able to be oneself before one's husband.

Although Charity did not look forward to convincing her mother of the equitableness of this plan, she had determined that she would choose her husband today. Yes Michael Poppy would be just the thing. The thought made her stomach clench with doubt.

14

The day after the Drummond Picnic, Charity took tea with Julia, the new Baroness Fawkland. No matter the trouble in Charity's heart, Julia could see through it. The truth was, Julia was practical and could understand things with an uncanny ease. Julia would help her make a decision. Julia would know what to do. At least, Charity knew she would feel more settled when she was finished with tea with Julia.

"Thank you Harrington." Julia said as her butler admitted Charity to Lady Fawkland's Bath home.

"Will there be anything else, Baroness?"

"Have Mrs. Harper bring tea in the morning room," Julia requested politely

"The house looks wonderful," Charity commented as she entered. "I cannot believe you just arrived at Bath and you already are all settled."

"Well, I do have the highest paid butler in Bath," Julia said with a little smile. "He does earn his salary. All of the staff are eager to please since Lord Fawkland and I took up residence here for the summer. After all they were hired to care for a country miss, and here I am a lady. In truth, I think they are more proud to serve a baroness than I am to be one."

Charity laughed at Julia's frankness. She knew her friend was still nervous that she would not live up to her new title. Charity assured Julia that there could be no finer baroness, nor a finer house.

Charity paused at a new display. Last year the paintings that had graced the walls of Julia's summer home depicted the sites and streets of Bath, many lovingly painted by Julia herself. Now, several key works had been replaced with new paintings, no less lovely, but they instead displayed a lush countryside.

"These paintings, are they yours?" Charity asked.

Julia nodded proudly. "Lord Fawkland thought we might move some of the Bath scenes to the barony and some of my newer works here so I might always feel myself at home."

"They are beautiful," Charity complimented her, pleased that her friend had found happiness in her new role.

Julia fairly glowed when she spoke of her new husband. Charity only wished she might feel that same joy. The two women spoke of Bath and of paintings, and Charity simply enjoyed her friend's company while tea was served. Julia always made her feel better and today was no exception, but eventually, the topic came to the subject of men, and Charity's troubles.

"At the opening ball, Lavinia said you were walking

the gardens with James Poppy." Julia raised an eyebrow. "And then again at the Drummond picnic. Are you considering him, Charity?"

Charity lifted a shoulder and placed her cup carefully back in its saucer. She had not thought how it might look from the outside.

"I did walk with James, but only to get a breath of fresh air." Then Charity spilled the entirety of the story to Julia: the fight with Lord Wentwell at the ball and how miserable she had been since. While she spoke she fiddled with her napkin and gloves in her lap.

"But is he not a rake?" Julia asked. A footman brought in biscuits fresh from the oven, and Julia thanked him. "That will be all," she told him.

Charity waited until the footman had left them before she answered. "I suppose he is a rake. He denies it, but what man wouldn't in the face of a disaster like Miss Danbury."

Julia shook her head. "It is true that all the *Ton* is twittering about Miss Danbury, and she has removed from Bath. Still I would advise against basing your decision solely on rumor." Julia offered Charity the plate of biscuits, but Charity refused. Her stomach was in knots.

"That is so," Charity said. "I know I let my tongue get the better of me, but if it is true Julia, I could not accept him, not with a bastard child. No one would expect it of me. You understand as much." Charity continued to worry at the napkin in her lap.

"I do, Charity. It is not an easy decision, when you do not have all the facts."

"But it all worked out right in the end, for you, Julia."

Julia looked over her cup at Charity. "It worked out better than alright," she said with a smile.

"What I mean is you were forced to consider much the same." Charity took a sip of tea, although it had gone cold.

"Of course. You know I would never be one to advise you to marry a rake no matter how handsome or titled he may be. If he is false...that sort rarely changes simply because he is wed," Julia cautioned. "Such men do not stop prowling. In fact, they may be more despicable to their wives than they ever would be to a woman they were trying to court. After all a wife has little recourse."

"My thoughts exactly," Charity said, setting the cup back in its saucer. "The fact that a man could be such a cad and get away with it makes me boil. A woman could never act so."

"Obviously," Julia said as she poured herself a bit more tea. She looked a question at her friend, but Charity declined the offer of more tea with a shake of her head.

"I cannot offer assistance on the matter," Julia said. "As I do not know the gentleman well and neither does Lord Fawkland. Your other friends know him better, Lady Beresford and Lady Amelia. Have you spoken with them?"

Charity thought of Reginald and James. They trusted Wentwell, but dare she trust a man's opinion on such a sensitive topic? She asked Julia. "I don't know what to believe."

"Well then, my friend. I must give back the advice you

once gave me. If Lord Wentwell is a rake, in truth, then you must simply choose another."

"You are right, of course." Charity agreed after a few moments pause.

The two women sipped tea in silence for a spell as Charity tried to get the sight of Lord Wentwell out of her thoughts.

"What other prospects have you?" Julia asked finally.

"I told my mother I have been considering the Poppys," she told Julia.

"So you do like James?"

"I like the family. I have no sibling as you do, Julia, no one to rely on or care for. If I were to marry one of the Poppy brothers then their sisters would be my own."

"Which one?" Julia questioned. "James or Michael?"

Charity sighed. She had been considering Michael Poppy, but she kept trying to find another option. Such hesitation was not really conducive to a happy marriage was it, she wondered.

"I know James better than Michael, but James is near promised to Flora Muirwood, and Michael has shown interest in courting me, so I guess, Michael." Charity shrugged. "I do not know that it makes a lot of difference. Either way, the Poppys would be my family."

Julia sat her cup distinctively into the saucer, at once every inch a baroness. "It makes a great deal of difference which brother," she said sharply, and Charity remembered her friend's conundrum last summer with the brothers Gruger.

Charity bit her lip as Julia continued. "New siblings are one thing Charity, a husband is quite another." She sat back in her chair. "I think you should get to know Michael better; then decide what you feel."

Julia was right. Charity could not say that she knew more than a handful of things about Michael. Lady Shalace was not pleased when Charity told her she wished to consider Michael Poppy as a suitor; as a husband. But if she were in love Charity was sure she could persuade her mother to agree to the match, especially if she convinced her father first. Of course, she wasn't in love with Michael Poppy, but perhaps she might fall in love if she got to know him better.

"I suppose I should get to know Michael better before I make a firm decision; that is true." Again Charity sighed. "It is only that Michael is so stoic and rooted."

"He is a good man, Charity." Her friend said in a softer tone. "I do not think he would ever bring you unhappiness."

"But would he bring me happiness? The man hardly ever smiles."

"Michael is just shy. If anyone should be able to bring him out of his shell, it would be you, Charity, much as you have done for me. After all, you and I get along swimmingly and I have been called quite dire."

Charity smiled slightly as she raised her teacup to her lips and then put it back down.

"And broody, and melancholy." Julia persisted. She waved a spoon as if it were a paint brush in her hand.

Charity laughed outright them.

"No longer," Charity said. "I think married life agrees with you."

"It is love that agrees with me," Julia said with firm

conviction. "You shall see." She set the spoon in her saucer.

"So you think Michael is a good choice?" Charity asked bringing the conversation full circle.

"I certainly can't answer that, Charity," Julia said. "It may be so. Only you can answer that question. Only you can know your own heart."

Charity frowned and then brushed the creases from her face with a soft hand. "I do not think I love either of them, at least not yet. Not the way you love your Lord Fawkland, or the way Lavinia loves her Captain Hartfield. Oh Julia, how should I know?" She leaned across the table, anxious to hear Julia's advice.

Julia looked thoughtful for a moment before she answered. Her eyes misted, like they did when she was considering a particularly tricky bit of a canvas, and Charity knew she was putting her whole self into the answer. "When you feel as though your heart will break should he refuse your affections. When you feel as though you may die altogether should you never see him again. That is how you know, Charity. That is the man you are meant to be with, because you cannot bear the thought of being apart from him."

For an instant, Lord Wentwell's penetrating green eyes flashed through her mind and Charity nearly felt the heat of him and smelled his scent. She thought of how miserable she was at the opening ball after their argument and these weeks since. The ache in her heart was real. The pain not yet dulled enough for her to hide her feelings.

"There! You see!" Julia said catching sight of Charity's

expression. "You already have some feeling for the gentleman. I think you just need to get to know him." Julia reached across the table and caught her friend's hand. "I am so happy for you, Charity."

Charity's face colored. She could not tell Julia she had thought of Lord Wentwell and not Michael Poppy.

Julia was right. She could not love a man without knowing him and rake or no; she knew the sort of man Lord Wentwell had shown himself to be. No good could come from dwelling upon their argument or their estrangement. She would focus on Michael Poppy. She would give him a chance to court her and she would get to know him better. She vowed that she would do so. Future potential or no, the history of their families owed him that much at least.

Then perhaps one day she might have a husband who looked at her the way Lord Fawkland looked at Julia or the way Lavinia looked at her captain, and on that day, she would share their joy.

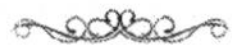

15

Several days later Lady Charity awoke with a lighter feeling in her heart. Father had promised to join her for an outdoor concert in the park, which was something so remarkable that it drove all thought of trouble from Charity's mind.

Her heart swelled whenever it seemed her father was inching closer to recovery. A hint of his old self could bring a light to Charity's eyes like nothing else. The evening prior Charity had complained that she might have to sit at the park without a gentleman to keep her company.

Father had made a joke about attending as her partner to sit for the musicians under the shade of the grove of trees. Charity had leapt at the offer and begged him to keep it. To her surprise, he had meant the words in earnest and the promise was made to be kept the following day.

"I have already accepted an invitation," Mother said.

"You cannot go," she told father, and the earl objected vehemently.

Charity had not seen the two of them have such a row in an age. She was upset that they were fighting, but the very fact that her father had the presence of mind to engage in the argument was cause for celebration.

"Do you remember the opera?" Lady Shalace said.

"What about the opera?" Father asked. "I have not been to the opera in an age."

"You are right," Mother said. "And do you know why? The last time we were at the theater, you insisted upon obtaining a playbill. You left me and Charity to go and get one, but you came out a different door and assumed that we had left the theater and so you abandoned us."

"I did not do that," Father argued. "I would never leave you unattended."

"Yes. You did. Then you went off with a group of strangers, and told them your friends had abandoned you. You asked if they might give you a ride home?"

"I see there was no harm done."

"No harm! Charity and I were in a panic, looking for you without appearing to look for you."

"I do not remember this," Lord Shalace said shaking his head angrily.

"My point exactly," Mother said.

"Who brought me home?" Father asked.

"I have no idea. I am only glad you remembered where you lived."

"Oh pshwa," Father said turning to Charity. "I don't remember that at all. You know your mother has the gift of making much out of of nothing."

"Indeed. We all have some forgetfulness," Charity said softly, trying to smooth matters.

Charity understood that her mother was worried that Father would have one of his spells, but Charity reminded Mother that he had been in good spirits since they came to Bath. The weather and the waters always agreed with him. This was Bath, not London.

"Besides, Mother," Charity said. "You know we cannot hide him away for days on end. Members of the Peerage need to see him sometime, or there will be talk."

Lady Shalace nodded. She had no wish to try to explain how the earl of Shalace was still doing the work of the realm when he did not know who he was from one day to the next.

"Perhaps the waters of Bath are improving his state," Mother said, "but it is not a cure all."

Father blustered and Charity took his part.

"Mother, you must admit, it certainly seems that his mind is clearer of late." Charity argued. When he might have gone off on a tangent and fallen prey to some delusion after only a half an hour, now his conversation seems more clear and his propensity to make untoward comments more controlled. Why, Charity thought, he might sit for an entire session if he understood the goings on. Charity had not seen her father so improved for a long time. She felt as if her Father had been returned to her.

"He wishes to go, and he has not voiced his own opinion for an age. He seems so much better. Do you not think so?"

"Perhaps."

"Please Mother. I know you are worried that he will say something out of sorts in front of someone of import, but I will not leave him out of my sight. Truly, keeping him indoors is as likely to cause rumor as allowing him this outing. We should have no reason to interact with anyone and yet, he will be seen listening to the music. It will soothe him."

"I suppose I have no say in this," Lady Shalace said at last, wringing her hands nervously. She would have cancelled her engagement, but after the argument, Father forbade her to come with them to the concert. Besides, others would wonder why Lady Shalace was begging off, and she could not plead illness if she went to the musicale.

"I suppose you will just get agitated if I come with," Lady Shalace said to her husband.

"I am escorting my daughter," he said. "And only my daughter." Father spoke with his old authority.

THE FOLLOWING MORNING dawned bright and beautiful. Lady Charity called to a servant in the hall to see if the earl still felt well and intended to keep their appointment. She had just finished splashing her face with cool water when it was confirmed that the carriage had already been called and Lord Shalace's man, Robert Benton needed only tie his cravat to complete his preparations.

Charity flew through her morning ritual so as not to

make her father wait. She would give him no opportunity to change his mind.

"My lady" her father's manservant greeted her with a nod. "Shall I call for a lunch of three to be set in a basket?"

"No," Charity bit her bottom lip with barely restrained glee. "Just two, if you will. Father shall be my chaperone this day, and I, his."

Her father's man looked uncertain with the arrangement, but knew better than to question Lady Charity. A lunch was prepared and a blanket provided on which they might sit while listening to the soothing musical tones of Bath's most popular string quartet.

It was a beautiful day and the park would soon be teeming with those who had come to listen, and so Charity was impatient to be off. She bid her farewell to her mother, who was off in the opposite direction to meet her ladies. One of Mrs. Thompson's friends had a promising second cousin, twice removed, that just might have potential as a match to her daughter. He was the eldest son of a Viscount. Mother tried to tell Charity of his virtues, but she barely heard her mother. She was so excited to be going on an outing with her father.

"Do not be late, darling," her mother warned while wringing her hands. "You know that he tires shortly after his meal. He shall need his rest."

Rest, Charity thought. The special code they used to refer to keeping Lord Shalace from making a fool of himself in public. Charity knew that the outing must be kept short, lest he allow his mind to wander. It was one thing for the Peerage to think that her father had short bouts of illness. It would be quite another for them to be aware that his mind was addled.

"Are you sure you feel well enough?" Lady Shalace inquired of her husband as they prepared to leave.

"Shut up, woman," her father growled. "You are my wife, not my jailor."

"At least he remembered which of us was his wife," Charity whispered and her mother nodded nervously. Her mother shook her head and looked to the sky as if it might provide some enlightenment

"Do not worry, Mother," Charity replied, "I shall be careful. We will not engage in conversation with others, only so much as is necessary. People will see Father with his daughter and that is all. Plus, Father shall have a wonderful afternoon. If he grows *weary* we shall return home at once. I am well aware of his tendencies. If he thinks that I am you, well, I shall feign a headache and we will return home, posthaste."

Charity's Mother had grabbed her gloves and a lace parasol, placed her lips to her husband's forehead, and preceded them to the door.

"Go," the earl said, shooing his wife out the door with masculine brusqueness. "You are hovering like a mother hen."

Charity was determined that she might prove herself capable by suppling all of her father's needs for an ideal afternoon. Perhaps, he might be tempted to another outing once he learned what fun might be had. Charity was determined to prove to all of the members of her family, including herself that she was capable of taking care of her father.

The ride to the park could not have been more ideal. Lord Shalace looked out the window at the streets of Bath and commented on how refreshing it was to be touched by the healing waters. He pointed out various landmarks that just a week ago he would not have recognized. His daughter nodded in response, her face dominated by a smile that could not fade. She was beginning to think that, perhaps, there was something to the rage about the mineral water. Her father was definitely better. Bath had healed her father, of that there was no doubt. Her heart was filled with joy.

Charity had chosen a soft blue day gown, the color of the rippling waters with which she felt newfound solidarity. She thought of the sea as she donned it and nearly removed the garment for another, but the color did much to draw attention to the brilliance of her eyes. Of course, the dye of the fabric paled in comparison.

Jean had piled her hair atop her head in the hope that a breeze on the back of her neck might provide some reprieve to the heat of the day. Charity felt exposed. The back of the dress was cut near as low as the front, leaving the breadth between her shoulders bare for all to see. It would help her to remain cool, yet she was now beginning to second guess whether she might have been better off to choose some gauzy shawl to tuck into the frame of the gown so that her skin might not be so readily available for viewing.

"Your skin is clear and pale," her mother had told her. "There is no reason to go hiding it on a day such as this. Simply remember your parasol to shade you from the sun. Do not leave it behind. Use it."

“Of course,” Charity agreed as she pulled on her wristlet gloves.

Now, seated upon the blanket that their footman had laid before his departure, Charity wondered if she might have been too hasty in her preparations this morning.

“My dear child,” her father mused as his clear eyes scanned the crowd, “I feel a sudden vigor, as if something remarkable is to happen to us this very day.”

“It is remarkable in itself that we are able to enjoy this concert together,” Charity replied. She would never cease to be grateful for this moment, in all its rarity.

“Soon enough I shall be giving you away to another gentleman,” Lord Shalace said. “Then you shall not have time for picnics and musicales with your father.”

“I shall always have time for you, Father,” Charity said.

He shook a finger at her. “Wait until you have a husband to care for...who will be the lucky man?” He frowned as if wondering if he should know the answer to this question.

“I am sure I do not know.”

His face brightened. “Ah, still making them wait, I see,” he teased. “You must be kinder to the poor gentlemen,” he laughed.

“I shall, Father. I promise.” Charity said as she looked out to the crowd, prepared to play a game with her father, of guessing which unsuspecting fellow might be the one. She soon realized that her father was serious. His eyes searched the crowd for familiar faces. If an introduction could be made, Charity was certain that he would not allow a moment to be missed. She was not sure allowing her father to introduce her to a suitor would be a good idea. She had hoped they would have little interaction with others.

"What is this, Father?" Charity said. "Have you finally begun to share Mother's thoughts that I should be married with all haste?"

"Only if my daughter takes pleasure in the project," he replied. His fingers squeezed her own. His strength was much greater than Charity had come to expect. Again, she felt her belief in the waters climb ever higher.

"Father," she smiled in return, "I would marry this day if it would bring you happiness."

"Do not marry for my joy, my child," he muttered. "Though, I will not deny that I would like the day to come while I still have some days to my name."

"Do not say such things!" Charity cried. "You are renewed, I can see it. You shall have many more days, of that I am certain."

Lord Shalace nodded as if he was considering his agreement, but did not say a word.

"Have you still no preference?" he asked of his child.

Charity lifted one pale shoulder and allowed it to drop. A vision of Neville Collington flashed through her mind, and she cursed herself for the thought.

"You have thought of someone," Father said. "Do tell your Father. It is my privilege and my honor to choose a husband for you."

"To be honest, Father," she murmured. "I had considered James Poppy for but a moment."

"But no longer?"

"No."

"What changed your mind?" her father asked. "James is a decent fellow. He is not quite so well off as your mother might prefer, but your fortune will be more than enough to ensure that you never go without. If you love him, you should have my blessing."

"He is in love with another," Charity said with a smile. She was joyous at the revelation, and her father was confused by the reaction.

"You seem quite happy for having lost a suitor."

"No. He was never truly a suitor, and I love them both. You remember the Muirwoods?"

Her Father frowned considering. She did not want to tax him with trying to remember, so she went right on with her thought, hoping that he would simply let the confusion go and capture something new. "They shall be most happy, I think. I only hope I can find such happiness."

The crease in his brow grew deeper. He could not understand. Charity feared that he had lost his moment of clarity. She sought to bring it back, by explaining.

"You see, Father," Charity explained. "I do not love James Poppy; and he loves Flora Muirwood. I believe she loves him too, so I am happy for them. However, you are right, James is a decent fellow and so I had considered him as someone who might bring me, if not a lifetime of happiness, at least no sadness or pain."

"I see," her father replied as he bit into a cucumber sandwich that he had just unwrapped with nimble fingers. Charity gave silent applause for the feat. He had yet to spill food on himself. She hoped she could take him home with his cravat intact.

She smiled happily. This was turning out to be a wonderful afternoon. She had her Father back from the fog that plagued him.

"I am happy that you are not hurt by his loving another," Lord Shalace spoke with a mouth full of food. His lack of care harkened to the weeks and months even, spent isolated from society. Charity glanced about, but there was no one to see him. She would not point out his error. Instead, she allowed him to eat and speak on.

"Not in the least," she promised.

"It is a shame," Lord Shalace mused. "James is a steady fellow. I feel that we might have got on well together."

"Mother would not rejoice," Charity laughed. Her father joined her, for there was truth to the words.

"Especially not with James being the second son. What of the other one?"

"What other one?" Charity inquired, but Father went off speaking as if she had not questioned him.

"Perhaps if James were to inherit..." Lord Shalace agreed. "As the second son to a family with more children than means, I fear he will need to marry a Lady of fortune if he wishes to remain in fashion."

"His brother will not leave him destitute," Charity assured. She understood her father was speaking of Michael, and she was overjoyed that he actually remembered the Poppys well enough to remember James and Michael were brothers.

"No?" Lord Shalace asked. "What of his brother's wife? Shall she approve of her husband distributing their fortune when she has children of her own that should be put before some aunt or uncle or other?"

Charity had not thought of such things. She guessed that Michael would never marry a lady that did not agree with his support of his family. Perhaps that was why he was so dire. She considered the brooding fellow for a moment.

"Perhaps she will bring a fortune of her own," Charity offered. "Then Michael might not need argue for their fortune, for the lady shall have her own."

"He should have to marry a lady of great wealth," Lord Shalace replied. "One as rich as you, or more."

"I have given the thought consideration," she informed her father.

Her father looked up with a grin. The prospect of a husband to his daughter pleased him.

He ate the rest of his sandwich and grinned through the food. "James will make a fine match," he said, "though your mother will not approve."

"Not James, Michael." Charity chewed her lip. Father had confused the gentlemen and repeated himself. It often made for an awkward exchange when others were about, no one was here with them now. Charity was used to her father's mind wandering, so she gave him a gentle reminder that they had been speaking of the elder brother, Michael and explained, to refresh his memory.

"Ah yes," her father fudged. "Well, they are so similar in features that I had mixed the names." In truth, the brothers looked nothing alike, barely passable as siblings. Charity knew it, but would not correct him. She allowed her father the out. He then began to go on about Michael being the second son, which he was not, and she was forced to sit in silence as he prattled on about the baby.

"What baby?" she asked at last.

"Why, Francesca of course!"

Charity sucked in her breath. Francesca was having her first season. She reminded her father of this, but he was inclined to argue the fact, so Charity let it go. What difference could it make if he thought Francesca Poppy still an infant?

She thought it was time to go home. She broached the topic to her father, but he refused. "I want to listen to the music," he said.

As long as they sat still and quiet, she supposed there was no harm.

Charity looked up and groaned.

"What is it?" her father asked. If she had been thinking, Charity would have claimed she was unwell and they could have left, but she did not.

"It is Lord Wentwell, Father." She gave a pointed look at a group several yards away but made no other gesture that might reveal of whom she spoke.

"The cad?" her father asked without hesitation, for Charity had complained much about the Earl of Wentwell in his presence, without much expectation that her father would remember.

"I shall give him a piece of my mind," Lord Shalace said, struggling to his feet.

"No," Charity admonished.

"Is he not the cur who has broken your heart?"

"No," she began again, trying to calm her father's ire. "He means nothing to me."

"But that is he? Is it not?"

"The same," she nodded. "There, with the linen jacket and the fair redhead upon his arm." She could not keep the disapproval from leeching into her voice. If she could shake the man, she would.

"He is not quite so menacing as you had described," her father observed. "I had quite expected him to boast pointed teeth and the ability to lure a lady to her grave with a wink of an eye."

"He is just so," Charity murmured. "Only, his dangers are hidden beneath a slippery façade. Lord Wentwell should trick you just as well as shake your hand."

"Wentwell, you say?" Her father frowned, a puzzled look coming across his face. "I know him. He is not a bad sort of fellow," Father said. "He has a shrewd eye, despite how far that eye might wander."

"Why would you say that, Father? He is loathsome."

Of course her father would say such things about someone Charity abhorred. Perhaps in his mind's eye Lord Shalace had created some goodness in Lord Wentwell's character. That was it, she determined. Her father had imagined more to the man than she had provided. He had, of course, had many hours to think on it when left to his own devices. Father easily made up untruths in his weak mind.

"There is nothing more," Charity said with relish. "He enjoys the pursuit of women. Once he has achieved his ends, she is cast aside so that he might find his pleasure elsewhere. Ruined or no, he could care naught."

"I could not blame the man for that," Father said.

"Father!" Charity admonished.

He began to launch into a tale and Charity blushed. “Father,” she chided. “That is not proper discourse for a lady, especially not your own daughter.”

He frowned but grew quiet, allowing a piece of cucumber to roll down his cravat.

Charity unobtrusively picked the offending food from her father’s person and she changed the topic for the object of their discussion had wandered too near to risk gossip, and she did not want her father to be agitated. “Are you getting tired, Father? Shall we go home?”

“No. I want to listen to the music,” he told her. As the musicians struck up a new song, Father told her about a concert that he had attended years ago. She listened with half an ear, glad that he was happy and enjoying the music. They settled themselves comfortably and listened as the musicians struck their chords and eventually her father nodded. His eyes had begun to drop closed, and he seemed less interested in the conversation or the music.

16

Charity was pleased for the chance to extricate herself from his interview, but she was glad that his spirits might rebound. She turned her attention to the music, which she had heretofore little time to enjoy. She was occupied with seeing her father comfortable.

Now, she looked around at the crowd. Charity realized that Lord Wentwell and his party sat not far from them. Drat! What ill luck that he would be so close, she thought. She fanned herself, both to dispel the heat and to allow herself the opportunity to chance a covert glance at the earl from beneath the cover of her fan. Five ladies and two gentlemen sat alongside him. Each of the ladies, save one, had her face turned up towards the earl. Charity watched his lips move as he spoke, his smile flashing bright teeth and his laughter rolling over the area. The ladies laughed too. Charity huffed from behind her fan. Her eyes were narrowed and if any could see beyond the screen they would have witnessed and unladylike scowl upon her face. She should not be bothered, she reminded herself.

She turned back to notice her father had awakened from his short nap, and was searching the pockets of his waistcoat.

"What is it, Father?" she asked.

"I have lost my vial," he said.

"What vial?"

"My vial," he said angrily. "My vial! I need it."

Charity was uncertain what it was her father wanted and then it dawned on her. "You mean your water? From the Pump Room?" she asked

"Yes. Yes. I should like a dip."

"You mean a sip," she corrected.

"I know what I mean, woman," he said in a loud voice. She hushed him, but he grew angry with her.

"You forget yourself, Emmeline," he said.

Charity froze. He had called her by her mother's name. This was not good. This was not good at all. Lord Shalace was standing now, fully intending to go off on his own to find his water. She had to stop him.

"I have not given you leave to call me by my given name," Charity said haughtily. The words seemed to take the wind out of his sails. If she could keep him from publicly calling her by her mother's name perhaps she could get him home.

He seemed even more agitated and Charity resorted to wringing her hands around her fan.

"Please sit," she whispered. "Calm yourself."

"I am calm," he shouted.

Several others who were nearby sent annoyed looks their way.

"I shall retrieve it," she said in desperation. "Just sit. I will only be a moment."

Lord Shalace sat back down, but looked a little restless. "Will you sit?" she said. "I shall get your water."

"Get it? I want a dip."

"Very well," Charity said again. "Just sit quietly. I shall only be a moment." There were sellers who were not far away. She could see them at the crest of the hill. If she could just get to them and back, all would be well. "I am only going over there," she said.

Charity gestured over to the far side of the park where a merchant was pedaling small containers full of the healing waters. Charity knew that her father liked to sip the drink and it did always seem to improve his spirits. Perhaps it might allow him to continue to enjoy the outing. Charity wanted nothing more than to make him well. "The water will be just the thing," she said.

"That would be just the thing," he smiled up at her. "I should like nothing more than a quick splash."

Charity looked from her father to the merchant. The merchant's booth was not far away and, though she might not normally have done so, Charity decided that the situation called for her to make the short journey on her own to retrieve the tonic.

"Yes. Yes. I shall return in a moment's time," she promised her father and gestured to the stall only a short walk away where he could watch her the entire journey. "Just there," she repeated. He nodded, his head appearing heavier by the minute. Maybe he would fall asleep. She wished she could be so lucky.

Charity stood and grabbed her father's purse which would contain the coin she needed to purchase the vial of water. She knew not if the miracle waters truly worked, but if they helped her father at all she would avow herself a believer from this day onward.

She continued to glance back over her shoulder at her father as she picked her way through the crowd. He was leaning back upon his arms and seemed quite comfortable in his leisure. Charity smiled. She would set him to rights in a moment and all would be well. Still, they would be wise to be on their way. She would plead a headache when she returned. They would soon be safely home.

A deep voice behind her said her name and Charity jumped with alarm.

"My goodness!" she exclaimed. When she turned to see who had addressed her, she added. "Oh, it's *you*," with a barely contained snarl.

Lord Wentwell offered her a bow, but she had no time for him. She tried to push past without even a by your leave.

"Wait," he said catching her arm.

"Let go," she snarled. Charity knew that she should not be so short with the gentleman. But it was for her father that she was abrupt. She must get back to him with his tonic in all haste.

"Just leave off," she said walking away.

He followed her.

"Lady Charity I must apologize for my behavior. I

should not have spoken so harshly as I did at the ball. Certainly not to a lady, but I understand if you are still upset with me."

Lady Charity sighed as he turned to leave. With a soft word she called him back.

"Wait," she said. "Thank you. I am sorry I was short. I am not going far." Lord Wentwell dropped into step beside her and remained silent as they joined the line awaiting their purchases. Charity wrung her hands together around her fan, twisting it unmercifully. "My father..." she whispered.

"How is Lord Shalace faring?" Wentwell asked. "Is he feeling better since he has taken the waters?"

"For a short while, but he is not well," Charity admitted, though she knew no reason why this gentleman deserved any such explanation. "This morning he was almost his old self, but now he is tiring and.... Well, I was thinking that some water might renew his spirits. At least, I had hoped..."

"You should never lose your hope," Lord Wentwell replied. His sincere tone and kind eyes caught Charity off guard. "Those we love deserve every moment of our effort on their behalf."

"You tease me..." Charity added, suspicious of his all too appealing approach. Flirtation she could handle because she was prepared for it. His kindness caught her off guard.

"You may not believe me, but I do understand. No matter what you think of me... I am not without loved ones of my own."

He was right, it was hard to believe. It was difficult to

imagine that Neville Collington cared for anyone other than himself.

The topic of her beloved father's degeneration was a sensitive one, and Charity could not believe that Lord Wentwell had any idea what kind of hurt she felt in her heart. She could not of course, unburden herself to one such as him. He who left ruined ladies in his path would only hurt her, and her father if he knew the extent of her father's illness.

"My father seems to do better after taking the waters," she explained with a level of candor that she had with few people, let alone this stranger. "I thought that a small vial might rejuvenate him so that he might finish the concert. He does not get out as often as I would like."

"It is very kind of you to look after him," Lord Wentwell offered. Charity turned her face to look up at him, expecting a grin that revealed that he was mocking her in some way. Instead, she found only open approval and something else that she did not wish to name for it might easily be mistaken for admiration.

"Thank you," she whispered, overcome with feeling at the compliment. She could not say why his approval mattered, but it had, greatly.

"Many would have hired a companion."

Charity nodded absently, thinking Mother had considered a companion, but that would only leave another knowledgeable about the earl's condition, and both she and Charity decided that was an unnecessary risk. Only a few trusted servants understood the state of affairs, and it was best that way.

Charity chose her vial, a small bottle that hung from a

strip of leather. She thought that her father might like to carry it round his neck so that he might always have the drink available.

Lord Wentwell paid for the drink before Charity had the chance to count the coin from her father's purse, as she was unused to such financial matters. She looked up at him baffled. She wondered why he was being so kind. As Charity prepared to say her farewell, determined to return to her father as soon as possible, she scanned the crowd for her father's form spread upon their blanket.

Except… the blanket was empty.

There, in the middle of the crowd sat the empty length of cloth. In the few moments that it had taken her to make her purchase, her father had disappeared. She scanned the crowd with panicked eyes. He was nowhere to be seen.

"Lady Charity, are you quite alright?" Lord Wentwell asked when he observed the fear that was written upon her features and she clutched his arm.

"My… my father!" she cried. Without another word Charity took off at a run to reach her blanket. She cared not what anyone might think of her race through the crowd. He father was missing and the world was spinning around her in chaos as she began to understand the dire situation. This was the opera all over again, and this was worse. This time she did not even have her mother at her side.

Lord Wentwell was hot on her heels as he skidded to a stop at the edge of the blanket.

"Perhaps a servant has taken him for relief," he offered.

Charity shook her head. “We were here alone. It was meant to be our special day.”

“Whose foolish idea was that?” Lord Wentwell snapped as he scanned the crowd. The benefit of his height allowed him a better view of the occupants of the park.

“Do you see him?” she asked. Charity wanted to grab Lord Wentwell by the front of his coat and shake him until he found the direction of her father. Her fear was overwhelming, and she had no one else to turn to save this man at her side.

With pursed lips, Lord Wentwell shook his head. “No, but he would not have gone home and left you.”

Charity thought he might have tried to. He had done so in the past. She thought of the opera, and her mind refused to focus in its panicked state. She could not make herself think, but think she must.

“I cannot imagine what disaster would have enticed him to leave you unescorted, but I shall help you find Lady Beresford. I believe she is here. I saw her earlier...”

“No,” Charity blurted. “You do not understand.”

“Enlighten me,” Lord Wentwell said crossing his arms over his broad chest.

She paused. Dare she confide in Lord Wentwell, of all people? What choice did she have? “My Father has moments. He wanders off. He has a...” she groped for a word.

“As he did at Covent Garden several months ago,” Lord Wentwell said.

Charity’s mouth went dry. Sweet heavens, he knew.

Her mind went completely blank. She did not know what to do.

Lord Wentwell raised an eyebrow. "Do you think he would have called for a carriage?"

Charity held up her father's purse in explanation.

"Lack of coin is no impediment. He is an earl. Let us hope he has not gone far," Lord Wentwell added.

Charity wrung her hands around her fan, twisting it violently. Where would her father have gone off to? If his mind had fallen back into its state of confusion he would be lost for certain. There were days when he did not recognize his daughter's face, how could he recall the path through the streets that would return him to their residence?

She tried to keep herself calm. The last thing that she wanted to do was raise an alarm and cause a scene at the park. Father would be shamed if his mental incapacities led him to be spoken of as if he were an invalid. His condition was not widely known, at least, not the extent that it had taken hold of him.

"Come," Lord Wentwell offered his arm. Charity took it without hesitation. His ability to take charge of the situation was just what she needed at the present time. "I shall have my driver take you home," he explained. "If your father appears there, send word straight away. I shall beg a second seat from my good friend Lord Barton, when I find him. I know he and his sister are here somewhere. I will make a round through the park and look for your father."

Charity shook her head. She could not leave the park without her father. She feared what it would mean to face her mother's censure when she had created such a horrible disaster.

"Oh," she cried. She covered her face with her hands, glad they had reached the row of carriages in the lane and her agony could not be seen by the crowd. "I shall never forgive myself. What if he is in danger?" She looked up at Lord Wentwell with wide, pleading eyes. The thought crossed her mind that she might never see her father again. How would he find his way home if he did not remember who he was? Tears flowed freely down her face.

Again, Lord Wentwell offered to send her home. Charity hated the thought and argued vehemently to remain with Lord Wentwell during his search.

"You cannot," he said patiently. "First it is a wonder no one has noted our walking together unchaperoned, or your upset, and secondly, someone must check your house for your father. It is possible he had the presence of mind to call a carriage, and he is already home, safe."

Finally, she was forced to admit that someone did need to check the house and make sure Lord Shalace had not simply gone home. She nodded and accepted the offer. What had seemed like the promise of a perfect day had turned into a disaster.

Charity allowed herself to be handed into the carriage. "If he has returned home, I shall send word." Another day she might have thought about how the sensation of heat on her elbow the lingered long after Lord Wentwell removed his hand. This day, however, she could think of nothing but her worry for her father. He had once been a savvy, intelligent man who could walk these streets once and memorize the crossroads. These days those moments were few and far between. Now, he was more like to get lost in their own house while looking for a slipper that was on his foot. Charity twisted her fan unmercifully in her hands, and the abused item snapped between her fingers. She tossed it aside, and leaned out the carriage door.

"Lord Wentwell," she said as she turned a tear-streaked face to the gentleman. "Please find him."

"I shall." The gentleman nodded and closed the door between them. With a sharp call to the driver, he sent the carriage on its way. Charity felt the wheels lurch forward, and she looked out of the window, anxiously hoping she might catch sight of her father. It was all that she could do to pray and prepare for whatever explanation she might give her mother.

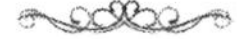

17

When Charity arrived at their spacious townhome in the main district of Bath, she was both relieved and worried to hear that her mother had yet to return. What might happen if the countess heard whispers of the search? Charity would be in a world of trouble. At the same time, she had none to share her panic with save Jean, who wanted to rally the servants to spread out through the town in search of their master.

"We mustn't," Charity replied. "Lord Wentwell is searching. We should not wish for this tragedy to become common knowledge."

"I shall tell Robert," Jean said earnestly.

"Tell him to be discreet," Charity warned. "And we should call for the physician."

"Of course, milady."

Once the message was sent to the physician, and

Robert was off to help Wentwell search, the ladies agreed to wait by the front window for the arrival of... anyone.

An hour passed and then two. Charity could not help but think that too much time had passed. Something must have gone wrong. Charity's mother did not arrive which either meant that she was marshaling her forces or still unaware of the trouble. Charity was not sure which she wished were true.

Charity munched on a biscuit but the sustenance did little to calm the knot that had twisted in her stomach. Jean, was surprisingly calm, as she did her needlework. Charity stood and paced. At least, Jean had all the appearance of one who was waiting patiently for any news.

"Perhaps I should send another note to Lord Wentwell asking... well," Charity admitted, "I am not sure what to ask but this waiting is unbearable. I should rather plod the streets myself than sit by a window and watch the world fall to ruin around me."

"All shall be right in the end," Jean murmured but her words held no conviction.

"Perhaps he has come to harm," Charity worried. She was well past the point of tears. "It shall all be my doing. I shall never forgive myself"

"You could not have known," Jean replied. "Do not carry this burden, my lady. I assure you, he will be found. You must have faith."

Charity perched on the edge of the chair beside Jean, but she could not settle herself. She looked out of the window, as if she could will her father home.

AFTER NEVILLE COLLINGTON had Lady Charity safely in the carriage, he scanned the park, looking for Lord Shalace. He had heard of maladies of the mind which affected older people, but he had never been exposed to such until today. He was sure he would be able to find the gentleman and bring him home. After all, he dealt with his brother, Edmund, and the earl was a good deal older and no doubt less recalcitrant than his own brother. Certainly, he was less robust. The man was elderly. How difficult could it be to find him and bring him home? But first he had to find him.

The thought of Lady Charity's joy at her father's return sustained him as he walked through the park, looking high and low. The concert was nearly over by the time he once again met Reg and Patience along with the Beresford brothers and Lady Amelia. Since he had not yet found the earl, he enlisted their help. Samuel Beresford stood immediately, but his brother Percival expressed some dismay that the earl may not be able to do his duty in parliament and noted that Lord Shalace had been absent from the stately body for some time due to his illness.

"A malady of the mind is troubling," Lord Beresford began.

Neville wondered if he should have been more discreet. This was exactly what Lady Charity had hoped to avoid, but Samuel Beresford smacked his brother on the side of the head and ordered him to take their wives home and leave the business of finding the earl to them.

"The man has a bit of forgetfulness," Samuel Beresford said. "Do not make a mull of it, Percy."

"We shall be the squires to your knight," Reg told Neville.

Lord Beresford grumbled, but his wife made him see that there were quite a number of members of parliament who were absent for much less pressing reasons.

"Besides Beresford, it is not like he is always in such a state," Reginald added. "Why just yesterday I met him at the Grand Pump Room and he was fine. He asked about you in fact."

"It is no different than a man in his cups, and we all know, there are some members of parliament who imbibe far more than they should," Samuel Beresford said. Lady Beresford was clinging to her husband's arm, anxious to go home, and Percival capitulated.

"I suppose," Lord Beresford agreed, but he accompanied his wife along with Lady Amelia, to their carriage, leaving Samuel and Reginald to help Lord Wentwell with the search for the Earl of Shalace.

Already much of the crowd had dispersed to return home and prepare themselves for the evening's events.

"Where could the man have disappeared to?" Reginald asked as their servants gathered the blankets and picnic items. "Just take it all home," he instructed. "And Lady Charity's as well. We will sort it later."

"I am sure I do not know where he has gone," Neville said. "I have made my way through the crowd twice, but I have not laid eyes on the man. He seems to have disappeared into thin air."

"Lady Charity must be distraught," Reg said.

"She is," Neville agreed.

"Where would a man of his age and sensibility choose to go?" Reg asked.

"I would find a drink," Samuel Beresford said. "It is deuced hot out here even with evening coming on soon." Samuel began walking in the direction of the pubs and evening entertainment. "I'm parched. I am sure he was feeling quite the same."

"We need to find him before full dark," Neville said concerned.

"Don't worry old chap," Samuel said slapping Neville on the back as they walked. "We will find him and you can return him to your little bird safe and sound."

"She is a lady of the *Ton*," Neville said smartly, his eyes narrowed at Samuel's insinuation.

"She is a woman all the same," Samuel said sipping from the flask that he had carried to the picnic.

"Careful Beresford," Reg said. "I think this one is different. If you insult her, you may find yourself on the wrong end of fisticuffs."

Samuel guffawed. "Wentwell? I don't give a tinker's damn. I can take him," he teased. "I have done, and that was when he outweighed me. Why now, he would split his fancy pants with one good swing."

"He doesn't have a good swing," Reginald teased. "He is no fighter."

"Leave off, Samuel," Neville said. "Both of you in fact. She is more than a lady. She is a daughter and she was distraught. This is her father we are searching for. We must find him and soon, before he hurts himself or the gossips get ahold of this rare tidbit."

"Indeed," Reg intoned, and the men began a systematic search of the grounds, and then the pubs.

The gentlemen had gone in and out of no less than six pubs but to no avail. Neville and Reginald refused to imbibe, but Samuel was half sprung, saying that they could not enter a pub and not patronize the establishment. It was rude.

They were practically at their wits end when Samuel spied the man. With a guffaw and a broad gesture. "Look at that fool in the fountain," he said, breaking into laughter.

Then they all saw that the man in question was indeed, the earl of Shalace, sitting not in a pub, but on the edge of a fountain. He had removed his shoes and stockings and had his feet in the water, which was certainly not for bathing. He stood, not at all steadily in the fountain. His trousers were soaked to his knees.

"Fiend seize it," Reginald intoned.

"Hurry," Neville said, "before someone recognizes him."

The threesome rushed forward, but they were already too late. Mr. Crafton peered nearsightedly at the earl. "Shalace? Is that you?"

"Oh course it's me," the earl said stumbling forward to catch Mr. Crafton by the lapels to steady himself. He nearly pulled Crafton into the fountain with him. "Do you know me?"

"No he doesn't," Wentwell said getting between the men.

By then, the three gentlemen had reached the fountain. "Get his shoes and stockings," Neville demanded as he and Reg man-handled the earl out of the fountain. "Let's get you home," he said to the earl.

"Do I know you?"

Samuel collected the stockings and wrung out the wet, before picking up the shoes while Mr. Crafton intoned that the *Ton* would surely stop talking about how drunk he was when they heard about the Earl of Shalace bathing in the public fountain.

Samuel stood with the shoes in hand, shrugged in the direction of his friends, and gave the man a sharp push. Crafton fell backwards into the fountain himself.

"Must have had you as an example," Samuel Beresford said. "Or are you still so ape drunk you wouldn't know your own mother, Crafton?" Samuel asked as he dumped half the contents of his hip flask on Mr. Crafton's head and left him to make his own way out of the fountain. "Waste of good whiskey," Samuel muttered as they moved away from Crafton. "But I doubt any will believe ill of Shalace from Crafton now."

"Good Lord! Who is that in the fountain?" Lord Cornishe asked of the gentlemen as he came out of the pub.

"Crafton," Wentwell answered as they frog-marched the earl away from danger.

"Is he tossed?" Lord Cornishe asked.

"Drunk as a wheelbarrow," Neville intoned as they marched the earl away.

"Wait," Shalace said dragging his feet. "I didn't get my drink."

"I think you have had quite enough to drink, my lord," Reg intoned. "You are already quite foxed."

Once they were out of Cornishe's view, Samuel thrust his hip flask into the earl's hand. "Drink up, man," he said. "Knowing your wife, I think you are going to need it."

Shalace took a drink from the flask and sputtered. "That isn't water," he said.

"No, it is not," Samuel agreed. "It's the finest Irish whiskey. Enjoy it, Shalace. And you, Wentwell, you owe me." He pointed a finger at Neville.

The Earl of Shalace took another drink from the flask. "It is very smooth," he agreed smacking his lips in appreciation.

"Nothing wrong with this man's head that I can see," Samuel intoned.

"What were we celebrating, gentlemen?" the earl asked as they attempted to usher him into the carriage. "Or is this the wake? Is someone getting leg shackled?"

Samuel guffawed. "Perhaps Wentwell, there," he said.

"Who are you marrying, Wentwell?" the earl asked turning to Neville.

Neville hesitated but a moment. "Your daughter with your permission, and hers," Neville said.

"Why of course, Wentwell," the earl replied with a laugh. "A wife and daughter? How drunk do you gentlemen think I am?"

"We need to get him home before anyone else sees him out of sorts." Neville gave him a push. "Let's go, Shalace."

"No one is going to think anything but that he is in his cups." Samuel said. "He shall not be the only gentleman who spent the afternoon at the musicale imbibing."

The earl balked at getting into the carriage. The gentlemen could have picked him up bodily and put him inside, but they paused to hear his protestations. "I don't know you," he said pointing a finger at Samuel. "Wentwell who are these men?"

"How it is that he recognizes you," Reginald said, but Neville shook his head. "I think he is mistaking me for my father."

"Oh," Reg said realizing that Neville's father had died when Neville was a boy. This must be a strange experience indeed.

"Of course you know us," Neville said.

"Oh, I think you have your work cut out for you, Wentwell," Samuel said.

"Shut it, Beresford."

Samuel chuckled and they managed the situation of getting the old man into the carriage without further incident. Since the earl did not believe that he was married, they finally convinced him that he should go to speak with his lady and offer for her on the spot.

"I am not sure I am putting forth my best foot," the earl said uncertainly. He suddenly discovered that he did not have shoes nor stockings on his feet and it was with much ado the gentlemen managed to get both onto his now rather dirty appendages. Nothing could be done about his sodden trousers, but with a few more swigs from Samuel's flask he was convinced that his "Sweet

Emmeline" would have him wet and bedraggled as he was.

"Sweet?" Samuel mouthed behind the earl's head.

Neville shrugged, he doubted any called the Lady Shalace sweet, but the earl continued, "Sweet and voluptuous. Miss Lovell loves me, you see, and I love her and no bloody conventions are going to keep us apart."

"I am sure Miss Lovell will be delighted to accept your suit," Neville encouraged the earl.

"If she doesn't," he said. "I told you before Wentwell, I shall just kiss her senseless. If she is mussed enough there will be no question of our marriage. She will have me or no one, and the *Ton* can kiss my arse."

Neville choked at the man's cavalier attitude. "But surely, only if she truly wants you," he said.

"Of course, but I am aware Miss Lovell has only the barest connection to the gentry, but you must agree Wentwell, there are ways around the constrictors put upon us by our standing; that is if the lady wants to be caught."

The men in the carriage were stunned to silence at his raffish language.

After a moment, Neville cleared his throat. "You forget yourself, Shalace," he said softly, but the unguarded comment made him think that all those years ago, regardless of rumor, it was not Miss Lovell who caught the earl, but he who had caught her and made her his countess, The Lady Shalace.

The rest of the carriage ride was made in silence and Neville could not help but compare Lady Charity to her mother, the Lady Shalace and not unfavorably. The lady was not the man catcher his mother and indeed the rest of the *Ton* thought her. It was clear that Lord Shalace loved her, and was still in love with her after all these years. He didn't just pick a young pretty bride and she did not trap him for a title. Neville smiled. If love could exist between the cantankerous Lady Shalace and her failing earl, at their age, then love was possible anywhere. It gave him a warm feeling inside and hope for his own lady.

He felt strangely closer to his own father after speaking with the Earl of Shalace, no matter that he was not completely lucid. It was clear that the two men, his own father and the Earl of Shalace were friends. The families had not remained friendly after his father's death, and no wonder. The wives were not. His own mother thought Lady Shalace was a social climber, but he now knew that was not true. He wondered if Lady Charity had much of her father's brusque honesty. It was the polar opposite to all he had thought of Lady Shalace, and in turn her daughter. He had misjudged Lady Charity, to his embarrassment.

"If you have this under control, Wentwell," Samuel said, "Drop us back at the park so we can pick up our carriages."

"We can follow you if you think you may need our help," Reg offered, but by then the Earl of Shalace was nearly snoring his head lolling onto Neville's shoulder.

"I think I can manage the man," Neville said.

"Ah, but can you manage his daughter?" Samuel asked.

Neville grinned in the darkened carriage. “I think so,” he said.

“Well. Good luck, old man,” Reg said giving him a clap on the shoulder. “Don’t let her get away,” he whispered.

18

Lady Charity was still waiting by the window when a carriage pulled to a stop in front of their gate.

"It must be Lord Wentwell!" Charity cried. It had to be. Anyone else would mean something terrible had happened. She sent a cry to the heavens that the carriage belonged to the gentleman and he would have her father inside.

The carriage door opened and Charity's guess was confirmed as the first pair of fine boots that descended the steps belonged to the lanky body of Lord Wentwell. He unfolded himself from the interior and then turned back around to help the other rider down the stair.

"Father!" Charity cried. The window had been flung open and her father looked up in confusion at her word.

"Emmeline?" Lord Shalace replied as if he thought Charity were her mother. "My dear, I have come to beg your hand." Lord Shalace grinned. "Wentwell here has encouraged me to come state my intent. I have come to do so before it is too late. You see, there are many a dashing fellow wandering around that might turn your head, and I love you to distraction and if you will have me, I shall make you my wife."

At this point Charity, who had rushed from the parlor to the front door, was standing on the top step staring down at her father in all of his delusion. "Father," she repeated. She has never been so happy to see him, although he did look a bit bedraggled.

Her father's eyebrows drew together and his head tilted to the side as if he were confused by her reply.

"Miss Lovell," Lord Wentwell said with a pointed tone. "Perhaps you would like to invite us inside?"

"Yes. Yes. Of course," Charity said, realizing that her father was still lost in the past and they could not converse on the step.

Charity could see that she must do so. She cleared her throat and swung her arm wide to offer entry into the townhouse. The pair of gentlemen strode by her as if nothing were out of the ordinary. She realized that her father's trousers were quite wet from the knees down, and he was nearly dripping on the foyer floor. Aside from that, he smelled of whiskey.

Lady Charity had sent for the doctor as soon as she had returned home from the park. Due to that preemptive measure, the physician was currently taking his leisure in her father's rooms. Charity sent a servant to retrieve the man immediately that he might inspect her father's condition. She invited the gentlemen to sit in the parlor.

Once her father had taken his seat upon the couch, his weariness began to take hold. As his brain struggled to continue the delusion, he grew more and more confused. Eventually, his eyes drifted closed and his head fell back to the seat as he fell into dreaming.

"Doctor Porter," Charity approached the physician with concern, "will he be alright?"

"I believe so," Doctor Porter replied. "What he needs now is rest. He has had a trying and confusing day."

Charity nodded and directed the servants to put the earl to bed. She could not help but think that she was incredibly lucky that her father had been found and returned unharmed, and she owed that luck to Lord Wentwell, who had found him and brought him home. No matter what she thought of him, Lord Wentwell had gone out of his way to help her and she was grateful.

"No more excursions without proper help," the doctor added before he made his exit.

Charity nodded, suddenly exhausted from the day's events. She sank back on the coach and asked, "Where was he?"

Lord Wentwell explained how he had found her father. "He had removed his shoes," Lord Wentwell confided. "I believe he may have chosen to bathe in the fountain if I had not found him."

"Lud!" Charity rubbed her forehead. She had the beginnings of a headache.

"In any case, he is home now," Lord Wentwell said.

How her Father had gotten to that fountain, such a distance from the park, Charity might never know. She was thankful that Lord Wentwell had been able to convince Lord Shalace to trust and follow him, and that he had returned her father to her. She was about to express her gratitude when the door to the hall burst open without warning and Lady Shalace stormed in to glare at the pair of youngsters sitting proud as you please alone in the parlor.

Wentwell stood immediately, but the damage was done.

"What is the meaning of this?" Lady Shalace cried. "I came back as soon as I heard. Mrs. Thompson warned me, Lord Wentwell had reduced another lady to tears at the concert, and then, she saw you with my husband; *my husband*, was seen off gallivanting with this... this..." she did not seem to have the proper word to describe Lord Wentwell; for any word that she chose would be an insult, and Charity's mother knew well enough to keep her tongue around a peer even when she was enraged.

Instead of continuing the tirade, she turned on her daughter. "I wondered where on earth you had gone to, Charity, and now!" She turned towards Wentwell. "How dare you enter my home uninvited, and sit with my daughter unchaperoned. Next your mother will have disparaging words for my daughter, saying she wished to catch an earl. Well, I can tell you right now, that is not so. You will not ruin my daughter, Wentwell. You will not."

"Mother please," Charity began, but Lady Shalace waved her off.

She was fully the countess now, and there was no stopping her. She turned briefly to Charity. "I thought you should have know better," she snapped. "Go to your room at once."

Charity had no intention of leaving until the matter was settled. "It is not what you think," Charity said, but her mother would not be contained.

"Mother!" Charity began. She stepped forward, ready to defend Lord Wentwell, but she felt his touch at her elbow. When she turned her head, a slight shake told her that he did not wish her mother to know the truth of his heroism. Charity was confused by this. The truth would do wonders for his reputation but he seemed to want the opposite.

Lady Shalace lifted a finger and shook it under the Earl of Wentwell's nose as if he were a boy instead of an earl. "You may be an earl, but you are also but a fledgling in the ways of the *Ton*," she said. "I know their collusions, and my husband is an earl, more advanced and prominent than you are. Do not think you can best me. You cannot. If you think to breathe a word of this, a single word, you will not be able to dig your way out of the scandal I will pour upon your head. Earl or no."

"Lady Shalace," Lord Wentwell began in an all too convincing tone, "I have come to apologize for my gallivanting, as you call it. You see, the concert was quite a bore, and I, as is my nature, longed for a small adventure. I met with the earl, and am afraid your husband does not hold his liquor as well as he might have once done."

"Liquor!" Lady Shalace threw a look at Charity who gave her the briefest of nods. She watched her mother's countenance relax if only slightly. Her mother believed that Wentwell only thought her husband was drunk. Things were not as bad as she thought. Charity knew drinking was not the best pastime, but it was also not something which would keep her father from his earldom. It was an obsequious and virile endeavor which abounded among the gentlemen of the *Ton*. Her father would not be looked down upon for imbibing.

Lord Wentwell looked shamed faced. "I did bring the earl home, but he is quite in his cups, as I am sure you heard."

"Oh," her mother said, the wind taken from her sails. She shot another look at Charity, as if to say, how much does he know? Does he truly think your father was drunk?

"I was only informing the Lady Charity of the incident," Lord Wentwell continued. "I am afraid we took flight without notifying Lady Charity. In fact, I did not know she was left alone, unescorted. I assure you, she has spared me no lash of her tongue."

"I should hope not!" Lady Shalace spat! "To leave my daughter like that. The shame! On her own as well! You have removed a lady's chaperone from her care! If she had not been wise enough to return to our home she might have been ruined!"

"But I am not," Charity said.

"That remains to be seen, young lady," her mother snapped. Charity knew, now that Lord Wentwell had explained he only saw the Earl of Shalace drunk, and not in any way indisposed, she supposed that her mother would soon vent her spleen upon her for losing him. "Good day, Lord Wentwell," her mother said haughtily, effectively dismissing the man.

"I will take my leave now," Lord Wentwell agreed.

"That is right," Lady Shalace said. "Take your leave

and do not darken my door again. You bring nothing but trouble and rumor in your wake."

He bowed to them both. "Lady Shalace. Lady Charity," he said and then he was gone. Charity did not even get the chance to thank him properly and her mother had insulted him, when he had been nothing but helpful.

As soon as Lord Wentwell was out of the door, her mother turned on her. Leaning against the door as if the structure could hold her upright, she said, "I thought you had this under control."

"I did, Mother, I only left Father for a moment."

"A moment! You should not have left him at all. This could have been a disaster, and even as it is, there were rumors of that rake accosting a young lady at the concert, and then he was seen with your father."

"Accosting a lady?" Charity repeated. The word sent a tremor through her. "Who?" Her heart sank as she realized that she might now be the subject of rumor. Had someone seen her?

"I do not know," her mother said. "Apparently she was hidden by her fan. She had more sense than you, Charity. Her face was not seen with that wastrel."

"Yes, Mother," Charity said. She had no intention of telling her mother that the lady in tears was her, but it pained her to think that she was the root of yet another rumor surrounding Lord Wentwell. This one, was certainly not his fault.

"Who saw you home?" her mother asked tardily. Her eyes widened in horror. "Surely you did not take a hired hackney?"

"No, Mother," Charity said. "Patience was at the concert with Lord Barton." Let Mother think what she will of that. It was not exactly a lie.

"Good. Good," her mother said calming down somewhat. "At least they will be able to shield you from rumor. Lady Beresford and her brother are both pillars, and scandal would not touch them."

"Yes, Mother."

"You could learn from Lady Beresford, you know," her mother said, and with that, Mother went to check on Father.

CHARITY SPENT MUCH of the later hours persuading her mother to keep quiet about the whole situation. It was too easy for her mother to let something slip to Mrs. Thompson or Mrs. Sullivan. Charity's only defense was in protection of her own reputation, which of course her mother would defend to the end. Charity knew that her mother wished she could spin the tale for all so that her daughter was the victim of Wentwell's rakish ways, but she could not. The scandal might bring her daughter much pity, but with the pity would come ruin, so Lord Wentwell would have to be spared her ire.

Charity reminded her mother that it was best to not speak of the matter at all. If word got out, Father would be looked down upon for his infirmity, and anyway, Lord Wentwell had brought Father home with no more than a thought that the man had drunk more than his fill, and so it was decided that they would speak no more of it.

Several days later she tried to speak with her father of what had occurred but he had no recollection of it. He only recalled their conversation in the park. Charity supposed it was a blessing that he might have a happy memory to look back upon. She kissed his forehead and wished him sweet dreams. She and Lord Wentwell alone knew the truth of the situation and the burden seemed unbearable.

She needed to speak to Lord Wentwell, to thank him for his aid and to apologize for her mother's words, but there seemed no way to manage it, with her mother watching her every move. In the end, Lady Charity penned a letter of thanks to him, and apology for her mother's actions against him. She asked Jean to post it for her. She expected him to find a way to answer.

Part 4

Honesty

19

A week passed and Charity found herself escorted to more than one event by Michael and James Poppy. She received no response from Lord Wentwell. She began to think Lord Wentwell was still angry about the horrible things she has said of him at the ball. She had accused him of being a libertine. She did not know what had actually happened with Miss Danbury, or even Miss Macrum for that matter. True, he had been a gentleman and helped her with her father, but she had been a lady in distress, and he, as a gentleman would be honor bound to help her. But he would not be honor bound to answer her letter or indeed have anything to do with her, especially since she had insulted him. And then her mother had essentially thrown him out of their house. Charity sighed. Mother had been hasty in her judgement, as was she, Charity realized. She had judged Lord Wentwell too quickly.

Why would he write back to her? She had apologized

and thanked him via letter, and it seemed that he felt, their communication was at an end. He did not want to see her. If he did, he would have sent word. He had been so masterful in saving her father. Charity realized she wanted more than a simple letter of acknowledgement. She wanted to see him again, but he obviously did not want to see her. He did not call. Perhaps he would never forgive her. The thought made her distraught.

Michael had become ever more attentive to her, and it seemed that after the fiasco with her father, her mother was willing to accept any gentleman who Charity accepted. Charity did her best to get to know more of Michael. He would make a steady husband. He was practical and smart, but Charity could not help but think that it was rare to see him smile.

She made it her objective to show Michael how to enjoy himself. Once or twice she almost succeeded. Almost. She found herself comparing Michael's serious attitude to Lord Wentwell's happy one. No. She reminded herself. She would not think of Wentwell. If Lord Wentwell had wanted to see her, he would have answered her letter. Nonetheless, Charity found herself wishing she had not told her mother that she was considering Michael Poppy. That decision was also hasty. Her mother and the Poppy sisters were practically planning their wedding.

It occurred to Charity that she tended to make hasty poor decisions. She flew off the handle when taking a moment to consider might be a better choice. Hasty words had hurt her possible relationship with Lord Wentwell, and there was nothing she could do to fix that.

Hasty words had also hurt her friendship with Lady Amelia, and that issue had been sitting unresolved for almost a year. She could not repair the relationship with Lord Wentwell, but perhaps she could talk to Amelia. That would make her feel better she decided.

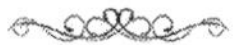

NEVILLE WAS certain that keeping a distance from Lady Charity Abernathy was the best course of action. She was too fine of a lady to be associated with one of his reputation especially after walking unattended through the musicale in the park. Rumor was not yet rife, but it could be re-ignited. There were moments when he wished it were not so, but there was naught that could be done for it now.

He knew he was a gentleman at heart. He would never truly ruin a lady of the *Ton*. Such were the sisters and daughters of his peers in parliament. Still, he had played his games; he engaged in witty banter and shocked the ladies, but he had never thought ruin would follow such action, until Miss Danbury, and Miss Macrum. He could lay at least part of the blame at their feet, but he was not innocent. He had flirted with both. He had played his part well and all the *Ton* knew him as a rake and nothing else.

When Miss Danbury's father had come to speak with him about her dalliance with his stable-master he had been shocked. He had promised to do what he could to protect the lady. He had never once thought that the *Ton* would tangle him in the embroilment.

It was now clear that Miss Macrum had dangled before his brother, but it was truly him she wished to catch, and Miss Danbury had no interest in either of them. Her passion for horses, was actually a passion for the master of the horse. He had been so blind, but when Miss Danbury's father approached him, he had thought only to protect Miss Danbury's reputation for the sake of her family. Her father hoped, that if she were not with child, a lesser match may be made next season. Neville did not even know if a child was possible, only that his stable-master had come to him later in the hopes of marrying the woman, and he had dismissed the man out of hand. Such dishonorable behavior was not welcome in his household.

Now Neville's own besmirched reputation had scattered the available ladies from him. It hurt to think that what he thought of as a game, had turned so serious. The *Ton* had convicted him of his crimes without judge or jury and he knew it was his own fault. He had embraced the libertine attitude because the ladies liked the danger, until it was real, in the sense of Miss Danbury. Then they avoided him like a leper. He had no recourse. He had cultivated the reputation. He could not shed it now.

He could of course wait a few years. The rumor would die down eventually, and he was not a female who needed to marry by a certain age. He could wait. The problem was, he knew that Lady Charity would not, and he had determined that it was Lady Charity he wanted for his wife. Why was it then, when he had played this game so well, he now found himself stalemated?

At first Lady Charity seemed determined to speak to him. She even wrote him a letter when her mother prevented any further interaction between the pair. Neville chose not to reply. He knew not what to say anyway. He could not be honest, for Lady Charity had already seen too much for him to allow her to learn more of his true person. To give her so much would be to give what he gave to Katherine. It would be heartache all over again. He held Lady Charity's letter in his hands and considered. He could write back to her, only what would he say? Was it fair to tie her name with his now? She would be suspect as soon as he did so, and he did not want to besmirch her reputation.

He could no longer play the game with her, because, he realized his heart was involved. Neither did he wish to deceive her by replying with a false pretense. So he had said nothing.

Now, he watched her from afar. Neville was certain that his observations went unnoticed. All, save his good friend Reginald, were oblivious to his interest in the lady. Reginald had a keen eye and was also the only person, save Samuel Beresford, who knew the truth of that day in the park.

Reg had encouraged his friend to be out with the truth of his feelings, but Neville thought that might only make the situation all the more confusing. At least, this way, Lady Charity could go on with her life without being mixed up in the mess of his. When Reg informed him that something of a courtship had developed between Lady Charity and Michael Poppy, Neville feigned disinterest.

Observation revealed that the pair was spending a great deal of time together. Lady Charity seemed to be focusing all of her attention on drawing the quiet fellow out of his shell. Her mother, for whatever reason, did not disapprove of the match. This would have been surprising except for the fact that Wentwell assumed the approval had something to do with ensuring that her daughter avoided him.

Lady Charity's mother was a shrewd woman with a keen eye. She would shepherd her daughter through life in order to achieve her own means, but she would not choose Michael Poppy. The family had little in the way of assets. No, Lady Shalace would not choose Michael, not unless the Lady Charity truly cared for the man. If that was the life she wanted for herself, why should he stand in the way?

A fire burned in his blood as he thought of her with Michael Poppy. He wanted her for himself, that was why, but he said nothing. He had no right to do so. To even be seen with her now, would bring dishonor upon her. Still the thought of her with Michael hurt.

Neville shook the image from his mind. He should not be so concerned with what Lady Charity wanted. It was clear that it could not, would not be him. This was for the best. He had no intention of marrying. He had done a kindness for the girl by leaving her alone. As the days passed he continued to keep his distance but, try as he might, he could never convince himself to stop watching and listening for her movements.

Lady Charity and Flora Muirwood were walking in the late afternoon upon the arms of the Poppy brothers. They had spent nearly every afternoon this week strolling through the extensive gardens that peppered the streets of Bath. Each day they chose a new route and, while it was meant to be different, Charity feared that this might be all that was left for her entertainment for the rest of her days. Charity tried to imagine what her life would be like if she were married to Michael and Flora were married to James. She had a hard time imagining the picture with appeal.

"Lady Charity," Michael drew her attention and then offered the same type of blue flower that he plucked every day for the past two weeks to offer for her pleasure. He had said that it brought out the color of her eyes. Perhaps that was so, but Charity could not help but long for more variety. Michael was all too predictable. She wondered if there was something that might be done about that. Perhaps she just needed to teach him how to be more spontaneous.

"Michael," she began with breathy excitement. The prospect of something different had renewed her energy. "Look! There is a path just there that we have not tried. We should take it and see where it might lead."

Michael looked around in an attempt to locate Flora and James. They were a ways ahead and not at all missing their companions.

To Charity's surprise, Michael agreed.

The path was overgrown to the point that Charity

could not make out the trail more than a handful of yards ahead of them. The trees formed a canopy overhead. The reprieve from the grasping fingers of the sun was a relief. Charity lowered her parasol and allowed the breeze to tickle her neck blowing the strands of hair that had escaped her neat chignon.

"Lady Charity," Michael stepped in front of her so that she might stop walking. He appeared distraught and Charity wondered if something were the matter.

"I have told you, you may call me Charity," she replied. If she was planning on marrying the fellow, she should be able to call him by his given name, and he hers. She took a deep breath. She could do this.

"Charity," Michael said, but her name did not roll off of his tongue with ease. He was more comfortable with formal address, even with those with whom he was close.

"What is it, Michael?" she asked. There was a fine line of perspiration upon his brow and she wondered if he was ill. She asked as much, but he just shook his head. Perhaps it was just the heat making him look so green.

"It is only," he began but allowed his words to trail away, his sentence unfinished.

Buck up, man, she thought uncharitably, and then she said with more patience. "What did you wish to say, Michael?" She, called him by his given name. It was not so hard. Lead by example, she told herself.

Michael still stood, tongue tied, biting his lip. She could make no sense of his behavior. Charity had learned that Michael Poppy did well with clear instruction. "Speak your piece," she demanded.

As predicted, he cleared his throat, straightened his

shoulders, and began again with what confidence he could muster.

"Lady ..." he grimaced when she gave him a pointed look. "Charity," he amended. "Our families have known one another for many years..."

"Yes," she nodded. "That, they have."

"I know that you have long thought of me as a cousin." For the first time Michael seemed uncomfortable. His loss for words was uncharacteristic because Charity had never known him to speak without great thought and preparation.

"Your family has always been very dear to me," she confirmed.

"Yes," Michael turned so that they were standing shoulder to shoulder looking out across the lush greenery. He seemed more comfortable if he was not looking directly at her. "It is for that reason that I wished to speak with you."

Charity had suspected for some time that they were approaching this conversation, yet she felt that it was far too soon. She had come to know Michael more. Of course they had seen each other often these past weeks. However, he still seemed an enigma. Each moment that she expected to break open his shell to reveal the layers beneath, she found yet another shell. He remained cool and collected, unswayable. Charity was certain that there was more to Michael Poppy than he let on, but she could not seem to access him. Perhaps one day she hoped that this conversation would bring her excitement, now it brought nothing but dread.

"I would like to speak with you about a very serious

matter," Michael began as if he were about to negotiate the sale of one of their prized hunters. "It is a matter that I believe you will agree is the next logical path."

"Michael…" Charity stopped herself from rejecting him outright. Was this not the ultimate goal? Even though she had not come to know as much as she would like about this gentleman, she would have her entire life to get to know him. Her intent for spending so much time at his side was to eventually reach this conversation. Then why did she feel as if she wished he had not spoken, or that they had not taken this isolated walk down the path.

"Lady Charity," his confidence seemed to increase when he was able to stick to his formal address. "I should like to ask your permission to speak with your father."

"Michael, I…"

"I know that he has not been well," Michael continued. "I have said nothing to save you the shame."

"Thank you," Charity said tightly. Yes, he had saved them embarrassment, but why did she not feel the same gratitude as she felt when Lord Wentwell had protected her?

"I shall have to speak to your eldest male cousin then as well, to ensure that the decision is agreed upon by one of sound reason," Michael continued.

Charity felt her hackles rise. "My cousin," she said. They had gone to great lengths to keep the news of her father's demise from her cousin. Still, she knew that he meant no insult, but this she could not allow.

"My cousin has nothing to do with me, or my marriage," Charity said haughtily.

"But as the one who will eventually hold the earldom, I think he does." Michael was merely stating the facts.

Even Charity could not argue the truth. However, she felt protective as she listened to him speak of her father's ineptitude. She could not allow him to continue. "Stop," she said. "My cousin has no say in my marriage. My father and perhaps my mother does, but no other."

"I am not as wealthy as I believe your mother to hope," he continued. "However, I have a keen sense of business and will do all in my power to continue your happiness."

"Business!" Charity interjected surprised.

"I know I am not wealthy, but with a bit of capital to fund a new shipping business, I believe that can all change. I shall be wealthy one day."

"Michael," Charity said. "It is not for wealth that I care to marry."

"I am pleased to hear that, though I assure you that my income is nothing to be ashamed about, and it will grow."

She realized that Michael had taken her statement as encouragement. Charity tried to remind herself that she should be encouraging him. Is this not exactly what she had wanted? The image of Lord Wentwell flashed through her mind and Charity was ashamed of the thought of another man at a moment like this.

The betrayal of her mind renewed her determination to focus on Michael. Perhaps that is what she needed to give her the final push to accept his offer. She felt sick at the thought. Perhaps the heat was too much for her.

"Lady Charity," Michael raised his chin, his face stoic,

and Charity half expected him to offer to shake her hand, if only he did not have his own hands stuck behind his back.

"I also am of the belief that a union of our pair would be most fortuitous, and I will argue for its execution. If you, and of course your father, will consent, I would like to make you my wife."

She couldn't do it. She could not say yes. She felt as if her tongue had cleaved to the roof of her mouth. She had wanted this, hadn't she? She would be sister to all of the Poppys. She would be sister to James, and to Flora. She would not be lonely. She would have a big family, and of course, money would be no issue. She may even be able to help with the younger Poppys' dowries. It would be the perfect solution.

"There is much to consider..." Charity replied when she finally found her voice.

"I have already weighed the options and I do believe that we would make a steady pair."

"A steady pair..." Charity repeated. Her determination was dwindling with every word he uttered. Was there not meant to be a proclamation of love? What of a promise of the future, a family, and years of wedded bliss? Were these things not to be spoken upon their engagement?

"Do you love me?" Charity blurted, much as she had asked James if he had loved Flora.

"I..." Michael appeared to be caught off guard by her question. He soon collected himself. "I believe that we shall get on well enough. In fact, couples that get on well often develop a deep sense of love and respect for one another."

"Develop..." she murmured. Then he did not, at this very moment, love her. Yet, he thought he could.

"Is it not too soon to know?" Charity asked. "Are we not to be certain before making a vow?"

Her companion found his own voice, which was suddenly quite forceful. "I have found no flaw and do believe that the depth of our emotion shall increase with time. I do believe that we might call this love, at some point, for I do care for you, and I am sure I shall not find another such as you."

"Such as me," she repeated. Someone with so much money, she wondered, or someone with physical attributes like passing beauty and youth. Charity thought over his words. They were nice enough but did nothing to make her wish to rush to the altar.

"If you would agree, I would announce our engagement," he said.

"Why now?" she asked. "Why not wait until we are certain? How can you be so sure when we still have much to learn about one another?"

"There are two reasons that I might provide," Michael began. Charity was shocked at his rational approach. Did he have any emotion in him? He would answer her question so that she might see, and agree with, his logic. "The first is that I can see no logical reason to delay. We shall make a fine match in every manner. I do not see how these facts will change with additional time. We might get to know each other more, but our compatibility will remain."

Charity nodded but pressed her lips together in a tight line. Was that not exactly what she was supposed to be thinking? If the aim was to wed Mr. Poppy, then what would a few more weeks or months matter?

"And your second reason?" she asked.

"The second, I must admit, is perhaps the most significant factor as to the speed of my determination." Michael turned to Charity and, while most men would have at least had the decency to appear shamed for the admission, Michael stated the fact as if it were nothing more than the arrival of the weekly chronicle. "My mother is anxious for me to wed. You know she is quite forceful. I had thought to gain a wife before the leaves turn color in the fall. The sooner, the better, I think. Mother would like it best if I made my choice before the month's end so that we might begin preparations at once. Then our wedding could coincide with my sisters' seasons, and we could save some expense, and since my choice is obvious I can find no reason to delay."

"I see," Charity mused.

They stood in silence for a long while as he waited for her to agree with his reason. He did not so much as take her hand. She felt it was the strangest marriage proposal ever.

"But you are not in love with me. Do you not wish to find someone you could love?" she said softly.

"Are you in love with me?"

"I do not feel as I imagined I would in love," she admitted.

"Neither do I," Michael said.

She looked down at the fan in her hand, and realized that she was not nervous. She was nearly as cool and collected as Michael himself. "Michael," she said. "I also thought I could find love with you; perhaps hoped I could." She looked up at him then. She owed him that. She faced him completely as she said the words. "I cannot marry you. I think I only realize at this very moment, that to marry without love, is a mistake, a mistake for both of us."

Charity watched a look of relief cross his face. For the first time she saw a side of Michael that revealed that he did care more than he let on. He did wish to find love for himself.

"I do not think that we would grow to love each other in the way that we would wish," she said. "While I admire you, and rest assured that I mean no insult to your person, I do not think that our match would be full of happiness. I cannot agree to a union that makes sense in the head, but not in the heart."

Michael nodded. He had been rebuffed and that must have hurt his ego, but he did not seem terribly upset by her refusal.

"I shall always consider you as a dear friend," she caught his hand and smiled up into his brown eyes. "I am sorry, I cannot consider anything more. I am sorry. I led you to believe there could be more between us."

Michael nodded. Still he had not spoken, so Charity placed her hand on his forearm and allowed him to lead her back up the path where they were soon joined by a frantic James and Flora.

"We have been looking everywhere for you two!" Flora cried. "We had thought you lost."

"We were just up the way," Charity gestured down the overgrown trail. Many a walker would have missed it for it blended well with its surroundings. Charity was aware that it would be the perfect spot for a pair of lovers to disappear without causing suspicion.

James and Flora grinned for the remainder of the walk. Charity wished to inform them that no agreement had been struck, but she could not do so without injuring her companion's pride. The lovers assumed that they knew what had occurred and looked forward to the announcement.

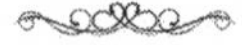

20

When Charity returned to her home that afternoon, her mother too seemed to expect a whispered confirmation. When she received none, Lady Shalace was distraught. Charity finally told her mother the outcome of the conversation. She could make no explanation for her refusal, other than that she did not love the gentleman. Lady Shalace would not be consoled and retired to her room without her evening meal. Charity could hear her mumbled cries about her *spinster daughter* echoing through the halls. Finally, she went to her mother's room.

"I do not know why you are so upset," she said. "After all, Michael Poppy is no particular catch. You said that yourself not a month ago."

"That was before you rejected every suitor out of hand."

"I have not," Charity said, but as her mother began

listing names, she realized that her mother was right. She had rejected quite a number of suitors. That was because a part of her was still hoping that Lord Wentwell would answer her letter. She knew it would not be so, but still, she dreamed of green eyes and strong hands helping her to alight into a carriage, while he promised that he would find her father. She dreamed of a man who would put everything aside for her, a man who made her heart beat fast and spoke to her as a person, not a contrivance, or a business deal. She realized that when Michael was squeezing out his bland proposal. He was everything Lord Wentwell was not, but Lord Wentwell didn't even want to see her or even speak to her. The thought made her want to cry.

It did not help that her mother was scolding her. "You are ruining your future, Charity. Eventually the gentlemen will realize that you will have none of them. Especially, now that you have broken poor Michael Poppy's heart. Word will spread."

"I have not broken his heart."

"I do not understand why you have rejected him, Charity. Just a few weeks ago, you were telling me why the Poppys were perfect, and now you are back to playing games."

"You should know about games, Mother," she snapped feeling annoyed.

"What is that supposed to mean?" Her mother demanded.

"I am not playing games," Charity said, sighing as she thought of Lord Wentwell, saying, *it's all a game isn't it?* The thought put her completely out of sorts.

"I am not," Charity repeated. "I am the one who wants an honest relationship. How can I find honesty if everyone is wearing a mask?" Charity complained. "You most of all, Mother."

"Charity, that's enough."

"It's true."

"Charity, I don't know what to do with you. Do you even want to get married?"

"Of course I do."

"Then why would you reject Michael Poppy when just a fortnight ago, you were telling me why I should consider him?"

"I don't love him, Mother."

"Then we are back to the beginning," Lady Shalace said. "You need to..."

"No!" Charity shouted. She wanted to put her hands over her ears. She could not hear one more direction, one more reason why she was a failure. "No. Just stop. I cannot. I cannot do this anymore. I can't be what you want me to be." Charity burst into tears, feeling like she would never measure up, not as a daughter or as a wife. "I will always be a disappointment to everyone," she said as left her mother's room racing for her own. She threw herself across the bed and unmindful of the disorder she was making of her dress. She cried until her face was a blotchy mess, and she did not care one whit.

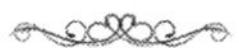

WHEN LADY CHARITY had cried herself out, she stood and washed her face. She did not know what to say to her mother. She was such a disappointment to her. She was a disappointment to everyone, most of all herself. She decided that she would go and visit with her father. Even if he had no advice for her, it was comforting to sit with him. Perhaps she would read to him. She knew he was going to take the waters later in the day, but she hoped that he would feel well enough to talk for a while.

She wanted to speak with him about her suitors since she could not see eye to eye with her mother. She fixed his blankets and fluffed his pillow and then sat beside him. First she told him about Michael Poppy's proposal and why she had to reject him, and she began to tell him about her feelings for Lord Wentwell, but he interrupted her, sharply. "I don't care about your dross, woman."

The statement struck to her heart. "Do you remember me?" she asked plaintively.

"Of course," her father said brightly. "You are the young lady who comes every day to read to me."

She sighed, and her breath shook with pain. "Father, it's me, Charity," she said. "Your daughter."

"Of course," he replied, but she wasn't sure he actually knew who she was. In a moment he demanded, "Girl, read me the Times."

"Father," she persisted. She needed him to know her. She needed her father. "Please, Father, I am your daughter. I am Charity."

"You are not!" he said. "You only think yourself above your station, and if you continue in such a manner, you will find yourself in want of a job. Do you understand me, girl?"

Charity blinked back the tears. "I understand, sir," she said.

"Now read the bloody paper or get out."

She wanted to run, but she stayed. Her lip quivered a little as she began to read to him, but after a few moments she got control of herself. It did not matter that he did not know her. She knew that he was her father. She read to him until his man came to get him ready to go and drink the medicinal water. She hoped it helped him.

Saddened and frustrated, Charity came back to her room, after her father left for the waters. Jean did not try to talk to her. She just brushed her hair until it shone and twisted it into a simple style. It was still hours before dinner and Charity was at loose ends. She decided to walk with Jean along the path to the shops.

"We will buy something beautiful," she told Jean.

"As you wish, my lady."

Her mother would be furious to be left behind, but Charity felt that Jean was chaperone enough, and she did not want her mother with her right now. It was a beautiful sunny day and she didn't want to spend half of it waiting for her mother and the carriage to be readied and the other half fending off her mother's barbs and trying to explain herself.

She looked at all the pretty baubles along the artist's market, and thought to buy a piece or two to cheer herself. She found some exquisite hand painted combs. "Which one do you think, Jean?" she asked, and Jean shook her head. "They are both pretty," her maid said.

Charity asked the seller to hold them because of course, she didn't carry coin. She would send one of the servants back for them. "Wrap them both for me," Charity had said, but neither of the lovely pieces made her feel better.

21

As she was walking home, she imagined the Earl of Wentwell calling upon her. That would not happen. She had dressed him down. He had helped her with her father, but he had not really spoken to her socially since the quarrel. He had not responded to her letter, nor had he acknowledged her in public. She thought perhaps the reason he had not replied was her involvement with Michael, but that was ended now. What might she do about it? Would another letter be too forward? Jean had said that it was in protection of her own reputation that he had not replied, and that she should be thankful for the consideration. Still Charity just could not understand why he could speak with every other female, reputable or not, besides her.

She found herself on a familiar street, nearing a familiar townhouse. Lady Amelia would be staying there with her Aunt Ebba while she was in Bath. The thought gave Charity pause. “Shall we visit Lady Amelia?” she asked Jean, not really expecting Jean to be a naysayer.

But Jean hesitated. “It is rather irregular to do so without prior appointment.”

“But you would like to see your friends, wouldn’t you?” Charity asked. “Your sister is still her upstairs maid is she not?”

“She is,” Jean said.

Charity had not seen her friend since the Duke of Ely’s funeral and she had barely spoken to Lady Amelia since their argument so many months ago. First Charity had stubbornly felt she was right, and then after Amelia lost her father, it had felt strange to speak to her once good friend with all that lie between them. Charity realized she had jumped to conclusions then too. Was that what she did with the Earl of Wentwell? Had she spoken out in haste and anger when the man was undeserving of her ire? Was he a better person than she surmised? Charity did not know. She only knew she deeply regretted how she had chastised Amelia and she wanted to fix something. She wanted to make something right.

She had alienated her friend with her sharp words, and although Amelia had been just as sharp, Charity felt the need to speak with her. The sad occasion of Amelia’s father’s funeral had not truly allowed them time to talk. It was instead a hollow empty occasion deemed necessary by society, but it was not the place for conversation. Anyway, Amelia had been devastated. Charity found herself wanting the easy camaraderie that she had once had with the duke’s daughter.

Perhaps it was her own father's condition that made her feel the closeness with Lady Amelia. The Earl of Shalace was at times as lost to Charity as Amelia's father was to her. So it was with sudden determination she stepped up in front of the townhouse. She knew it was gauche to call without first sending word, but Charity felt strangely compelled. She marched up to the door, and ignoring Jean's protests, knocked like a commoner. Her mother would have been upset to know Charity had done so. She did not care.

Lady Amelia was perhaps the only person who could understand her relationship with her father, since Amelia had been close to her own father. Perhaps speaking to Amelia would bring her peace. At the very least, Charity could mend the rift that was between them. That she could do.

The butler opened the door, and invited her into the townhouse. She stood for moment in the foyer with Jean, when the butler went to inform Lady Amelia who was waiting. The first moment Charity saw Amelia she knew her old friend would understand. Amelia did not even wait for the butler to announce Charity, instead rushing to greet her in the foyer. Amelia smiled and welcomed her friend with open arms, as if they had not quarreled at all and Charity went to her and returned her embrace to give solace as much as accept it.

"I am sorry to come unannounced."

"Aunt Ebba will not mind," Amelia said. "She has taken Phillip to the park. "

"And Captain Beresford?"

"He is out with his brother. It is good to see you, Charity," Amelia said.

"And you, Amelia. How are you?" She stood at arm's length holding her hands.

"I have been well." She said laying a light hand on her slightly rounded midsection.

"I mean, since your father's death. Oh Amelia, I cannot even imagine." Charity squeezed her friend's hands, feeling tears well in her own eyes, not for Amelia's father, but for her own. "He was such a pillar. How do you go on?"

Amelia sighed and moved from the foyer. "Come, and sit," she said leading the way to Aunt Ebba's morning room. Amelia called for tea, and smoothed her dress before she spoke. "It has been difficult since father's death, but Aunt Ebba is a tower of strength and of course, Captain Beresford."

"When Patience wrote to me of your engagement last year I could hardly believe my ears, and then the rumors of your uncle were just horrible. I told Mrs. Thompson and Mrs. Sullivan what Patience had writ. I hope I did well for you."

"You did," Amelia agreed. "You were a great help to me even though you may not have known it."

"You have my congratulations on your marriage," Charity said. "And the expected addition to your family."

Charity felt she had trapped herself in small talk. She had been full of purpose when she marched up to knock upon the door, and now it was so difficult to say what she came to say.

"Thank you. Samuel and I are most excited, although

it saddens me that my father will not know his grandchild."

At the mention of Amelia's father, Charity thought of her own and felt another pang of sadness. Amelia gave her a long look before she continued. "Still, I doubt you came to speak to me after all this time merely to congratulate me."

Amelia had the truth of the matter.

"No," Charity admitted gathering her courage. "That is not the only reason. I came to apologize and if I am able, mend the friendship we once held between us. I misjudged you, Amelia. I spoke out of turn and now those words cannot be swallowed again. I seem to do that quite often." She finished, thinking of Lord Wentwell and the disparaging words she had thrown at him.

"Oh, I know," Amelia said with a sad smile.

"You know?"

"I do not fault you for it," Amelia said. "You are just quick to anger, but you are also kind and generous to a fault."

"I am sorry, Amelia. I did not think."

"Of course you didn't." Amelia laughed. "You wear your heart on your sleeve, but that is why I love you so. You are bright bit of sunshine, surprising on a dull day."

"It is surely not dull," Charity said, but she understood Amelia's meaning.

The footman brought the tea, and Amelia addressed him. "Please take the service to the garden," she said, and the footman bowed slightly with the tea set. "We've decided to enjoy the weather."

"Right away, my lady," he said, and left them to their privacy.

"Let us take our tea in the garden," Amelia said. "We may not have many more clear days in the summer. We should enjoy the sunshine while we can."

"I do not want to dredge up old hurts," Charity said as they walked from the house. "But I must. I think I was jealous. You had the love of the *Ton* and were so effortlessly beautiful."

"Effortless? You jest," Amelia protested, but Charity continued undaunted.

"Mostly," Charity whispered. "You had your father, and mine was..." she swallowed heavily, the words catching in her throat. "My father is dying bit by bit."

Amelia said nothing. She just turned and hugged her friend. They stood that way for a long moment in the archway of roses which led to Ebba's spectacular garden. "I am so sorry, Amelia," Charity said.

"All is forgiven, Charity. Long ago forgiven," Amelia said. The girls walked along the garden path behind the townhouse, and it was as it once was when they were younger. All of the anger between them fell away. Charity confided to Amelia about losing her father at the concert and of Lord Wentwell gallantly returning him to her.

"At least you have found him again, Charity. Perhaps with care he will recover."

Charity shook her head. "You know these thing do not get better. They get worse. You lost your father quickly. I am losing mine slowly. Every day he slips farther away," Charity whispered. "I cannot bear it." Soon tears were streaming down both of their faces.

"You will bear it because you must," Amelia said. "Though it hurts just the same." Both girls walked along the path and sniffed, patting corner of their eyes with matching handkerchiefs. "But remember, your friends are here for you: Patience and myself most especially."

"Are you truly?"

"I am," Amelia promised.

"But you have chosen Captain Beresford..." Charity said, forcibly squashing the pang of jealously that rose in her breast.

She and Amelia sat the garden table, and Amelia reached for the teapot to pour. "I suppose I did choose him," Amelia said with a faraway look, "but he is nothing that I thought I would have chosen. He has no title, no money to speak of, and he is not polished or suave, but in the end I found I was in love with him, and that has made all the difference."

"I never would have thought of him, Amelia. He always appeared to be such a ...scoundrel," Charity finished with a wan smile. She put her attention on her tea, stirring in the cream and sugar.

"Perhaps he is," Amelia said un-offended, "but perhaps he is *my* scoundrel, and I love him nonetheless." Charity could see the sincerity in her friend's face. She did indeed love the naval captian. Charity turned away, suddenly filled with sorrow. How would she ever find her own love?

Amelia who was ever more perceptive than others thought, caught Charity's hand across the table. "Oh, Charity, you will find your true love. I know you will. Do not fret,"

"No. You know me too well, Amelia I have myself in a state."

Amelia passed a plate of cinnamon cakes and Charity took one.

"Over Michael Poppy?" Amelia asked.

Charity nodded. "I have refused him." She sat poking her cinnamon cake with a fork until it was quite demolished. "Oh Amelia, my mother threatens that if I don't marry soon, I will be a spinster. I am not cut out to be a spinster."

"Of course you aren't," Amelia said.

Charity continued to worry the cinnamon cake. "I do not want to be an old maid, but I cannot see my way clear. I do not want to be alone, and I fear I have led Michael on." She paused and looked up at Amelia. "I supposed, the Poppys are much what I thought I would have with the Duke of Ely."

"However so?" Amelia asked tipping her nose just a bit into the air, at having her Father compared to the Poppys.

Charity put the fork aside and picked up her tea. She sipped it thoughtfully. "I mean the Poppys are not wealthy and have no titles, but they have a wonderful family that I would love to be a part of, much like I once hoped to be a part of your family, Amelia. We could have been like sisters if things had been different."

"If things had been different," Amelia agreed. "Truly, but you will always be my friend, Charity. We cannot choose our family but our friends are always our choice."

"You say you are my friend, and I believe you, but it is

so different now. Now that everyone is married. Oh what am I to do? I cannot be alone, Amelia. It terrifies me. I cannot be the maiden aunt. I have no brothers or sisters. I will be the poor relation in my cousin's household and I cannot be a governess. It would not suit me at all. You know my mother and I barely ever see eye to eye. Can you imagine us sharing an apartment in my cousin's house?"

"Then it is important that you marry," Amelia said softly.

Charity shook her head.

"I know it is hard," Amelia said. "Believe me. I know, but a woman alone in the world, even a daughter of a peer, is still a woman alone."

"There is no one," Charity said.

"What of the Lord Wentwell? You mentioned he aided you at the concert. He is rich, titled...You always said you would not marry a pauper. He certainly is not."

"He is a rogue," Charity said with disparity. She picked up the fork again, and put it down.

"So I have heard," Amelia said. "But a handsome rogue, if a bit slight for my tastes, and somewhat of a dandy if I understand."

"He is not a dandy," Charity interrupted. "And not everyone judges a man by how many stone he weighs nor how strong he is. Just because Samuel Beresford is a behemoth does not mean everyone thinks such a large man is handsome."

"So you do think Wentwell is handsome?" Amelia said.

"I admitted no such thing," Charity said. "He is a cad and a reprobate."

Despite her harsh words, Wentwell knew the truth of her father's illness and had kept his own council. Disregarding their quarrel, he had come to her aid at the concert. He had not even accepted thanks for the deed. Instead, her mother had further reprimanded him. Charity reminded herself that despite his kind action the man could not be a gentleman and have thrown over Miss Danbury.

"Lord Wentwell has ruined Miss Danbury," Charity said, her anger at the man reigniting. "Then once he achieved his ends, he cast her aside."

"Those are heavy claims to lay at his feet."

"All the *Ton* knows it," Charity said as she sipped her tea.

"As they knew the truth of my father?" Amelia asked.

That gave Charity pause.

Amelia sighed. "Ruined or no, why are you so distressed over the state of Miss Danbury? It is regrettable yes, but you seem to take Lord Wentwell's supposed involvement as a personal affront. My dear Charity, one might think you were jealous of the man's attentions."

"Jealous!" Charity scoffed. "Hardly. I am relieved at any distance I can manage," she said more for herself than Amelia. "I am merely angered at his audacity."

Amelia gave her a slow, pointed look and Charity quailed under her friend's knowing gaze and she picked up her now empty cup to hold because it gave her something to do.

"Perhaps I have developed a poor habit," Charity admitted with a shamed expression. "But it is not what you might think."

"Oh?" Amelia replied.

"I only meant that I should not allow his misdeeds to plague me so, or allow myself to wish that he might be better."

"Do you wish him better?" Lady Amelia did not seem surprised by her friend's words.

Charity hoped that Amelia might mistake her blush for the effect of the heat of the day. If Lord Wentwell had been a different sort of character, then he had every other attribute that would draw Charity to him. However, his flaws could not be overlooked and so she would try not to imagine a different, more respectable version of the man.

"I always wish the best of everybody, Amelia," she replied "For his own sake, and Miss Danbury's at the very least." Charity sat her cup on the table with an unladylike clink in her saucer. "If Lord Wentwell had any gentlemanly feeling, he would right the wrong and offer for Miss Danbury." The words dropped into Charity's heart like blocks of ice.

"But then he would be lost to you," Amelia said softly.

Charity balled the napkin up in her lap. And there was the rub. Charity realized with a start that she was jealous of Miss Danbury, not of her position, obviously, but of the idea of her as first in Lord Wentwell's affections. That another woman may have enjoyed the full effect of his wit, his smile, his burning green gaze, his kisses, his touch wounded her deeply. The kiss that Charity had so longed to take back in the streets of Bath taunted her, and she fairly burned in her seat, whether from anger or desire, she did not know.

"It matters not. I am looking for an honest man, and a kind one. I do not think Lord Wentwell is either."

Amelia took a sip of tea and eyed Charity over the cup. "I must admit, I barely know Lord Wentwell, but I remember Father said both he and his brother were in the war, as Wentwell's own father before him. I know he has been the Earl of Wentwell since he was eight, and a peer has little censure. If he was going to sire a bastard, he would have had ample opportunity to do so, but as far as I know, as far as anyone knows, he has not. In fact despite his reputation before this business with Miss Danbury, there was little that was said of him that would have caused true scandal, except that he was once engaged." Amelia broke off with a frown.

"Engaged," Charity repeated wide eyed. "Did he breech the promise?"

"I do not know the details, only that the wedding did not occur." Amelia sat her cup in its saucer and paused thoughtfully. "Still, he is also good friends with Lord Barton. I think that speaks to his character."

"But if he is a rake," Charity protested. "After what happened last year with Julia..."

"Oh pish posh," Amelia interrupted. "You are not Julia. You are not a shy little miss. You never were. You are the daughter of a peer. If you want Neville Collington, then you shall have him, rake or no."

The thought that she could have Lord Wentwell as her own made her heart soar, but the idea that he could love another broke that selfsame heart. That he could cast off her love without a thought, brought a pain that was sharper still, leaving Charity both envious and indignant on the lady's behalf. That is if Miss Danbury truly was his lover, a small voice reminded her and Charity felt a flicker of hope.

"How do you know me so well, Amelia? How did you know it was Lord Wentwell all along?"

"Because James has always been more like a brother than a suitor, to you, and Michael would bore you to tears, and because I too know what it is to fight ardently against what is in your heart, when your heart already knows what it wants. You have been searching for the man you love, Charity. That man is right in front of you. It is Neville Collington."

Charity's heart swelled in her chest. Amelia was right. She felt she may have loved Lord Wentwell from the first time she danced with him, without knowing it. She had been a fool. She desired honesty from a man, but she had not even been honest with herself. Instead, she realized she had jumped to conclusions again.

"I have become used to judging him, and that is my error," Charity admitted. "I am too quick to search for flaws and allow them to ruffle me. It is neither the practice of a lady nor of a charitable heart."

Oh, but if the rumors are false... Charity thought. "But Wentwell must hate me. He will never forgive me. I said such awful things, Amelia."

"I do not believe that is the case," Amelia said, smiling at Charity. "It is easier than you think to forgive someone you care for deeply, no matter what may have been said."

"First," Charity said, "I have to apologize to Lord

Wentwell. Oh but how can I? Mother threw him out of the house, and forbade me to even speak to him."

"There is always a way," Amelia said firmly. "I promise you we shall find it."

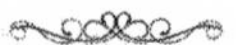

22

Lord Wentwell had been uncharacteristically withdrawn for days. Reginald had warned him. The word was that Michael Poppy was going to make an offer for Lady Charity Abernathy's hand. The pair had often been seen together, each time causing Neville a strange burst of jealousy that he could not contain and so he kept his distance.

Why would she not marry Michael Poppy? He was respectable, smart, and the Poppy holdings had nearly doubled in the last ten years, thanks to their son's effort. There was some talk about the Poppys now engaging in business, but there was no actual proof of it.

Michael was on the fringe of the *Ton*, and of course, he was wanting in one way which a daughter of an earl would surely notice. He had no title. However, Lady Charity did not seem as upset by the lack of that feature as many of the other ladies that Lord Wentwell had encountered. Perhaps it was because she was in possession of her own wealth. Perhaps she loved the dull lout? Whatever it was, she spent quite a lot of time with Michael over the last few weeks.

Reg said that even her mother approved, in all her prickly plotting. Save the formalities, it had seemed settled. The thought sent Neville into a fit of melancholy. It was true that as an earl and a gentleman, he had no need to hurry into matrimony, but the same was not true for ladies. If Lady Charity indeed married the Poppy sap, she would be lost to him. He tried to tell himself that it made no difference; that one woman was just the same as the next, but his heart would not agree.

A knock on the door of his office brought Reg to visit. Neville signed the last of his notes and placed them on the corner of his desk for the servants to take out to post.

"To what do I owe this visit?" he greeted his friend with a clap on the shoulder. "What mischief have you and your sister done?"

Reginald laughed. "This is not about me," he informed his friend.

"Oh, heavens," Neville groaned. "What have I done now? Tell me the new rumor."

"I still do not understand how you stomach it," Reg shook his head. "Why do you allow the gossips to carry on so? You should just make it known that you are innocent of all their ridiculous claims."

Neville shrugged. He cared not what anyone thought of him save those in his closest circle. They knew the worth of his mettle. Nothing else mattered.

"There are no rumors about *you* to report this day," Reginald informed him.

"Whom do the gossipmongers aim to destroy?" Neville asked.

"Not destroy," Reginald continued in his vague fashion. "I can also confirm from the source that it is no rumor, but truth."

"Out with it," Neville said. "I have no use for your guessing games."

"I have news from my sister..." Reginald began. "Patience says..."

Neville felt his heart stop. "I do not wish to hear it," he replied.

Reginald was aware that Lord Wentwell harbored some feeling for Lady Charity. Still Reg looked all too pleased with himself and Neville wondered why he would boast of Michael's union when he knew it would bring his friend nothing but pain.

"You shall hear it," Reginald continued.

Neville waited with his hands pressed flat against the writing desk. He had been preparing for this moment for several days now, yet he still did not feel ready to hear the words that it was official.

"She refused him." Reg stood rocking on his feet, his lapels held tight in his hands. A grin was on his face.

Neville did not even hear for he was too lost in his own thought.

"I assumed she would, Michael is a fine gentleman and will make an honorable husband," Neville replied.

"Are you daft?" Reg laughed. "Did you not hear my words? She refused him!" It was all that Neville could do to wait in silence for the explanation. "They parted on good terms. Both agreed that there was no depth of feeling there, and Charity was adamant that she should marry for love. She does not love Michael Poppy."

Lord Wentwell wanted to shout for joy, but he just shook his head. He had not expected such news and had no idea how to make sense of it. She had refused him? Why? He could not help but allow hope to bloom in his heart. If Lady Charity did not love Michael Poppy then perhaps she might have some feeling for him. Or, if not, then there might at least be a chance for him to convince her that he was worth her consideration.

He swore in a low tone.

"Are you not happy with the news?" Reginald asked.

"Of course I am," he replied. "It is only that I have spent so much time allowing myself to be spoken of as the type of man that the Lady Charity would never consider. Now I fear that I will be unable to prove myself worthy of her affections."

"You had best get to work then," Reg said. "Charity will have many after her heart. There are many men, with better reputations than you, who will attempt to woo her."

"But not with a title, nor more coin," Lord Wentwell said.

"She cares nothing for money. She has never felt the loss of it, and I do not think she even cares for a title."

"Then what does she want?"

"Love," Reginald said. "She spoke long and with much depth on the subject to Lady Amelia, about her relationship with Samuel Beresford. And when she knew she loved him."

"Your sister told you all this?" Neville asked. It seemed

a strange conversation for a brother and a sister, but he did not really know of such things. He only had a brother, and neither he nor Edmund were like to share feelings like a couple of women.

"No, not Patience. Samuel," Reginald confessed.

"Samuel Beresford!" Neville was surprised.

"Lady Amelia told him that Lady Charity had come to see her, and she asked Samuel if you had an entendre for her," Reginald said.

"And Beresford told her, yes?"

"Why yes, of course he did."

"He had no right."

"Good God, Neville, you are the only one still in denial. Follow your own advice why don't you?"

"What advice?"

"The advice you gave Shalace. Go and talk to the woman."

"I cannot," Wentwell said.

"Oh, Poppycock," Reginald said.

Neville laughed aloud.

After a moment Reginald realized they had been speaking of Michael Poppy, and he laughed with his friend at the unintentional joke, which soon degenerated into further jokes about Michael Poppy's anatomy.

"I shall only hope the lady looks upon my suit with *charity*," Neville said wiping tears of mirth from his face.

"I hope that you will soon be able to tell me that all your conversations with the lady *went well*," Reginald quipped.

"I shall truly hope that she will favor me," Wentwell said, sobering a bit, "despite my reputation."

"Wentwell, I am sure she will have you. Just go and speak to the lady. If she loves you, she will have you bedraggled or no, and at least you have your shoes."

"That I do," Wentwell agreed.

Later the next afternoon, Patience arrived for a visit with Charity. The ladies were to ready themselves for afternoon tea at Aunt Ebba's home.

"It will be just like old times," Patience promised. "You and me and Amelia..."

"And, of course, your gentlemen," Charity added. Patience promised that Reginald would pick them up at the Shalace townhouse and escort them to the party. Charity thought it nice that her friend had thought of her and offered to include her in their party, that she might not be forced to arrive alone, or worse, with her mother. Instead, her mother was off to play cards with Mrs. Thompson and Mrs. Sullivan.

"Charity! We are going to be late to tea," Patience complained. "You know how Amelia is when we show up late. She will be in a temper all evening."

Charity huffed. "She will just have to be in a temper then," Charity said. "I am not yet ready."

"Will you be ready directly?" Patience asked as she hovered over Charity's shoulder.

"No. I'm afraid not." She had taken too much of the day moping, but her father's words had upset her, and she wanted to wear one of the new hand painted combs. Jean was engaged to redo Charity's hair. For that reason, her hair was still straight and loose down her back. There was no hurrying the hot iron and with the heat of the day, her curls were stubbornly insisting to go straight. Charity called over her shoulder, in a very unladylike way. "Go ahead without me, Patience. I will have Jean accompany me. It is not far, and I like the walking in the sun." She supposed she did it just to spite her mother, but it was also kind for Jean. Charity knew that Jean was friends with some of Aunt Ebba's servants and always appreciated the time to visit.

"If you are sure. Please do not be too late," Patience said, taking her leave of her friend and hurrying to the stairs. She paused and a light appeared in her eye. "I know! Why don't I have Reginald come back for you?" Patience said clapping her hands together with the thought.

"An excellent idea," Charity said, even though she would have rather walked.

Patience went downstairs to where Reginald was waiting to escort her and Charity to Aunt Ebba's home, and left with him requesting that he come back for Charity.

Charity stood up from Jean's ministrations and took in her appearance. The leaves painted on the comb went wonderfully with her new dress. It was the palest blue in color. The sleeves were capped just over the curve of her shoulder and were made of the same gauzy overlay that stretched from the high waist down to the floor. She adored the dress, it was the height of fashion, and even Lavinia would approve. She pulled on the matching silk Spenser jacket which had a high neckline embroidered with tiny purple flowers, added some wristlet gloves, grabbed the matching parasol, and moved to the stairs.

She paused at the top of the stairs when she noted that their butler was talking to someone standing in the doorway. Assuming it was Reginald, she moved quickly down the stairs, speaking as she descended, with Jean at her heels.

"It is alright, Peters. Please show him in. Lady Beresford said that she would send him back. No doubt my mother just did not want me walking. Isn't that right..?" She gasped suddenly as the figure stepped into the foyer more fully and Peters closed the door behind him. It was the Earl of Wentwell! Charity had to consciously close her mouth, because she was sure it gaped open.

He bowed low to her and smiled as he stood up. She had not laid eyes upon him in several days, certainly not since before her refusal of Michael. His looks had improved in that time, if that were at all possible. His bearing seemed more straight, his confidence and charm a new level that she had yet to witness. It was as if he were prepared to charm a duchess and yet, here he stood in her foyer.

"Indeed. It is unbecoming for a young woman to go strolling about without a proper escort. I am happy to oblige."

"Lord Wentwell... I... We..." Charity remembered her manners and she returned the bow with a slight curtsey of her own, the color flooding her neck and cheeks, unbidden her hand reached out to his and Lord Wentwell kissed her gloved hand in greeting.

He stepped aside and offered his arm. "I would be delighted to escort you."

Charity hesitated another moment. He was being very proper, considering their last meeting. Had she not said to Amelia that she wished to apologize to the man? And she did wish it so, but how to get to the topic.

Something inside of her thrilled at his arrival. He was here. He had not answered her letter, but he was here now. She was all jitters at the thought that he had come to see her, searched her out, and made the call. She could not really refuse him especially after just allowing Peters to invite him in... And she should not walk alone.

She never got the chance to speak to the man after the disastrous afternoon with her father and the subsequent tongue lashing by her mother. Now she felt particularly tongue-tied, but she pressed on. The apology must be made.

She looked at Jean who stood ready to walk with her. There was a coy grin on the maid's face. Charity did not wish to consider that perhaps Jean knew Charity's heart better than she knew herself. "Jean, I..." she began, but she did not need to say more. Jean grinned at her. "Enjoy your outing, my lady," she said with a slight curtsey and a twinkle in her eye.

Lady Charity's heart was beating a fast tattoo. What should she say to him? Should she bring up the fact that he had not responded to her letter, or should she apologize again now that she was in person before him? Her mind was all a whirl. She found her fingers clutching her fan, and consciously loosened them before she broke another of the fragile objects.

As the two stepped into the sunlight on the street, Charity let the fan drop to the ribbon around her wrist and opened her parasol. She lifted it over her head to shade her face from the heat of the sun. The earl stepped up beside her with his arm bent ready for her to take. She hesitantly placed her hand on his arm and he tucked it into the crook of his elbow. They walked down the steps together and nothing ever felt so right, and yet they walked in silence. It seemed as if neither of them knew where to begin.

"I received your letter," he said at last.

The silence stretched, but Charity could not call it awkward. She breathed in the scent of him, and reveled in the feel of his solid masculinity next to her. "I'm sorry I did not answer it," he said.

"I thought you did not accept my apology," she blurted.

"Of course I did." He said. "I just..." he paused at the door of the carriage.

Charity looked at the conveyance. "If you don't mind, I would rather walk," she said. "It is not far and it is a beautiful day."

He nodded and gave instructions to his driver and then took her arm again. A thrill went through her at his touch. Michael Poppy never made her feel this way, like she was floating on clouds. No one ever made her feel this way, only this man. Everything was right with the world. The birds were singing; the roses were blooming, the cobbles under her feet were smooth and perfect.

"Yes, it is a beautiful day," Lord Wentwell said.

"Although the beauty of the day is out shown by the beauty at my side."

"You are too kind," Charity answered automatically and then she clamped her mouth shut and the pair moved down along the street in awkward silence. Was he sincere, or was the compliment just a convention? Charity searched for a bit of conversation. Other than the weather, she was at a loss. Her stomach was in knots and her heart was racing. All Charity could think of was her sweating hands. She was glad she had gloves on. She wouldn't want him to notice her most unladylike perspiration.

"That is not what I meant to say," Lord Wentwell said.

She frowned at him. "You did not mean to complement me?"

"No. I mean, yes. Of course, you are beautiful, but I say that..." He broke off.

"To all the ladies," she finished with a grin.

He looked sheepish. "I do," he said. "Or rather I did. I was going to say, *so glibly*, but I no longer want to speak so."

Charity scrunched up her face in a quizzical look and he explained. "I want to shower you with complements every day, Lady Charity, but only you."

"If that is true," Charity said. "I do not understand. Why did you not return an answer to my letter?"

"I guess I was at a loss for words."

"You? I do not believe it," She laughed gently, but he was suddenly serious.

"I wanted to say something honest, and I found I did

not know how to do that. I have always been full of artifice, but just this once, I wanted more."

"I have heard tell that it is honest artifice," she said.

"I wanted honesty, true honesty. I did not know how to begin. I still don't. I have hope that you will teach me," he said softly.

Charity's heart swelled in her chest. She realized what the difference was between him and all the other suitors. She was in love with him. She was in love with Lord Wentwell, and she was walking with him. Her heart began to sing. She never wanted this moment to end.

They were about half way to Aunt Ebba's townhome, and Charity was afraid that she would lose this moment with him, and he would disappear again. She groped for a common topic, another time when they could see one another.

"Do you know the Atherton's well?" She asked after a few moments. "Will you be invited to the wedding next week?"

"I am," he said. "But from the Beresford side."

"I still cannot believe the turmoil from last year. You knew the duke, of course," Charity said, feeling a bit more on solid ground, but realizing that she was not saying any of the things she wanted to say to him, and there may not easily be another chance.

"Of course. Not personally, but through parliament. Terrible business that." He shook his head. "I can hardly believe it. I do know the Beresfords though. Their riding master taught me to ride as a boy. Do you like riding, Lady Charity?"

She was a passible rider. She was not sure she wanted

to go riding with him. She wanted to be at her best, and that was not on horseback.

Charity screwed up her face with the thought.

"I love the way you get that quizzical look on your face," he said.

"Mother says it causes wrinkles."

"I shan't mind," Lord Wentwell said.

Charity looked at him suddenly. Was he planning to be with her when she had wrinkles? She could not speak. She stopped in the road and looked at him. His green eyes were very dark and his hand warm on hers. He tightened his grip slightly, and Charity had the feeling if they were not in the middle of the street, in the middle of the day, he might have kissed her. Instead he said, "I wish to call upon you."

"I would like that very much," she replied, but her thoughts went to her mother, and the fact that the countess had practically thrown Neville Collington from their house. Well, Charity would just have to figure something out. She would tell her mother she would truly be a spinster if she did not allow Lord Wentwell to call. That was it. It would be Wentwell or no one. While they stood there lost in one another, she noticed Lord Wentwell's carriage had pulled up beside them on the road. It had pulled slightly in front of them and a servant in well-cut livery jumped from the carriage and ran up to the earl.

"My lord," he bowed low, and then stopped waiting to continue.

Neville glanced at Charity and saw her interest in the

young man. "Yes, Danvers. What is it? Why are you chasing me down in the street?"

Danvers shifted from foot to foot clearly in distress over something. "Lord Wentwell, your mother begged me to find you in haste. It's your brother..."

Charity felt Neville's arm tense beneath her hand, and she saw a muscle twitch in his neck and jawline. He glanced at her.

"I apologize, Lady Charity, but I must insist on seeing to my brother." He made a gesture toward his man. "Danvers shall see you to the party. I offer you the most sincere of apologies, but we must continue our stroll at a later date. I will call upon you."

"Yes, of course," Lady Charity said.

Charity found that she was happy at his offer to court her, but inside her mind was screaming, No. She did not want the earl to go so soon. This was not the way this conversation was supposed to go. They were supposed to speak. Now, it might be weeks or months before they could speak again with her mother so against his suit. She dug her heels in. She would not lose him again.

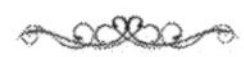

23

"Wait!" The word was out of Charity's mouth before she thought what word should follow it.

Lord Wentwell turned to her expectantly, and she stood tongue tied. Charity wondered briefly, what had happened? She was curious as to what cause would create such urgency. Was his brother hurt? Any of those questions would be rude in the extreme. She searched for another.

"Is it far?" She asked.

"No. Just up the way," Lord Wentwell replied with a gesture.

"Perhaps we shall make it a side trip. Then you might still see me to the party." Charity offered. She would like to see where Lord Wentwell lived and, more than she cared to admit, catch a glimpse of his personal life, and they could continue the conversation in the comfort of the carriage or perhaps after he dealt with whatever problem his brother caused. It occurred to her that perhaps only his brother was in residence at his home. There would of course be servants, but that was not the same as a chaperone. "Would it be proper?" She asked.

Lord Wentwell seemed surprised and pleased by her offer to come with him to his home. He nodded. "My mother is at the house, so there will be little room for scandal."

If she went with him, she could perhaps find out more about this enigmatic man, or she could be ruined. He was still considered quite the rake. She recalled the way he had treated her father and the care that he took with her reputation that day, and she knew she could trust this man. Anyway, she might not get another chance to speak with him. That decided her.

"Then I will accompany you," she said.

Charity felt a thrill of excitement at the prospect of joining Lord Wentwell on this adventure. He seemed worried and so she did her best to contain her pleasure. She wondered what it could be that would cause him to abandon his flirtation at just a word. Was his brother often in trouble? She would not ask, no matter how curious she was. It would be rude.

Lord Wentwell helped Charity into the carriage. He climbed in and sat beside her.

"I do apologize, and I beg your forgiveness for delaying your visit," Lord Wentwell said.

Charity was more intrigued than worried about her tardiness. Charity inclined her head politely. "Is something amiss? With your brother I mean?"

Lord Wentwell looked at the concern and interest in

Charity's eyes. He didn't answer at first, and Charity wondered if her question was too personal.

"I do not know how much you know of my family. There have been rumors of course."

Charity remembered. Several years ago, there was some to do about the war and Edmund's return from it. She was younger then, and the war seemed far away. She didn't remember the details of the gossip, so she just shook her head. "If all gossip were true," she said, "I would never have gotten into this carriage with you."

"Quite so," he said. "In any case, my father expected my brother and me to join the military for a time and so he bought us each a commission."

"I did not know that," Charity said. "So you were in the war?"

"I was." He did not elaborate, so she did not press him. She nodded. "Sounds like something my father would have wanted if he had had sons."

Lord Wentwell put his hands on his knees and took a deep breath. "We were separated of course. I was spared the true horrors of war. Edmund was not. When he came home, it was like he could not leave the war behind him. He startles sometimes and I think in his mind's eye, he is back there. He has never been the same since. My mother can do nothing to calm him. He does not often recognize her during his spells."

"I see," Charity said. She reached out and put a gloved hand on his and when the earl turned to her, his face was grave.

"There are times I think I have lost my brother completely. Most days he is quite his old self. Then other days, he is exceedingly violent and is a horror to be around."

Charity felt chills move down her spine. She had not known. No one did as far as she was aware. What a horrible family secret, and now she was unwittingly part of it. She saw the concern in Lord Wentwell's face. Whatever part of him was the roguish flirt was gone in the concern he had for his brother.

"I understand," Charity said. "My father is not violent, but you know there are days when he does not recognize me. It is painful."

"I'm sorry," he said, and she felt his sincerity.

"Has your brother hurt anyone?"

His countenance darkened. "No, but of course that is always the fear. More often than not, he hurts himself." He chanced a glance out the window as the carriage seemed to slow. "We are nearly there. I do apologize for getting you involved. I will leave you in the care of my mother if you do not object, while I calm my brother."

Charity nodded. She realized that in spite of what she once thought, she and Wentwell were decidedly alike, at least fate had given them similar crosses to bear. "I am sure I will be quite comfortable with your mother," she said.

Lord Wentwell allowed a smile to touch his lips. "I warn you, you are not like to be comfortable, Lady Charity. One day she is anxious for me to marry to secure the line and the next she is sure that no woman is worthy."

"One must excuse the love of a mother," Charity said with a wry smile as she thought of her own difficulties with her mother. She felt even more of a kinship to the man beside her.

The carriage stopped and Lord Wentwell hopped down offering her his hand to help her. Once they alighted from the carriage, he led her quickly inside and rushed across the grand entrance room to a parlor where an older woman sat in a plush chair with needlework on her lap. Charity stood by his side.

"Mother! Forgive the intrusion. You know the Lady Charity Abernathy, of course. Would you please see to it that she is entertained while I see to Edmund?"

The elder woman gaped at her son and Lady Charity, but finally nodded, waving absently for Charity to take a seat near her, but Charity hovered uncertainly near the doorway of the parlor, until the woman fair shouted at her.

"Sit girl" and Charity sat perched uncomfortably on the edge of a chair. The woman then turned pleading eyes to her son.

"It is bad this time, Neville. Do be careful. I have called for the doctor as well, and Danvers tried to get some laudanum into him, but it only spilled on the floor."

Lord Wentwell nodded as a loud crash rang out from some far corner of house. He gave the women a short bow and rushed from the room.

Charity sat in uncomfortable silence. She commented on the weather, but received little response. She ventured to ask questions about the large home, but was ignored. About this time, one of the servants entered with tea, but Lady Wentwell ignored it. Charity knew it was not her purview to pour. She felt terribly ill at ease. She then tried to venture a question about Lord Wentwell, at which point his mother put her needlework down and looked at Charity with piercing green eyes. Charity couldn't help but notice they were the same extraordinary green as her son's.

"I have no interest in getting to know you, young lady. I know your mother and that is enough, Although you have grand aspirations for my son, I will have none of it."

"Grand aspirations," Charity repeated. "I am an earl's daughter."

The woman looked at her askance, and Charity felt a blush coming to her cheeks. She did not know why. Charity sat back in her chair and stared at the older woman. Well, it looked like both she and Lord Wentwell where going to have to deal with their mothers.

"He has asked to call upon me," Charity said loftily. "And I have given him my permission."

"Your permission?" the lady said.

"Only after due consideration of course. He is a rogue and a shameless flirt," finished Charity.

"But he is an earl and rich," the Dowager countered.

"And I am an earl's daughter and wealthy as well, such does not speak to one's character."

"How dare you come in here on the arm of my son and then insult him?"

"Inviting rumor seems to be your son's pastime, not mine."

"So you are free of rumor?" the dowager asked. "Except for the Lovell name," she added.

"The *Abernathy* name is as revered as the Collington name," Charity retorted and then clamped her mouth shut wondering if she had said too much. Lord Wentwell's mother had a barely bated grin that seemed determined to cross her face, despite her best efforts. She seemed pleased with Charity's response, as if she had yet to meet a lady with a bit of spunk to her. Charity did not wish to argue with his mother, even if it seemed to raise her in the elder's esteem. Instead, she lapsed into silence, and after several minutes Lady Wentwell returned to her needlework. The tea sat cooling in its pot.

In the silence, the women heard crashes and muffled yells from somewhere in the house, causing both to lean forward in their chairs. Then there was silence. Charity counted the seconds and Lady Wentwell looked as if she could sit still no longer. There was a muffled sound and then a loud crash which seemed to make the entire house shake. The lady jumped to her feet with amazing alacrity, for one of her age, exited the room, following the sounds.

Lady Charity followed the countess to the room where the two brothers were locked in a struggle. Danvers tried ineffectively to pull Edmund off of Lord Wentwell while Edmund screamed something about fire.

Charity noted that Edmund had the same tensed jaw as his brother, when he was upset. Edmund's nostrils were flared and his eyes wild, his dark hair mused. Charity caught her breath. Already a bruise was appearing on Neville's cheek and his brother seemed not to recognize him or by his coarse language, the fact that there were ladies in the room.

"Edmund!" The countess spoke with authority, but Charity had eyes only for Lord Wentwell, who looked to be having the short end of the fight, with the combination of his brother's size and the fact that Neville did not want to hit his brother. It was obvious that Neville was trying to hold him still, while calling his name, over and over again, but the plan did not seem to be working, and Danvers seemed to be of little help.

"Oh!" Charity called rushing to the brothers' side. She was not sure how she could help, but she only knew she must. She had no idea what she did, but Edmund's eyes seemed to clear a bit as she spoke.

"Please, sir, be still. It is alright. You are home."

He spoke to her in a hash smattering of French, "*Sortez l'enfant! Avant que les soldats viennent.*"

She realized that he was telling her to get the child out while he held off the soldiers. What was he thinking? What child? She wondered, but instead of saying her thoughts, she remembered how she humored her father to keep him calm. She only said. "We are safe. We all are safe. Look around you. You are safe here with your family."

Edmund did look around and had a moment of confusion, but he stopped struggling against his brother's hold as he took in the furnishings of his own house. The tension went out of his body.

"Let him go, Neville," his mother said and Neville did so. Danvers also stepped back.

Edmund rubbed a hand over his face. "I'm sorry," Edmund said, sinking to the floor. "I'm so sorry. I did it again, didn't I?"

"It's okay, brother," Neville said laying a hand on his shoulder. "It's okay."

"No. It's not. You should lock me up before I hurt someone. I hit you again, didn't I, Neville?"

"You didn't know what you were doing."

The countess came forward and lay a hand on her younger son's shoulder. Charity felt supremely out of place in the family moment. "How did she bring you back to us?" the countess asked with a shrewd eye. "Think Edmund. Tell us what happened. Something Lady Charity did made a difference. It turned you around."

"Lady Charity," Edmund said with a groan, as if he just realized she was there. "I cannot. It is too awful for feminine ears."

"What did you do?" the countess asked Lady Charity.

Charity shook her head. She wanted to help, but she did not know what she did. "I do not know," she said. "I was doing nothing, but what Lord Wentwell was doing. Asking him to be still. That is all."

"No. What happened, Edmund?" Lady Wentwell asked. "Think. She touched you, and..." his mother began, but Edmund shook his head.

"No. She didn't touch me, Mother. Praise God, or I might have hit her too. I was back there in the fire and pain and the smell of death, blood and gunpowder, but then, I smelled lavender." He looked up a light in his eyes. "It was her perfume. It was the lavender. It was such a shocking scent. It did not belong in war. There was woman beside me and she could not be where I was, and then I could see the room again, the furnishings, and I knew what I had done." He covered his face with his hands.

"You should rest, Edmund," his mother said. "Danvers, have the physician see him in his room."

"Right away, milady," Danvers said.

"Yes," Edmund agreed standing and he let Danvers lead him away.

"It always takes so much out of him," Lord Wentwell commented as he rubbed a hand over his face.

A red mark marred his cheek and Charity wondered if he would soon have a black eye. Charity took a step towards him with the intention of touching him, and then realized how improper that would be. She didn't want to give his mother any more reason to think she was improper. She froze within steps of going to his aid.

"If you would give me a moment," Lord Wentwell said, gesturing to his uncharacteristic disheveled appearance. "I am truly sorry to have gotten you involved in our family drama, Lady Charity. I must ask you to please not share what you saw with anyone. There is enough fodder for the gossips. As far as anyone else knows, my brother is simply ill from recent travels."

Charity nodded. "I would not break your trust. I shan't tell a soul, but I'm afraid the eminent bruise on your face may speak for itself regardless."

Lord Wentwell inspected himself in the glass at the far side of the parlor. "Hmmm... Yes. It is rather worse than I first thought. I shall have darkened my daylights." He turned and flashed her a grin. Even with his battered features, Charity still thought him exceedingly handsome, and she could not help smiling back. "I shall think of something," he said. "Perhaps I got into a match of fisticuffs over a pretty lady. The *Ton* will love that sort of story."

Charity heard his mother groan in frustration at his storytelling. It was clear that she disapproved of his ploy, for whatever reason, to be known as the most uncouth gentleman of the land.

"I do apologize," he repeated in all sincerity. "Might I play host and invite you to join my mother and I for dinner? As it is, your date for tea is well past fashionably late."

"Oh!" Charity squeaked with the thought. "Amelia and Patience! They shall be frantic, wondering where I am," Charity said.

"Oh they know," Lord Wentwell said. "Or at least they know that you were in my company. Who do you think sent me to escort you?"

"Oh," Charity said again a blush filling her face at the implications.

"I imagine they will make our excuses, separately of course," Lord Wentwell said. "They are our friends."

Charity blushed all the more. "But they will still be frantic," Charity said softly, but for a different reason entirely, she thought. "I should send a note with my regrets."

"Do you think that will help?" Lord Wentwell asked eyebrow raised.

"Not a bit." She bit her lip. "Perhaps it would be best if you would take me home."

Lord Wentwell nodded. "As you wish."

As Charity gathered her reticule, she realized that she had vials of the mineral water as well as lavender water with her. She had decided on the day after her father's near disastrous excursion that she would not be without some recourse again. She paused and dug through the contents to find the correct bottle, and hesitated but a moment. If she did this she would be tacitly agreeing that her father was not well. She turned to Lady Wentwell who had been chaperoning them with quiet competence.

"I know that this is a most unusual gift, a half filled bottle," she said holding up the vial, "but the lavender water seems to calm my father, and help him to sleep. If it will help your son, and Lord Wentwell's brother, I should like to gift it to you."

Lady Wentwell raised an eyebrow. "I have misjudged you, Lady Charity, and I am sorry you are not staying for dinner so that we might become better acquainted. You are not the lady I thought you to be," she said taking the vial from Charity's hand. "I shall send my regards to the Lord and Lady Shalace," she said loftily. "Perhaps dinner shall have to wait for another time. I hope that your parents will accompany you on your next trip."

Lady Charity gave the woman a curtsey, all the while thinking how would she manage to get her mother to read Lady Wentwell's missive much less accept an invitation to Lady Wentwell's home.

24

Ten minutes later, Lady Charity was seated in the carriage with Lord Wentwell once more.

"Do you mind if we go the long way and take a drive past the garden? I always find the ride soothing," he said. "I could use a moment of calm."

Charity nodded her consent, and Lord Wentwell directed the driver the route to take. Her own head was reeling with today's events. Still, she thought it could not matter much if she was any later, she was already quite beyond excuse, but having seen a much deeper side to man she had previously discounted, curiosity got the best of her.

"Might I ask a personal question, Lord Wentwell?"

He nodded sagely.

"You have painted yourself as a flirt and a rogue. I have seen with my own eyes how you have bounced from one maiden to another leaving rather horrible rumors in your wake..." she paused and stared into his deep green eyes, "and yet, you have never been ungentlemanly with me, and tonight... The depth of your commitment to your family... I admit I am puzzled."

NEVILLE SAID nothing for a few minutes, but he realized that he had already trusted Lady Charity with the biggest secret of his family.

"You will think me a fool, I fear," he started. She frowned, but he continued. "I am not so flippant as the picture I present. I love my home. I care for the people of my estate. I thought someday I would marry to further the line, but I was in no rush. I see no reason to hurry fate." He thought of the disastrous Miss Katherine Dubois, but Lady Charity was nothing like her. He could trust the lady with his heart.

"I see," said Lady Charity, although the situation begged more explanation.

"So I decided to do whatever I could to push the young ladies away. If I could make myself disgusting enough in character, even my money, my title, my appearance should discourage matchmaking and the like. I assumed that the dowagers would warn their charges against me, and I would be free."

Lady Charity burst out laughing, and then covered her mouth embarrassed by the unladylike loudness of it.

"What, pray tell, is so funny?"

"You thought the ladies would actually listen to their mothers and their chaperones?"

"Why yes. Of course, I thought so. It is in the nature of women to obey...their fathers....their mothers...their husbands." His own grin quirked as he thought of the irascible Lady Charity. "I believe I may have misjudged women kind in general."

"Verily," Lady Charity agreed, still giggling. "Silly man."

"What is so silly about not wanting to be leg shackled to one... you do not love?" Lord Wentwell asked. He bit his lip. It was too soon to be speaking of love. He planned to be at least forty before he even considered the idea, but the idea was there, blooming in his heart.

"Nothing," Lady Charity said sobering. "Nothing at all. I hope for the same for myself." She looked at him through her lashes, and he thought, he could love this woman. Perhaps he did love this woman. She was so unlike Kathrine or even Danbury.

"I do believe the rumors got quite out of hand," he said. The specter of Miss Macrum's lies sat there between them, but neither acknowledged her part in the scandal. She did not matter. She could not matter.

CHARITY WATCHED a myriad of emotions track across Lord Wentwell's face. He looked out of the window for a moment and then back at her, as he spoke. "I have never heard so many untruths strung together. It became quite alarming actually," he said.

"Untruths?" Charity asked. "All of them were untruths?" Her heart beat fast as she thought of Miss

Danbury, and Lady Amelia's succinct sum up of the situation. *If he were a gentleman, and the lady had his affections then he would be lost to you.*

He quirked an eyebrow. "Pray, of which did you wish to inquire?"

She felt her face burn as she plowed on undaunted, "I mean....Miss Danbury? The word is, she is ruined." Her voice dropped to whisper.

Her heart beat fast. Would it change? Would the world change for her if he had a bastard child? Her heart climbed to her throat. She hoped that she had it in her to forgive him, but Julia's words flashed through her mind. *Once a rake, always a rake.*

She twisted the fan in her lap. A man who did such, was not a gentleman. She breathed, and stilled her roiling thoughts. She laid the fan purposely aside, and just listened. She knew that what happened before their meeting was beside the point. There was only this moment. And then he answered her.

"And Miss Danbury might well be," he said matter-of-factly. "But not by me."

Relief flooded her. She looked up into his green eyes then, and believed him. The atmosphere of the carriage became quite serious, and Charity felt a bit lost. What did one talk about after such a conversation?

Every judgement that she had ever made about the man had been thrust out the carriage window. It had all been a ploy, a ploy to protect his own heart because, deep inside of him, he was nothing like the image he portrayed. He was, she now realized, the best and most faithful of gentlemen.

"I heard tell that you were once to be married," she murmured.

He stiffened.

"I'm sorry," she said. She knew immediately that her curiosity had taken the conversation too far. She should not have spoken, but she did want to know. She wanted to know everything about this enigmatic man, but perhaps wringing all the secrets from him in one night was not the best strategy.

"Bloody Reg and his sister," Lord Wentwell muttered low enough that she might pretend she did not hear the coarse language, but she found that she liked the sudden heated passion. He was not so cold a creature as he pretended to be. She remembered that he had once said the male was a creature of cool and calculating logic and a woman a creature of emotion. She had proved that assumption wrong, in a horribly hurtful way, but she had proved it so nonetheless. Still, he clung to the idea, and she understood why.

"It was Lady Amelia who told me, of your past engagement. But yes, she most likely heard the tale from Lord Barton's sister," Charity revealed. "I believe she made an attempt to excuse your behavior, that I might look beneath the guise and see more."

"Yes," Neville said, "Reg will do such things. In fact, I see evidence of Reginald's fingers all over this."

"You are not cross with him?"

"Not at all," he smiled. "Not if it is preventing you from being set against me."

"Here I am," she replied in a breathless whisper.

"Yes," Lord Wentwell seemed similarly affected in his

ability to breathe. "I suppose it is best you hear the truth from me, than from rumor," he said. "The lady that I was to marry was named Miss Katherine Dubois," he continued. "She was young, beautiful, and all too skilled at convincing me of her love."

"Did you love her?" Charity asked. She knew that the question would be improper to most, but they now shared a kinship and, besides, she needed to know.

"I thought that I had," he said with a shrug. "I was mistaken. Fooled by the art of deception."

"I had no idea."

He took a deep breath as if clearing his head. "It was a long time ago," he explained. "I was young and not so knowledgeable. I only wish that I knew then what I know today." He closed his fingers around her gloved hand, his fingers warm against hers.

Charity was confused by his words but he said nothing further. She was afraid to press for she was beginning to realize that the more that she learned about Lord Wentwell, the more she was drawn to him. Every detail circulated about the *Ton* was false, a creation of his protective barrier. She had to pick apart the rumor bit by bit to find the truth. She was beginning to see that there was much more to him than met the eye and, what was hidden, was a puzzle that she longed to solve.

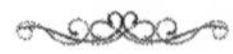

NEVILLE SAT BACK and watched Lady Charity for a few moments as he realized she was indeed serious. She had taken his word and placed her trust in it. He would never have expected such a gift and vowed not to misuse it. In that moment, he knew that she was a different kind of woman, an honest woman in every sense of the word. He had suspected it from the moment he saw her and she had chided him, and challenged him to be better. He had watched her lips tremble as the weight of her future weighed on her. Now, as she learned the truth of him, he could see that it had turned her world upside down.

"I have acted the fool," he said. "And I have hurt people. I thought of what you said to me many times. I have played with women's hearts. I did not know how fragile those hearts might be until lately." He thought of his own heart, and how hurt he had been by the *Ton*, and most especially by the lady beside him when his own reputation, a reputation that he had cultivated, kept her from his side. "I did not think people would so easily believe the worst of me, especially the ladies."

"I do not believe they do," Lady Charity said, and when he meant to disagree, she continued. "They think the worst of themselves."

He frowned. "How so?" he asked confused.

And blushing she replied, "They ask themselves, if they were in Miss Danbury's place or a similar situation, would they be so sorely tempted."

The blush on her face, and the grip she had on her fan spoke volumes to him, and he smiled a secret smile that made him feel warm inside.

She did not look at him, but he looked very carefully at her, memorizing every nuance of her face, the thought that she would want him made his heart sing.

They sat in companionable silence the rest of the way

to her home, and Neville wondered at her ability to be so still when most women found silence daunting. The footman opened the door and he alighted first. He helped Lady Charity to the ground and walked with her to her door. Neville led Charity slowly. He did not want to part from her.

He bowed low over her hand and kissed it tenderly. When he stood back up, he lifted a hand to her face and restrained himself from kissing her there on the front step, instead he cupped her chin and stared into her eyes. She reached up, unexpectedly to touch the forming bruise below his eye. Her touch was tenderness itself, and then she let her hand drop to her side.

"Had I known earlier what I know now, Lady Charity, I would never have chosen to play the game I played. I would do naught to upset you." He knew he had hurt her, however unintentionally.

"It can still be undone," she whispered. "You need only allow the truth to come to light."

He paused a moment and then continued. "Your father gave me leave to court you," he said. "But I do not believe your father was entirely clear about my identity at the time. Still, I believe, asking your cousin for permission would be a mistake."

"Lud yes!" she exclaimed.

"And so, I think you are a lady who knows her own mind. I would like to call upon you, to court you with intent to marry."

Charity felt her heart leap for joy, but she nodded her assent coolly. "But has that not been what we have been doing, Lord Wentwell?" she asked with a twinkle in her eye.

"How so?"

"I know your family secrets; you know mine..." she quipped.

"I've met your mother; you've met mine," he countered, and Charity blushed embarrassed.

"Oh, but I have never apologized for the way my mother treated you, or the awful things I said at the opening ball." She said. Her hand went to her mouth.

"There is nothing to forgive," he said. "That was a lifetime ago, Lady Charity, and your mother was only protecting you." He took a deep breath. "I hope to convince the Lady Shalace, that I am not a complete libertine. I might ask you to ease that path."

Her lips quirked up in a smile. "I will," she promised.

"Then, until the morrow," he said with a bow. He turned with a grin. "Will it be too early if I arrive before noon?"

"I shall have breakfast set," she promised and with that hope in her heart, Lord Wentwell was back in the carriage and it was pulling away.

Lady Charity stood watching it for a minute before entering the house. It was quiet, which meant her mother was still out, and her father, agitated earlier in the day, had retired for the night. Charity also retired to her room and spent the evening reading and waiting for her mother to return from her card playing with Mrs. Thompson and Mrs. Sullivan.

She contemplated the events of the afternoon and

wondered how she might smooth the Earl of Wentwell's way with her mother. She was not quite sure what she would tell her mother about Lord Wentwell, only that she must do so.

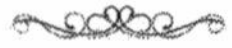

25

The conversation with Lady Shalace did not go half so badly as Charity expected. Her mother paced the floor of the parlor and railed at her for changing her mind from the numerous available peers that she had presented, to James Poppy to Michael Poppy and finally to the Earl of Wentwell. When Charity finally exasperated, said, "What do you want me to do, Mother? I can't be you!"

"Oh Charity," her mother replied. "I never wanted you to be me. Quite the contrary, I only wanted one thing for you, Charity. To be happy. That is all I have ever wanted for you." She came to Charity and put a hand on her shoulder.

"You do not care about the rumors?" Charity said, looking at her mother, and sizing up her feelings.

"I do," Her mother said grasping Charity's shoulders. "I know how it feels to live your life surrounded by rumor, to fight your way through every event and know that even your closest friends are most likely close to you because they wish a scrap of gossip, not because they care about you."

"My friends care about me," Charity said.

"Good," her mother said pacing away again. "I am glad, and I want you to have a husband who cares about you too. That is of the utmost importance." She turned to face her daughter. "A woman alone in the world is a frightening prospect."

"A husband that I love," Charity urged.

"A husband that loves you," Lady Shalace corrected. "It is more important that he loves you, than that you love him, and this is even more paramount now that your father is ill and cannot protect you."

"I think both are important," Charity said.

"And so you have found this paragon, have you? At Lady Amelia's tea."

Charity blushed, thinking she never even made it to the tea. "I have found him," she said. "But you have to let him court me," she said.

"If he is who you wish, Charity I will consider him. Who is the gentleman?" Lady Shalace sat on the settee and looked up at Charity awaiting her response.

"Lord Wentwell," Charity said.

"The rake? Oh Charity."

"No Mother. He is not a rake. The *Ton* has branded him so, but it is not true. Surely you see how wrong the *Ton* can be. Surely you know this. They wronged you all those years, Mother. I know it. I know that you love Father. No one thinks it is so, but I see the truth of it, just as I see the truth of Lord Wentwell. Let him present himself. Please Mother. Give him a chance to prove himself worthy of my love."

"You love this man?" Lady Shalace said, shaking her head.

"I do."

Her mother pursed her lips, and Charity wasn't sure which way the conversation would go, but she knew how to swing it to her favor. "I have a confession to make," Charity said.

Lady Shalace looked at her, a frown of worry crossing her usually smooth brow.

"It is about the concert. When Father had his episode..." She sat beside her mother then, and took her mother's hand in her own. Charity took a deep breath and relayed the entirety of the incident, including Lord Wentwell's part of it. When she was finished, her mother had a better opinion of Lord Wentwell. Charity did not tell her of the incident with Lord Wentwell's brother. That was not her story to tell.

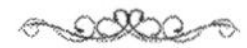

26

The following morning, Lord Wentwell arrived at Lady Charity's home at the earliest possible calling hour, and as promised, she had breakfast set. He decided that, he was not going to let the young lady out of his sight until she was safely his. He could not ask her to marry him so soon, but he escorted her to every event for the next week. Whispers followed him, as whispers always followed members of the *Ton*. Of course the first of those rumors was how he got his blackened eye. The most prevalent idea was that he had engaged in fisticuffs over a young lady. Of course, since Lady Charity Abernathy was the only young lady he had escorted in the past six days, rumor held that she was the lady in question.

"I do wish I had been left out of your rumors," Lady Charity said without venom. "But I suppose you cannot help it. Rumor sticks to you like flies to ...sugar," she said sweetly. With that, she informed him that she had let slip to a gentleman dance partner that Lord Wentwell had not engaged in fisticuffs at all. He had simply run into a tree branch and was too embarrassed to tell the tale of how he got his black eye.

"Surely you did not," he said. He was just a tad annoyed at the thought, and then he smiled. "They will believe anything, will they not?"

"I think they will," she said and suddenly, it became a game to see who could make the most outrageous claims.

"I heard it was a carriage door," he told her later in the night as they shared a waltz. "I apparently am quite clumsy."

She giggled and told him that she had heard he had been attacked by a highwayman, fell down some stairs and was kicked by a horse.

"A horse? Surely not." He frowned. "You do not think it had anything to do with the previous rumor about my stable-master do you?"

Charity shook her head. "You did manage to put that rumor to rest, I think." At Charity's urging, he had given Miss Danbury and his stable master three good mares, and a young stallion and sent them on their way to the colonies. Her father, the baronet was boasting that his daughter was marrying a man with land, if not a title, but that was yet another rumor, growing more with the telling. Still, some of the *Ton* insisted that Miss Danbury had run off with the stable-master. At least Lord Wentwell's name was absent from the latest rumors about Miss Danbury.

As the dance ended, Lord Wentwell stood, still holding Lady Charity's hand and asked, "What on earth was I doing, that I was kicked in the face by a horse?"

Lady Charity collapsed into giggles and Lord Wentwell just shook his head. There was no explaining rumor.

Reluctantly, he let Charity go, to dance with Colonel Ranier. Neville was not happy that he had to let her dance with others, but even married couples rarely danced with each other. As much as he wanted to keep her to himself, he had to be satisfied with only two, or perhaps three dances per event. He had managed to enlist his friend's help to be sure that she did not dance with Michael Poppy...just in case she had any feeling for the man after all.

Now, Lady Charity was dancing with Lord Beresford who was already married to Charity's good friend, Patience. Neville could finally relax.

"You know," Reginald told his friends as Neville paused for a drink. "Captain Hartfield says wagers are being taken that your wedding will be celebrated before Christmas. I told Hartfield, you shall not make it until Christmas. I think you will not make it to the end of the summer. What say you, Wentwell?"

"Hmm?" Neville said. He was busy watching Lady Charity dance the quadrille. She and Lord Beresford had joined Flora Muirwood and James Poppy. He wanted to be sure that none of the gentlemen became overly friendly with her. It was irksome that he could not dance every dance with her.

"Shall I take that bet?" Samuel asked, "Or are you going to dither around for another month or two?"

Neville glanced back at his friends.

"You have not heard a single word, have you?" Reginald asked.

"I have not," Neville agreed. "So sorry."

"End of summer latest," Samuel said to Reginald and I'd give odds on it. Reginald agreed, and then Reginald danced with Miss Macrum, who was doing her best to wheedle a dance from Wentwell. Behind Miss Macrum's head Reg shot Neville a look which said he was definitely going to pay for Reginald's rescuing him from the strumpet.

THROUGHOUT THE SUMMER, Lady Charity had managed to avoid the busy body Miss Macrum, but today, Miss Macrum had become bold and Charity was annoyed with her constant insinuations. She knew it was not ladylike to confront her, but when she next tried to speak to Lord Wentwell, in Charity's presence, Charity exchanged a glance with Lord Wentwell, and took the lady's arm. For a moment, Miss Macrum tried to pull away, but Charity held fast, digging her fingers in so that the lady must follow or look rude.

"Won't you excuse us, Lord Wentwell," Charity said with a coy smile "I want to introduce Miss Macrum to two of my dear friends," she said.

Charity marched right past Patience, Lady Amelia and the Beresford brothers. She walked past The Baron and Baroness Fawkland and The Captain and Mrs. Hartfield. Instead, Charity stopped in front of Mrs. Thompson and Mrs. Sullivan. "I want to introduce you to Miss Macrum," she said to the ladies. "You remember when she was all mixed up with those rumors of Miss Danbury and the stable master."

"I do," Mrs. Sullivan said with a gleam in her eye.

"I had nothing to do with that," Miss Macrum exclaimed.

"Of course not," Charity said. "But like Miss Danbury, you are marrying for love, are you not?"

"Oh, I'm not marrying," Miss Macrum said giving Charity a narrowed look, "unless I marry an earl."

"But I thought you were in love," Mrs. Thompson said wide eyed. "Did Lady Charity not just say that she was in love?" she inquired of Mrs. Sullivan.

"Miss Macrum just said she was not marrying," Mrs. Sullivan replied. "Not ever?" Mrs. Sullivan directed her question back to Miss Macrum. "Surely you are not one of those bluestockings, are you?"

"Terrible things," Mrs. Thompson added. "But you are not one of those I think. No. Now do tell me, who is this gentleman you love? I think it is so romantic to marry so low, below your station, don't you, Mrs. Sullivan?"

"So you were the lady who was involved with that stable boy?" Mrs. Sullivan asked.

Miss Macrum choked. "I'm not," Miss Macrum interrupted, suddenly frantic, but Mrs. Sullivan talked right over her, "Or was it the stable master?"

"I thought it was the groom," Mrs. Thompson said. "The stable master moved to the colonies with the other strumpet."

Miss Macrum choked, but Mrs. Thompson patted Miss Macrum's back gently. "It's okay, dear," she said. "We can't all marry earls."

"As long as you love him," Mrs. Sullivan said.

Charity turned when she realized Lord Wentwell was at her elbow. "The waltz is about to begin," he said. "I believe the dance is mine."

"Oh, do excuse me," Lady Charity said sweetly to Miss Macrum. "I'm sure Mrs. Sullivan and Mrs. Thompson will keep you entertained."

Miss Macrum looked positively trapped. Charity smiled all the way to the dance floor. She took Lord Wentwell's hand and they began the dance. "That was masterfully done," he said as he twirled her around the floor.

She laughed up at him thinking she would not lose this man. "I thought I should remove temptation," she said.

"There is no temptation," he told her. "But I am glad you decided to give Miss Macrum a bit of her own medicine."

As they danced Charity got lost in Lord Wentwell's green eyes, and soon realized that Lord Wentwell had danced them out onto one of the patios so prevalent in Bath. The cool evening air was bliss after the heat of the day.

FOR A MOMENT CHARITY could not speak. Lord Wentwell had taken her gloved hand in his. His hands were so fine: long fingered, and the nails manicured. He gripped her hand firmly but not too tightly and began rubbing his thumb along the inside of her wrist. The movement sent shivers up her spine. There was something about that grip that spoke to her of masculinity. His was a hand that would hold her forever, and melt away the shadows of her heart. He was looking at her so seriously, and she realized, this was the moment.

This was the time, when he might ask her to marry him, and she would say yes. I shall marry you, and all she asked was that he promised to be honest with her and she should do the same.

"I am all butterflies," she said.

"As am I," he admitted.

She laughed, a soft feminine sound.

"In your quest to share your own feelings, Lady Charity, you have denied me mine," Lord Wentwell said, "But I must speak."

"I thought that gentlemen were all the cool collected logic and not given to flights of fancy," she quipped.

"I was wrong to say it. And when I am wrong, I admit my misdoings."

"I too have been wrong about you, Lord Wentwell, You are not a rake. Not truly."

"Hush, woman," he said. "You will ruin my reputation. Shall I prove what a rake I am?" He leaned in to kiss her, making her heart sing and her blood rush to her head. She felt dizzy with the passion of it. When she could breathe again, she said, "But you are not so callous as you would let on. You do have feelings."

"Feelings," he said and he kissed her again.

"You deny them, but you are not so cold as you would have others believe."

He held her a bit apart then and looked at her. His so green eyes bored into hers, and Charity thought to look down, unable to bear the intensity of his gaze, but Lord Wentwell took her chin in his hand and turned her face up to his, rubbing his thumb along her lower lip.

"I did not tell you of my feelings, indeed, I have denied them even to myself. It is not easy for a man to admit to such things."

Her lips quirked in a smile. "Oh, so Lord Wentwell has found a game he will not play?"

"Not so," he said. "I have only found that the stakes are much higher than I ever thought. It is true that I have often worked to keep the upper hand in a relationship. That is because, my dear Lady Charity, the truth of the matter is, I am afraid. I am afraid to lose this wager."

For an instant Charity almost spoke, to tease him, to say, the daring and dashing Lord Wentwell, afraid, but then she realized he was speaking the absolute truth, and she reached up to touch his face. How was it that he was so strong and so vulnerable all at the same time?

"You shall not ever lose me," she whispered.

"I have been afraid of showing my true self for a long time now. I did not believe that a woman could be trusted with such knowledge and so my initial intent was far from honest," he said. "I knew you were the most beautiful, the most engaging, the most interesting of my acquaintances, and I thought only to turn your head, but then, you met me quip for quip and challenged me to be a better man, and I realized my own life would be less without you in it, because of the person you are, Lady Charity Abernathy."

He moved his hand from her chin to her cheek stroking it gently. "You are not like any other woman I have met. You are Lady Charity Abernathy, buxom and beautiful, but more. You have a kind and generous soul, and you have healed mine, Charity. I want to spend all my days with you, grow together and grow old with you and fill our house with children so that you will never have a moment to be lonely. Say yes." But he did not allow her to speak. He kissed her sweetly, gently, and she smiled up at him. He did not even realize he had forgotten the most important part.

"You will have to do better than that," she quipped.

"I love you," he said.

"I think that you are really not at all good at this," she said screwing up her face in a quizzical expression.

"Please do not tease me," he said. "I want to do better. To see a woman as more than a plaything. To see her…to see you. As a person. A person I love. Just as you are. The only transformation I should want to make, is to change your name from Abernathy to Collington. Will you be my countess, Lady Charity, and let me play this game of life with you and only you at my side?"

"Finally," she breathed. "Yes! There is no where I would rather be than at your side, Lord Wentwell, *as your wife!*" She wanted to tell him that she looked forward to joining his family to hers, to having his children, growing old with him, no matter what that entailed, and indeed being his countess too. She wanted to tell him she could never be lonely with him at her side. He was the other half of herself for which she had been searching, but she never got the chance.

Before she could speak again, he swept her into his embrace with all the exuberance that she loved about him, and he was suddenly kissing her, kissing her with all the passion that she knew was inside of Neville Collington, rake extraordinaire, but he was her rake now, she thought as she felt his lips hot and insistent upon hers.

The scent of him filled her senses and made her both weaker in the knees and stronger at heart. She felt her soul fill with love as he kissed her long and deep. She tasted him, as he wrapped his arms around her making her feel sheltered, and protected and loved, and he deepened the kiss. As her body turned to liquid heat, she found herself with the railing at her waist. His hands had moved from her waist, to cup her and pull her close. She could feel every inch of him, and she wanted him with all her heart, but she managed to pull herself from the passion. Her body was trembling; her head swimming.

"No," she whispered against his lips. "Someone will see." She would not be embroiled in rumor. She would not prove his mother right. She would not be her own mother. She was herself, and she wanted something more.

He broke the kiss and looked at her with dark passion in his eyes. "I love you," he said. "What does it matter what someone else sees? What does it matter how the *Ton* twitters?"

"And I love you," she said, "but if I am to be your wife, I will not be the center of rumor. I have seen what this did to my mother. I will not be her."

"You are right, of course," he said, putting an agonizing space between them. He brought his hands from places unmentionable, and smoothed her dress with a loving touch. "You are right. I forgot myself, Lady Charity."

"So did I," she admitted with a glint in her own eye.

He stepped away from her then as he spoke, almost to himself. "I should get a special dispensation so we do not have to wait weeks until the banns are read. We have waited too long already."

"No," she said again. She felt bereft with the loss of his touch. "It will be hard, but we can wait knowing that we shall one day be in each other's arms forever."

He blew out his breath and straightened his oh so tight trousers and then his jacket, pulling the cuffs at the sleeve. "Forever," he said with a gleam in his eye. "Yes, it shall feel like forever."

She smiled up at him, as he took her hands in his. "Forever," he said again. "There is no one else for me, Charity and I can wait for you."

"There is no one else for me, Neville," she added as he leaned in and kissed her softly, sweetly, chastely, with oh so much tenderness, her heart was like to explode with love. His lips held all the passion inside of him. When he broke the kiss, and she could think again, she thought, I am not marrying a rake. Like Julia, I am marrying a good and kind man. Like Lavinia, I am marrying a man who loves me, and I love him. Nothing was more important than that. Then the thought appeared that she would have to wait nearly a month, while banns were read until she could truly have him fully in her arms. Dear God, she thought how had Amelia and Samuel survived her year in mourning?

"A month. It is not so long," she repeated, perhaps to convince herself.

"Forever," he said. He clasped her hands as if he did not trust himself to hold her in his arms.

"Forever," she whispered thinking a month was an eternity.

He rallied, and pulled her back towards the ballroom. "Come. We will be missed," he said, and although they were not quite ready to announce their engagement, Charity shared the news with her special friends, Lavinia squealed and hugged her, Julia promised that she would dance at her wedding, but Amelia and Patience just nodded sagely and said they knew all along that she and Lord Wentwell were made for one another.

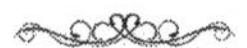

EPILOGUE

Neville smiled as he entered the dining hall where his wife to be, his mother and her mother sat over tea and papers. Having The Dowager Wentwell and Lady Shalace sitting down in a civil manner was an amazing chain of events.

"We were speaking of the wedding plans," The Dowager Wentwell said to her son.

It seemed to him that lately, no one spoke of anything but the wedding. His mother was in a state, and he wondered what the problem might be.

"The Beresford wedding was lovely." Lady Shalace said. "I do not see a problem having the wedding here in Bath. I know you would prefer London, Lady Wentwell, but I am sure it would be so much nicer at Bath Abbey."

So that was it.

"It is so old," his mother said. "I really would prefer London."

They differed on the venue for the wedding. He knew

he should just let the ladies be, but he also knew Charity wanted the wedding to be in Bath. "I do not think having the wedding in Bath will be a problem," Neville said, grinning at his bride-to-be.

"But you are an earl, and she an earl's daughter," his mother intoned. "I just thought London..."

"After all, Mother, you do know Charity is hoping to have her father walk her down the aisle. I think we should not wait too long," Neville said. "And he does well here in Bath. He can take the waters the day before and then rest rather than taking a long carriage ride. Bath it is."

Charity's mother chimed in. "I am sure it will be so much nicer to have the service at the parish here, in Bath anyway. All of Charity's friends are in Bath, and I am not sure a large London wedding is a good idea. We should keep this a family affair if we hope to keep my husband and your son calm."

Neville's mother harrumphed.

"Even the Bath Abbey is large," Neville said. "It is quite an aisle to walk." He sent Charity a questioning look.

"But the Abbey is the Bath parish," Charity said.

"Then I will make no objections," Neville replied with a smile at Charity. "If my bride truly wishes it, I am sure that the quieter church in Bath will be better for Edmund as well."

"As you wish," his mother said in a tight voice. She exchanged a look with her son, and Charity smiled down into her teacup thinking that Lord Wentwell had given his mother an ultimatum, be civil. Unfortunately Charity could give her own mother no such instruction, but she seemed to be on her best behavior anyway.

"I do hope your brother will be settled enough to come," Charity did not want to exclude Edmund, but it was taking fate in one's hands to expect both her father and his brother to get through the service without incident. She was glad that Neville agreed it should be a small family affair.

"Well if it must be in Bath, then we must make haste with the invitations, said Lady Wentwell. A number of the Peerage will still be heading back to London or still in Brighton and that is quite a ways to travel on short notice. It will be a hardship. I expect many regrets."

"I am afraid you are right, Mother. The inns will all be full to bursting," Neville said. "There always seems to be a crush at the end of the summer season. Perhaps we should try to move the date forward. I am sure I can get a special license." He gave Charity a wink.

"Absolutely not," Lady Shalace intoned. "With your reputation, Lord Wentwell, can you just see the tongues wagging if Charity is married under a special license?"

"I can recommend an inn in Upper Nettlefold," Charity said. "It is only a day's ride from Bath."

"I think that will quite do," her mother said with a smile.

"I see I am out maneuvered," The Dowager Wentwell said, pouting.

"And The Keegain Manor is not far from Bath either. I am sure the Earl of Keegain's sisters will want to stay there," Lady Shalace added.

"You do plan to invite them, do you not?" Neville asked.

"Of course," Lady Charity said, thinking of all of her friends and how she wanted them to share her special day, even though quite often weddings were only family affairs. "And Julia is my dear friend. I was going to ask her to stand up with me."

"Of course you will have all the Ladies of Bath surrounding you," Charity's mother intoned. "I am sure it will be a beautiful day."

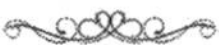

As it turned out, the day was not beautiful. It was windy and threatened rain, but nothing could dampen the joy in Charity's heart. She was marrying her true love. Her friends were all here, and her mother stood teary-eyed and told her how beautiful she was, before she hurried to her seat in the parish church. Charity felt beautiful in a gown of blue silk, with a blue silk hat, trimmed with flowers. The neckline was decorated with Brussels lace, so that it was not too revealing, and a fine silk Spenser jacket was used for church, along with wristlet gloves. Afterwards at the wedding breakfast, she could shed the jacket if she became too warm.

Her father stood beside her at the back of the church, while she peeked at her handsome husband who awaited her at the front.

Lord Wentwell was splendid in his shirt of white linen and white silk cravat. His black cutaway jacket was open to show his white silk waistcoat embroidered with blue and green leaves. He wore black trousers, in his customary skin tight mode which was all the fashion, black stockings and black pumps. Charity thought he looked marvelous. She could still not quite believe that this man would be entirely hers by the end of the day. The thought brought a blush to her cheeks.

"You look so like your mother," Lord Shalace said. "Beautiful and glowing with love." He patted her hand on his. "Are you nervous, Charity," he asked.

She smiled at him, exceedingly grateful that he was lucid today of all days.

"Not at all, Father," She cleared her throat. "Well, perhaps a little," she admitted. There is so much that could go wrong, she thought. It could pour down rain any minute. Thunder could crash, and Neville's brother could go into a frenzy. Her father could forget who she was and leave her alone in the back of the church. She had much to be nervous about, but not about the man she was going to marry. About Neville Collington, she had no doubts. He may be a rogue, but he was her rogue.

Her father, misunderstanding her nerves, said, "Do not be so, Charity. Wentwell is a fine man, like his father before him, honest and generous to fault. Stern, when needed, but at his core, kind. I venture he will make a good husband, and a good father for your children."

"Father!" Charity said aghast, but the thought warmed her heart. She thought of her children with those startling green eyes. She would have beautiful children if they all looked like her husband, and she admitted to herself, she too would offer them something in beauty and in wit.

"I hope you give him an heir," Father said, "and many daughters, as beautiful as their mother."

"Are you sorry Mother never gave you a son?" Charity asked suddenly.

"Only because you cannot inherit and I wished to give you the world," her father said. "But no, Charity. Not really. No one could have been more of a joy to me, no matter your sex." He patted her hand and asked, "Now, are you ready to meet your bridegroom?"

"I am," she said, as the thunder rumbled outside, and her Father took a step forward. She held her breath as the storm crashed, but Edmund stood tall and straight by his brother, and did not seem to be bothered by the loud noises. Perhaps, she thought, there may, one day be a cure for him. On this of all days, she wanted to believe in miracles, for the fact that she was marrying her true love was the greatest miracle of all.

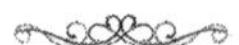

CONTINUE READING FOR A SNEAK PEEK OF...

The Forbidden Valentine ~ Lady Eleanor
by Isabella Thorne

1

Snow flurried down around Lady Eleanor Hawthorne. It clung to her eyelashes, her stylish hat and her fur cloak. Eleanor's boots were made of the finest smooth leather, but they were somewhat slippery and not very warm. She was up to her shins in snow as well, standing beside the sleigh with one arm wrapped around herself, and the other holding the draft horse's head. Her poor elderly driver, Mr. Arthur Junnip, was down on his knees in the snow, his grey head bowed as he sought to deduce the problem.

With his head beneath the sleigh, the driver's words were muffled. "One of the stanchions is cracked, Lady Eleanor. Rotten luck, that. Had 'em checked before the season and there was not a hint of rot on 'em." He sat back on his heels, and doffed his hat. "I am terribly sorry, but I cannot see making it back to Sweetbriar in this state. If it cracks clean through..." He let the thought hang. "I am sorry, Milady."

"It is not your fault in the slightest," Eleanor said. "You could not have seen that rock, buried under all this snow, and it is just a lucky thing old Mouse here did not stumble over it and hurt himself." She rubbed the horse's shaggy nose and he lipped at her glove, looking for treats. She edged closer to the horse, borrowing his heat in the cold wind.

Arthur got to his feet and brushed snow from his trousers. He rolled his hat in his hands. "I might walk back to the Albemarles' residence and secure a means of repair, but that does not solve anything, as I cannot be leaving you out in this weather with naught but a horse for protection."

The weather was nothing more than a snow flurry at present, but to Arthur any amount of risk was too much for Eleanor. She peered up the road in the opposite direction. It was difficult to see through the haze of falling snow in the low, failing light, but there was a golden glow upon the hilltop, less than half a mile's distance.

"What of that house?" Eleanor asked. She gestured towards it.

Arthur shook his head and yanked his cap back on. His ears were rimmed a bright red. "I could not go there, Milady. That is the Firthley house, as you well know."

Lady Eleanor sighed and stamped her boots, trying to bring some life back to her frozen feet. She slipped slightly in the wet snow and clutched onto the horse's mane to steady herself. The big gelding turned his head to look past his blinkers at her, and then stood stoically in the cold.

Eleanor's boots, like her clothing were quite

fashionable, but the boots lacked the fur lining to make them warm enough for the weather and the new leather soles were treacherously slippery. What had begun as a pleasant day of shopping in town had turned rather difficult. Her packages sat neatly boxed in the back of the sleigh, covered by canvas. She, however, was becoming quickly covered by snow.

"Yes, I do know it is Firthley Manor," Lady Eleanor said. "But I think under these exceptional circumstances, it may be reasonable to disregard the absurd feud of our families and ask for some assistance. I am certain they would lend a hand to a lady stranded in the snow. We are practically neighbors, after all."

She was referring; of course, to the feud between the Hawthornes and the Firthleys that had existed since before she was born. The original cause for the argument had never been adequately explained to her. Lady Eleanor suspected the reason for that was because neither of her parents actually remembered what had begun the whole affair, but were too stubborn to admit their ignorance. The feud had caused the odd tension in the local circles. Hawthornes would not attend, nor be invited to, events hosted by the Firthleys, and vice versa, and they did their best to avoid meeting at the social gatherings hosted by other members of society when they could. From everything Eleanor had heard, and she had asked about, the Firthleys were a perfectly ordinary family much like her own, and no one she asked had the faintest clue what had started all of the nonsense; or if they did, they would not tell her.

"If your parents found out I asked at the Firthley

house for aid…" Arthur tutted. He was clearly torn between finding help for Lady Eleanor as swiftly as possible and earning the ire of her parents.

Lady Eleanor, with sudden inspiration, proposed a compromise. "Well then you shall not ask at the Firthley house. I will. Here," she said, gesturing toward Mouse and passing Arthur the reins. "You take over this job and I shall find us some help."

This caused Arthur to turn as red as his ears. The loose, wrinkled skin at his neck trembled, but he came up beside her and took her spot at the horse's head.

"I do not think this is the best course of action, Milady" said Arthur, in a wavering voice. "Your parents will be livid."

"We shall not tell them, then. After all, they never speak to the Firthleys. How will they ever find out I went to their door? I shall return as soon as possible, Arthur. Perhaps you should climb beneath the blanket and try your best to keep warm. I do believe the temperature is dropping with the sun, and all this slush will turn to ice." Before he could come up with any more arguments against the idea, Lady Eleanor hurried off in the direction of Firthley Manor.

Hurried was too generous a word. Even with the aisles of snow smoothed down by the passage of other sleighs, it was treacherous going in the middle of the road, and her boots were not equipped for such travel. The snow was deep enough at the side of the road that her boots sunk in, breaking through the top layer of frozen snow. That gave her an awkward gait, but at least the snowfall was not high enough to cover her boots, and the deeper snow actually gave her some footing in the slippery slush. However, the drifts along the side of the road were large enough to wet the hem of her dress and cloak.

By the time Lady Eleanor reached the drive of Firthley Manor, she was warm from her exertion, and sweating in her layers of fur and wool, although her feet were still cold and the hem of her dress was sodden. She took a moment to straighten her clothing. Eleanor smoothed her chestnut brown hair back beneath her cap and brushed the snow from her shoulders with the back of her glove. It was the first time a Hawthorne would stand on the Firthleys' doorstep, in who knew how long, and she did not want to be the cause of a bad impression. Somewhat decent, but hardly looking like the lady of quality she was, Lady Eleanor Hawthorne marched up the drive and knocked at the door.

Eleanor waited. The sweat from her exertion began to dry, leaving her chilled and shivering. Just like that, all her warmth was gone. Her toes felt like hailstones in her boots. Eleanor knocked again. She could see a light in the entrance hall. Peering up at the house, one of the rooms above was also lit by what appeared to be a cheery fire, but there was no answer at the door. She huffed and knocked again. Briefly, she had the foolish notion that those within could somehow tell she was of the Hawthorne line, and were refusing to answer on principle. Of course that was absurd; she was so heavily bundled in winter clothing that it would be impossible to tell who she was unless they stood just in front of her. Still, no one answered.

Thinking of poor old Arthur, waiting and freezing with the sleigh, Lady Eleanor turned to go. Arthur would say it was all for the best that those within had not answered and she and Arthur would be forced to walk back the way they had come; to the Albemarles' house, over a mile away. Lady Eleanor shot a last, sullen look over her shoulder at the house, and picked her way down the front stair. The steps were treacherous with snow and ice and she clung to the railing.

"Oh, hello there," a voice called from somewhere off to the left. The sudden voice caught Eleanor by surprise, so that she did not see a patch of ice on the final step, directly beneath her foot. Her boot slipped and her feet shot out from under her. Eleanor lost her grip on the railing and landed quite indignantly on her bottom in the snow.

CONTINUE READING....

The Forbidden Valentine ~ Lady Eleanor

Want Even More Regency Romance...

Follow Isabella Thorne on BookBub

https://www.bookbub.com/profile/isabella-thorne

Sign up for my VIP Reader List!

at

https://isabellathorne.com/

Receive weekly updates from Isabella and an Exclusive Free Story

Like Isabella Thorne on Facebook

https://www.facebook.com/isabellathorneauthor/

Made in the USA
Coppell, TX
27 December 2019

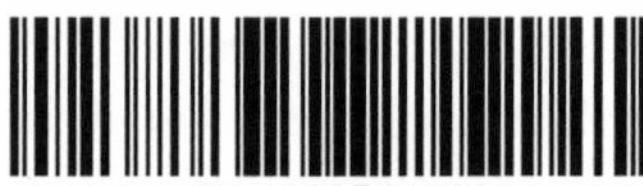